What birds can only whisper

What birds can only whisper

a novel by

Julie Brickman

TURNSTONE PRESS

Turnstone Press
607–100 Arthur Street
Artspace Building
Winnipeg, Manitoba
Canada R3B 1H3

Turnstone Press gratefully acknowledges the assistance of
the Canada Council and the Manitoba Arts Council.

Cover art: Untitled (oil pastel, 1985) by Allan Toews

Design: Manuela Dias

This book was printed and bound in Canada
by Friesens for Turnstone Press.

Canadian Cataloguing in Publication Data

Brickman, Julie

What birds can only whisper

ISBN 0-88801-214-4

I. Title.

PS8553.R433W43 1997   C813'.54   C97-920136-5
PR9199.3.B6934W43 1997

This book is dedicated
to the silenced
inside us all

Acknowledgements

For his generous and invaluable help with the process of sending out this manuscript, I would like to thank Rick Archbold. For his patient assistance with the particulars of life as a musician, I would like to thank Daniel Koulack. For their enthusiasm, love and support, I thank Molly and Leo Brickman, and Nina Brickman. For belief in me as a writer, I thank Samuel Stein. For help with French, I thank David Leitch. Other people helped at particular junctures: Susan Swan always offered a lead, a contact, a word of advice; Judi Denny provided secretarial assistance on early drafts; Philip Stern could fix any computer emergency.

For giving a new writer the experience of her dreams, I am profoundly grateful to my editors at Turnstone Press: Jamie Hutchison, who believed in the book and understood the vision I strived to reach; Manuela Dias, who extended deep, personal care and meticulous attention to every part of the process of publication; Patrick Gunter, who communicated his powerful enthusiasm for the worth of my book in the world. I wish every new writer could have such a wonderful experience.

For generous grant support in 1991 and 1992, I thank the Explorations Program of the Canada Council, my project officer Leutén Rojas, and the jury who gave me more money than I requested. I would like to express my regret that this program, so vital to the encouragement of new artists, has been cut from the budget.

Preface

When I first started to write this book, more than anything I wanted to give voice to the voiceless, in myself and in others I knew to be disbelieved, distrusted, silenced. To share, not the factual details, but the emotional truths of what I had learned about the silencing of the voices of the soul. Perhaps it was too great a burden for me to carry alone.

Yet, if I were emotionally on target – the goal I had strived for ten years to achieve – every person who had a history of abuse, especially if they had spoken to me sometime over the years, might identify with my heroine, feel that I had told their personal story, or part of it. This is the dilemma all fiction writers face. Any story that is psychologically true has the potential to expose someone's private, interior world.

It was a risk I had to take. My novel is fiction and the characters are not anyone I know. The one intersection I have been able to specify is in my use of the name "the Little One," so frequently used as a name or designation for a part of subpersonality as to essentially be generic.

Primo Levi in *The Drowned and the Saved* tried to answer the question so often put to him: why didn't the people in concentration camps, the *lagers*, rebel? They did, of course, but only a few and most lost their lives in the process. Levi wrote "Yet, in every case, one can see that it is never the most oppressed individuals who stand at the head of movements: usually, in fact, revolutions are led by bold, open-minded leaders who throw themselves into the fray out of generosity (or perhaps ambition), even though they personally could have a secure and tranquil, perhaps even privileged, life. The image so often repeated in monuments of the slave who breaks his heavy chains is rhetorical; his chains are broken by comrades whose shackles are lighter and looser." (p.159–160).

Lighter and looser, yes, but still there. As for the intersection with my own psyche, I could never have written this book without listening to the shattered voices in my own soul. Perhaps the silence of any one of us is ultimately the silence in all of us. It is to those silences, the ones we do not choose, that I have chosen to dedicate this book.

Solanas Beach, California
August, 1997

LOVE

1

She awakes early, thinking about a cardinal. She saw one perched on her neighbour's fence yesterday, but he flew away before she could get close enough to look. He was ruby against the early snow. She wanted to hear his song, though it was dull enough for a pretty bird. She dreamed about birds last night, an old dream from her childhood where she is flying away from trouble. The bed is hot as a furnace. She hears a whispery sound, rhythmic like breathing, muffled. The bed shifts.

The sound continues, low and undisturbed. She rolls over, props herself on an elbow, looks. The breathing figure is completely covered by quilt. She doesn't know who it is. She has never invited anyone to share this room, it is hers.

She slides from the bed, taking care not to jostle the slumbering figure. On the other side of the bed is the drawer where she keeps her knife. She drops to her knees, crawls over. A cool breeze fans her skin. She is naked. She never sleeps without clothes.

She opens the drawer. Her knife glints crimson in the ivory morning light. Its blades are folded, like still wings.

She unsheathes a blade, stands, peers into the bed. The figure shifts again.

Axel.

A mop of black, wavy, familiar hair protrudes from the quilt. It's Axel. How in the name of the holy mother did he get there? Axel. Christ, she might have stabbed him without looking. Her knees tremble as she shuts the weapon drawer. Her hands tremble as she slips into her bathrobe. Bathing, she tries to remember what happened in the night. Nothing comes to mind.

Back in the room, she leans over the man who is sprawled in a sleeping heap on her bed. "Axel, get up."

He pulls a pillow over his face. *I could tighten that pillow over his nose and mouth, one, two.* She joggles his shoulder.

Knobby fingers, their scent musty like seaweed, tickle her jaw and she rubs her chin along the palm behind them. He asks if he has time to shower.

"If you're quick," she answers.

Sipping her coffee, she hears him get up and start the shower. Too naked, she thinks, as she rummages through the kitchen for some breakfast food. People get too naked with each other. She pours the dregs from yesterday's wine down the drain.

"The Americans of waste, that's who we are." Axel is practising a new speech as he showers, exhorting Canadians to care about producing more garbage than any other Western country. While he pauses, Kendra dredges some oily peanut butter and a hunk of white cheddar from the fridge. He gave a speech like that the night she met him at the Earthsky benefit two years ago. She and Survivors were the main act. He was the stranger in the limp tweed jacket and faded jeans who mesmerized an entire amphitheatre with only words. The cheddar has nibble marks at the end, which she trims and saves.

Axel is arguing with himself, his voice travelling from bass to falsetto as he parodies questions he expects to hear from his audience and prepares his replies. "Maybe our volume is due to the

depth of Canadian purity" (she can see the grin) "which widens our zone of garbage and narrows our zone of acceptability." He claims he delivers his best speeches in the shower. She thinks their most successful conversations occur then, too. Just last week, sitting on the toilet lid with layers of plastic curtain, pounding water, and humid shower air protecting her from his lathered nakedness, she explained why she would still not sleep with him after two years. "I'm thirty-four years old," she said into the steaming hiss, "and I've never had a sexual relationship with anyone. I don't think I can. Not even with you."

Axel pads into the kitchen, towelling his hair. His wine terry-cloth robe hangs like an old sock. "Over the moat, and into the fortress," he teases. He is referring to her bedroom. "It wasn't immutable after all."

A vision of him, blue-tongued, swinging from a noose in the basement, crosses her mind. She places a pitcher of hot milk in front of him.

"Did you dream?" He smears peanut butter on a piece of brown toast and gazes at her with inquisitive eyes, lustrous icy blue prisms that break the light into a thousand pieces, like his curiosity breaks up the world.

"Yes," she nods, grateful for a subject she can talk about. "I turned into a bird, tinier than a sparrow, but larger than a hummingbird, small and swift and beautiful." A cardinal when she awoke. "I could fly anywhere. Not only in air, but through concrete, glass, storm clouds, anything. I think I could also fly across time and space, but I'm not sure. It's just a feeling. As if I could fly up and down my own life, and in and out different consciousnesses, my own and other people's too."

"And last night?"

"I flew for a while. Went skimming low and fast across some fields just to feel myself in flight. Then I came back and perched on a telephone wire. I think it was right outside the window." She pours some hot milk into her coffee. Axel taught her to do that.

"I used to dream that dream when I was a child. Night after night I'd fly off into that blue-black silent bird world." She can hear her own voice drifting, fading, speaking the language of dreams. "It was such an eerie world. I could catch an air current and glide like an eagle, only further, until I was floating on my back in space, watching the soft lighted pathway of the Milky Way." Remnants of the dream tug at her eyes, pulling them inward. She laughs abruptly. "I used to worry that I'd forget to come back. That when I did, I'd be dead."

"You certainly weren't dead last night."

His eyes would glitter like mucus-polished jewels if I forked them out.

"You were wonderful."

He means this as a compliment, she reminds herself desperately.

The jewelled eye prisms gleam at her from a fluffy bed of rice, a golden biryani.

He asks the question she's been dreading: "How was it for you?"

How can she tell him? Mutely, she shakes her head.

"I can't remember a thing."

2

Kendra's birth would have etched itself on anyone's mind, and she does remember it in formidable detail. She was born on the bathroom floor of an old farmhouse in the Upper Peninsula of the state of Michigan, the "You Pee" as it was known to the landproud folks who lived there. Karl, her father, did not believe Hannahjean, her mother, was really in labour, but thought she was faking just to cause him trouble when he was busy and tired from spring planting. So Kendra entered the world while Karl beat her mother on the bathroom floor, and her first act on the air side of the womb, after she had relieved her mother's pain by pushing herself out of the tunnel, was to not cry like a baby, which, she came to believe, was why she was named Kendra: Ken for the boy who didn't cry and dra for her vagina. In this manner she was only half a disappointment to Karl, who wanted a boy but liked her dra.

Five children followed, one per year: Kiki, Katie, Kelley, Kimmy (who officially changed her name to Kimberly when she became an actress), and Karl Jr., after whom Karl (Sr.) allowed

Hannahjean to stop her annual foaling, although he never stopped reminding her that she had produced the longest line of female progeny north of Traverse City, progeny for whom Hannah, smiling her wispy faraway smile, that omnipresent upturn at the corners of her lips (once late at night Kendra had sneaked into her bedroom to see if she slept with that quarter-moon smile), shopped, baked, canned and cleaned with absolute deference to Karl's pedestrian tastes and rabid, fluctuating moods.

It was Kendra's misfortune to be Karl's pet. Until Karl Jr., or Jerry as he came to be called, was old enough, Karl took Kendra everywhere, teaching her about wind and weather, water and soil, planting, harvesting, and heavy equipment, like tractors and loaders, backhoes and thatchers. By his side, she looked after the farm and fed the family. He even taught her to hunt, taking her deep into the woods where they would bag geese and ducks and watch for hawks in the treetops. In between chores, he played with her dra.

"He never did anything much," she told Axel, meaning he never had intercourse with her, "but he touched me a lot."

At the age of eleven with the help of Ellen Tremayne, the Eagle City Regional School music teacher, a Detroit-raised, Ann Arbor-schooled, hip woman of the sixties, who had moved back to the land by way of northern Michigan, Kendra discovered the guitar. "Buckets of talent," Ms (she insisted) Tremayne would tell her, and Kendra, wildly, heartthrobbingly in love with the first person who had ever encouraged her for free, played until she had calluses as thick as nickels.

Karl, though also her mentor, would be jealous of a passion he could not possess, so Kendra hid it from him and played only during lunchtime, free periods, and long sweet hours after school. When she was very late coming home, Karl beat her. He became obsessed with the notion that she was awash in hormones, boy-crazy, and out in the woods behind the school screwing incessantly, two, three, five at a time. Occasionally, driven nearly mad by these visions, he would race the old pickup, squealing on the edges of its tires, to her school, park around the corner, and stalk the back woods, ear cocked for the quick scuffle of adolescent sex which he would interrupt with a noisy tattoo of boot-stomping or a single rifle shot. It was only later that she connected these escapades with the worst beatings, the ones where he lost himself in a frenzy.

At seventeen, she got careless and made a mistake. The forty-two students of her class had decided to write their own graduation ceremony. They wanted Kendra to provide the music, because Kendra's music, from Childe ballads to Delta blues, had echoed in the corridors with their footsteps as they ran to the classes, clubs, and locker-side trysts of their high school awakenings.

Ellen Tremayne pushed Kendra to accept. Kendra had never performed, demurring every time Ellen brought it up, and Ellen did not want her to graduate without a taste of the stage. "Do it for me, Kendra," she urged, she who had never asked for anything. Running her thumbs along those nickel-plated fingers she'd acquired through hours hunched in the back of Ellen's classroom, headphones on her ears, guitar on her lap, thrilling as Billie Holiday and Bessie Smith wailed her soul's own blues, Kendra forgot about Karl and agreed.

Karl knew nothing of her music. Kendra padlocked her guitar and sheet music in a school locker, never listened to the radio at home, and sang in a flat murmur on birthdays and Christmas. She didn't think he'd come to graduation; though his own skills were abundant, other people's accomplishments brought him no pleasure. If he knew she was playing, he'd ruin it, so she adopted tactics to distract him. Some days she'd come home early, find him in the fields, and work by his side until sundown. Evenings, she'd watch a TV show with him and bring him cold beer. Small attentive surprises could keep him calm, but too many would raise his suspicions. At night she dreamed of exploding villages and napalmed children.

This is what happened: it is graduation night. The students, Kendra in their midst, promenade down the aisle in awkward pairs while Ellen Tremayne plays "Pomp and Circumstance" on the piano. In black-and-white gowns they queue like a choir into ascending rows on the right-hand side of the platform. Unable to look at faces, Kendra fixates on the polished mahogany surface of the grand piano, watching it spill brown rainbow lights onto the stage. A battered grey metal chair, her favourite from Ellen's classroom, sits empty and waiting between the piano and the speaker's podium. Beside it, her guitar case lies open, exposing its worn plush interior of flattened scarlet. At Ellen's nod, Kendra extricates herself from the choir. Something in her gait, a hesitation, a vagueness of rhythm, is still trying to hide. She gets caught in the folds of her gown and has to fumble and tug her way free. At last, she draws the guitar from its case, places it across her lap, and starts to tune.

A low growl reverberates through the silent auditorium. She barely has time to recognize his voice before Karl looms in front of her, his face iron-still. Without a word, she hands him the guitar. He settles it back into the case, snaps it shut.

Grabbing her hand, he leads her off the stage. He didn't even dress up, she thinks, foolishly revolted by his plaid lumberjack shirt. Hannahjean, two decades out of style in a black crepe sheath, is standing at the back of the auditorium, smiling her Buddha-like half-smile. Pandemonium breaks out behind them, which Ellen controls with the opening riff of a jazz piece.

Back home, Karl sets the case in front of the wood stove, hands her a hatchet. "Do it," he says. She draws the guitar out of its case for the second time that evening. With her first swing, she hears the strings screech, whine, pop.

Then there is nothing but the snap of dead, dry wood. It makes a dull crackle as it burns.

What birds can only whisper

Kendra packs hurriedly, silently, sliding whatever she can into Ellen's old canvas backpack. Jeans, sweatshirts, underwear, turtlenecks, sweaters, all rolled into tight balls so she can fit more. Warm socks, tights, jewellery, makeup. Fists of pressure pound at her temples. Shit, her hair dryer's in the bathroom, she'll have to leave it behind; she can't risk waking Karl, you never know when his frenzies are over. She can hear him snoring, a rumbling wheezy sound that shakes the rafters and sends nausea burbling up her throat. She has to leave now; there's no more time to pack. She grabs a photo of her sisters and one of Billie Holiday, stuffs them into a side pouch, and tiptoes out the door.

3

The wide Toronto streets are empty Sunday morning, and Kendra drives with the easy joy of someone who is comfortable with machines. Bright autumn sunshine streams through the bare branches and bounces from the sidewalks in tiny crystal rainbow shards that remind her of Axel's eyes and their night of lovemaking, which is nothing but a bird dream to her. To not think about that requires effort; she wants to get to the studio before the others and play some old English ballads to soothe the restless chorus in her head.

Baker's battered Tercel is angled across the corner space of the parking lot. Baker, who is never on time unless she's slept there. Kendra parks next to her, jogs the back stairs two at a time, though she still wishes she could have a few minutes alone.

Baker sits high behind her mauve drums, playing with gusto, while looking tiny and pale, almost ill. She greets Kendra with a flourish on the drums and resumes chanting her new story-song. Baker, too slight a container for her vibrant personality, should be big and conspicuous. Kendra gets the message, slides on a stool to listen.

What birds can only whisper

I went that day to a clinic downtown
cut through the people   circling round
past the bookstore, up the stairs
grimfaced   palefaced   determined air
doin' my duty   doin' what's right
("Not now babe. Time's not right.")
they sucked me clean   sucked me sterile
no more fetus   no more peril
to my relationship   new and feral

Baker will want music for this one. Kendra slips into a trance
of magnified senses, absorbs the cadence and rustle of the words,
the tones at the crest of the vowels, registers Baker's song in her
skin, her guts, her yawning dra.

He is glad: Let's celebrate!
while I feel I've sealed my fate
fecund   fertile   fruitful   bearing
pregnant   swollen   seeded   caring
all the things I cannot be
punished for eternity
Sahara   Gobi   Mojave
me

Kendra's faraway mind logs the thought *disaster*.

Nights up late I try to name her
Ursula Doris Jane my daughter
after all my favourite authors
two months old   already slaughtered
by her father long departed
who was sure he wouldn't want her
thought that we'd survive without her

We know how to kill them early
diaphragm   condom   cap and jelly
sever us from spontaneity
"Don't touch me!" I told him after
and each night I'd just roll over

Ursie's five now   rocks with laughter
I hear her footsteps   join her chatter
"Don't tell me
            it didn't matter."

Bleak lyrics about children spell disaster. Baker's melancholia surges or disappears according to the absence or presence of a male person in her life. Men are tricks, distractions she waves in front of her, like a conjurer's white hanky: look, audience, no rabbit, no balls to juggle, no emptiness, no depression, no black hole in the centre where love should live. So Gary Steale, who has been in her life almost six months, a record for Baker of the two-week, "this-one's-the-love-of-my-life" mad-passions, must have disappeared, stomped out probably, smashing to pieces the flimsy, jerry-built, perfect-family world that has never existed for her and never will, but which she's longed for since her diaper days when Jackson Baker began his revolving-door version of fatherhood, his out-with-the-blonde, in-with-the-gifts largesse that left Baker two years old and toddler-hearted for every slick-tongued, womanizing, woman-hating, crumb-dropping man who came her way. Under her pliant surface rages a core of black talent, a parallel Baker, who gobbles each insult and emerges stronger than ever, writing songs with a lyrical anti-male bitterness that speaks to millions of women and sells their albums around the world.

Kendra scrutinizes Baker to see how bad it is this time. Beneath the dark curls, her olive skin looks liverish, the pouch under her eyes an apricot shade of bruised. Kendra massages a skein of muscle along Baker's neck and shoulders.

"Like my song?" Baker exhales a long breath.

"Nope. Hate it." Kendra cringes at her unmodified bluntness.

"Fuck, why not?"

"The rhythm. *Bum ba dum dum. Bum ba dum.* I need loose lyrics to write anything decent." Kendra mocks the rhythm by drawing it out. "What can I do with that?"

"I've seen you write to much worse. 'Endless nights of parties, admirers flocking round,'" Baker hums a line from the title song of their first album. "So tell me what you really don't like."

"The story." Kendra fetches a chair, another battered favourite. This talk is going to turn into a purge or a confession. "I loathe women who martyr themselves for men."

"Millions do. Still."

"And every time it endangers the children."

"That's what the song's about."

"The song's about an embryo with a name. If I set that to music, it'll feed the great nineties abortion myths: that women suffer deep psychological scars from abortion. That embryos are small curled adults temporarily housed at the womb address."

"Open your heart, dammit. The song is about Ursula and the ghostchildren."

"*Ghostchildren?* Did I miss a verse?"

"Let me tell you about ghostchildren. I've been thinking about them for a long long time." Baker leans her face as near as a whisper. "They're the children women weep for. The ones we hear in the corridors who aren't there. Who cry in our nurseries, drink milk from our dry breasts, stamp their little feet with spirit. Who grow up, braid their hair, go to school, come home with stories they tell in high-pitched voices, but who aren't there." Her hands rub along her knees, rotate around her kneecaps. "They're the kids we wanted but never had. The ones we aborted or gave up for adoption. The ones we dreamed about, longed to have, or went to any length to have. The unborn, the stillborn, the uncarried, the miscarried. The ones who died of leukemia or choked in their cribs. The kidnapped or custodynapped; the runaways, the missing. All the children, named and nameless, who grew up as ghosts, gone but sleeping in the next room.

"Like my Ursie."

Fourteen years together and Kendra had no idea about Ursula.

Kendra and Baker met shortly after Kendra arrived in Toronto, both of them Americans, expatriates, lost in a country not supposed to be foreign. Baker was older, attending university, hanging around the periphery of a network of intellectuals whose concepts were not her own. Kendra was alone, in a rooming house, scrounging a living as a street musician. It was love at first sight.

Baker, a fourth-year humanities major, would come over with her favourite books, dog-eared and magic-marked, and read passages to Kendra late into the nights, giving Kendra the education she could not afford. Kendra, in return, liberated Baker's rage through a birthday present, drum pads, which Baker pounded morning and night, pulverizing the faces of Jackson Baker and his blond loves into meaty smithereens as she learned the rhythms of blues and trouble from around the world.

They started "Quillan and Baker" just because they enjoyed the sound of their collaborations. Baker's lyrics were angry, urbane, feminist, funny. Kendra's music resonated empathy. It was white women's blues they sang. Blues that told the stories of women's pain. And then laughed. Laughed from the inside. Laughed at each other. Laughed from that dark hole in the centre where love should live. They were surprised when other people liked their music, and accepted every invitation eagerly. The women's movement was strong then, and poor. They were billeted and fed, applauded and admired, though rarely paid. It was a time of such confluence between ideal and action, it accidentally eclipsed their personal misery and made everything seem possible. It was the time of their lives. At one such event they met

Lena, playing keyboards with a makeshift rock band, and invited her to join them. They had found another expatriate. Lena Farshady had arrived from Jamaica just eighteen months earlier. Angel was the only one who joined by audition. They were looking for a bass player and in strolled Angel, fifteen years younger than anyone else, blond, bland and utterly Canadian with her impossible way of being outrageous and restrained at the same time. "I don't know if we can use you," Baker had joked. "What will we do with our expatriate jokes?" Angel's reply told them all they needed to know. "I'm a sexual expatriate," she explained, "a visible lesbian. Agitating for a multisexual Canada."

They changed their name to Survivors and became a band.

Lena and Angel breeze into the studio. Lena is hugging her coat of white angora around a carafe of coffee and shivering as if the October weather were cold. She's never gotten used to Canadian winters, claims her skin is permanently calibrated for Jamaican temperatures. Behind her ambles Angel, her bomber jacket of soft black leather unsnapped to display her disdain for common human needs like protection or warmth. "I've got nipples as leathery as the soles of summer feet," she once told Kendra. A most Canadian boast.

The coffee is home-brewed and stored in a tall mirrored jug. A dozen of Lena's faces beam in silver slivers as she pours. Long brown Modiglianis. "We're celebrating," she announces.

Baker walks over to the kitchen to get some milk.

"We're going to have a baby."

The milk carton crashes to the floor.

"Are you pregnant?" Kendra directs the question to Lena. Angel is too much of a dyke.

"We've got a fertility referral."

White liquid pools around Baker's feet, as if the life were draining from her breasts. Thin white milkblood in a puddle.

"To the doctor with the biggest-sized brood." Angel's monotone crawls out between lips that hardly move. Upper Canada lips, Lena calls them. "I asked my daddy for the best." Daddy is Dr. Rillington-Downes, a surgeon who specializes in diseases of the bowel. Margaret Angelique Benoit Rillington-Downes, Angel, is a strange cross between Upper and Lower Canada. Baker maintains they should name the group after her.

On her hands and knees near the fridge, Baker makes slow circles with a J-cloth, wiping and re-wiping the milk from the dry floor.

"A success rate over fifty percent," Lena explains. "And that's for the infertile."

"Inflated by women who were popping the pill or sneaking in the diaphragm, trying not to have yet another kid," Angel adds.

Baker hoists herself out of the dry patch onto her knees. "You both going?"

Lena nods. "We want to keep everything in the open."

Kendra plucks at a string. There is never a home without secrets.

"With all those straight couples howling at the doors, do you think they're going to take a couple of dykes who play in a rock band?" Baker asks. "One who abandoned a child and a husband already? Another who wears her hair like the Statue of Liberty and looks like she just started a third sex? C'mon," she exhorts. "Do you want a kid or don't you?"

"I will have no family before I have the wrong family." Ice levels the melody of Lena's voice. "I compromised before."

Children, children. Kendra hunches over her guitar, rambling around its strings to find a phrase for the children: dead children, lost children, unborn children, ghostchildren. Lena has left her daughter in Jamaica, unwillingly. Baker has resorted to an imaginary one. Angel wants to be a father. Kendra looks at the others. "Let's play."

4

≁ ≁ ≁

She is lying in a sleeping bag, army green with a plaid felt lining, spread over a thin strip of foam on the floor of a cabin deep in the woods. Bare branches floured with snow rustle outside the drapeless window, and a pale winter moon casts a rectangle of dim light across the plank floor. The room is empty, except for the sleeping girl on her unzipped bag, its flaps of material open to her knees, her torso revealed like a half-wrapped gift. Now the girl, too, unzips from her sternum down to her vagina, a tiny hairless thing of flesh-coloured porcelain. Tendon and muscle and rib roll away, exposing the blue and rose of her guts. Her viscera stretch towards her heart, as plants towards the sun, or to provide a shield for its feeble beat. Around and beside and between all the organs oozes a translucent white slime.

Everything glistens, and is still, like a hyper-realist painting.

The dollgirl sleeps with her eyes wide open.

≁ ≁ ≁

Sweating, flopping under twisted blankets, hooked like a fish to the dollgirl, Kendra revisits the still face with the staring eyes, which fragments every time she gets close to it. She flips through images of children she knows: Lena's Cornelia, Cristophine downstairs, Allycia, Starr, Josie, Faye, the street girls with wise baby faces who hang around the studio, little tough-girls in studded boots and minis, who who who could she be? Lena's girl? Ursula? When the phone rings, the fragmenting image disintegrates completely.

Baker's mood shimmers across the line. Gary is back. She found the prodigal darling flung across her bed, exhaling sour, beery odours, and snoring in his explosive, arrhythmic fashion. A B-52 coming in for a landing, and her on the runway without earplugs, was how she once described these sudden rackety bursts that punctuated her nights. To show everyone the full extent of her trauma, she developed a snore imitation on the drums, a rattling, clanging crescendo she detonated whenever anyone was drowsy or inattentive. Kendra, defence-trained to pounce when startled, had nearly socked her with a knockout punch the first time she did it.

Baker regales Kendra with the details of her obeisance to this unconscious man, how she peeled off his clothes, kissed each millimetre of his unveiling skin, as if it were one of Jackson Baker's treasured gifts. Kendra wants to rattle the false joy out of her, Eve's apples down from the tree, to shout stop stop Baker, why're you falling for this pig manure, this man who shits words, this toilet-mouthed charmer who won't stay longer than a week.

"Sex inspires me," Baker exults.

"I'm glad you didn't say 'love.'"

"I don't know love. Just sex and them old penis blues."

This is part of an old joke between them. Penis blues is Baker's name for unspeakable pain, the source of every woman's deepest trouble.

They arrange to meet after Kendra goes for a run. Kendra

needs the sting of cold air to clear the who-ing from her head, the stench of yesterday's anxiety off her skin. She is soaked when she returns, but it's clean sweat, the perfume of effort.

Isabella's Library is a dusty maze of a shop, crammed with second-hand, rare and antiquarian books, bins of old music, records, and no one is quite sure what else. The regulars, who find the cafe in the back, try to keep it a secret, reserved for professors, artists, people in the know, but the proprietor gives away so many free samples, of books and pastry, that his store attracts people no one would speak to on the street. Baker is already in the back, riffling through an old book, drinking coffee from a chipped white mug. "You look awful," she says, as an invitation to talk.

Kendra recounts her dream to Baker, and its details reassemble: the cabin had two rooms, a kitchen, furniture; a pickup was parked down the lane; there was an outhouse with no door. It sounds like the cabin in the woods near Lake Superior where Kendra vacationed as a child, but it doesn't feel the same. It *feels* like her bedroom here, her fortress.

"Did you have a fight with Axel?" Baker asks.

"Axel doesn't fight." The knife episode wasn't a *fight*.

"You mad at him?"

"How could I be? You know what he's like." Axel is probably the only man Baker gets along with.

"Well, something happened. Dreams like that don't come from nowhere." Baker is a serious reader of psychology.

"Promise not to laugh?"

Baker snorts. The worse it is, the more they laugh.

"I think I'm afraid of sex."

Baker howls. "That's just occurring to you *now?*"

"Seriously. Axel's my first decent guy. He terrifies me."

"I know," she nods. "You can count on the assholes. They go away before we have to come up with anything."

"I don't want him inside me. Inside. Where I live."

"I loved that part with Linc." Baker shuts her book over a napkin she takes from the metal holder. "He didn't feel weird in there, but like he belonged. After I saw him, I felt like I could be alone for days and never have that sad, dark feeling, the one where your elevator's dropped to the bowels of the earth."

"But I feel good without Axel," Kendra says.

"When I was with Linc, I couldn't tell whose thoughts I was having, his or my own. I just had this clarity, this fearless bright beacon that shone around inside, highlighting my best thoughts. Now *that* was company."

Baker pushes a paper across the table, a new version of the Ursula song. It includes a little girl with braids and questions, the child who might have existed if Lincoln hadn't insisted on the abortion. It's much better. It has guts blended in with the politics.

"You have to tell me everything about her," Kendra says, "or I can't find the music."

Baker closes her eyes. "It began with little thoughts," she says. "If Ursie were alive, she'd be one week old today, two weeks, a month, six. I could hear her wail or coo or even just breathe. At a year, I made her a birthday party with gooey chocolate cake and one of those fizzy sparkler candles."

Kendra is starting to see Ursie, a pudgy brown cherub with pizazz in her eyes.

"We began to do Christmas and Thanksgiving, sometimes Easter, always Mother's Day. I took her to zoos, and playgrounds, parks, libraries. Then came the dolls."

"Your collection."

"Dolls aren't obvious. Not like buying children's clothes, or tacking up clown paper."

"You'll have hundreds of them soon."

"It's a passion. To find the dolls I picture in my mind."

Kendra hums snatches of melody. Ghostchildren are ethereal yet textured, almost grounded by the knowledge of Ursie.

"You remember how I was when Linc left."

Kendra remembers. Baker had tried to fuck away her misery with thugs, greasers, desperadoes, the worst of male slime, and dared to bring them to the studio.

"I remember trying to stop you."

"Ursie got me out of it," Baker says.

"Is that what happened? I could never figure it out." Baker had insisted using the studio helped her get rid of them pronto. They always talk about The Next Time, she had grimaced. They think if you fuck them you're going to want to see them again.

"The day Ursie was born," Baker says, "you know, due, supposed to be born, I couldn't let anyone touch me."

"I wish I had known."

5

Axel has returned from the north. He and Kendra are meeting for dinner at a Mauritian restaurant on Roncesvalles near where he lives. They haven't spoken since he left, their easy patterns unchanged.

Kendra has some free hours. She collapses on the bed, more exhausted than pre-tour rehearsing warrants. Her blood feels watery, her limbs massive, thick, bloated. She sets the alarm in case she drops into sleep and drifts. She thinks her body is moving but isn't sure. Her awareness has dimmed as if her mind has slid far back from centre stage. It's more like her body is being moved. Her legs rive, her hips gyrate, *bam, bam, bam, bam,* tears gush down cheeks that must be hers, stone cheeks. *Little bitch.*

What the hell was that about? Dazed, she staggers to the bathroom. A long shower might clear her head. The water pummels down as she scrubs every inch of her skin. Was that a memory of sex with Axel? Her body felt like it was thrown all over the bed, yet the sensations are starting to fade. Even her scalp feels sweaty and unclean. She tilts her head backwards, lets the water stream through her tangled hair. Cool water, like evening rain, splashes over her, and she massages her head like a dog clawing its coat. Maybe it was only a dream.

White cords, khaki shirt, runners, the soapstone earrings Axel gave her last Christmas. Bronze gloss on her lips, streaks of blush along her cheekbones, brown mascara, the sweetness of a squirt of Shalimar, the safety of her army knife in her purse. She surveys herself in the mirror. She's 5'7 1/2" but tells people she's 5'8", and with her lean frame, they believe her. Her legs are firm from running, but her arms look flabby, and her chest sunken. She needs to get back to the gym. Her hair, dark auburn with glints of red and gold, came out frizzed instead of wavy and looks as if it's cut above her shoulders. And her eyes are odd, more out of alignment than usual. The right one, which is blue, looks nearly half an inch higher than the green one. As if they belong to different people.

Axel has two newspapers and a magazine spread in front of him at a corner table. A beacon of a smile lights his face when he sees her, and she releases the breath she didn't know she was holding.

He pounds an article with his pointed finger. "Look at this environmental slime from our prime minister again. Have you noticed how his mouth disappears when he lies?"

Kendra laughs. Nothing has changed.

"It's not enough that the scientists invent language so obscure that no one can understand it. We have to listen to politicians intone the words, which ought to alert everyone to how meaningless they are. Listen to the oxymorons in this one article: 'safe toxic waste,' 'old reforestation,' 'distilled acid rain.' And here's a new one: 'ozone plug.' I keep waiting for one of them to talk about faecal counts as organic." He slaps his palm against his forehead. "Sunshine, air, forests, water, all unsafe now. Do you realize these were the realms of the gods and goddesses of all animate mythology?"

"Bad trip, huh?"

"Not great. It's tough to explain fish with tumours to the people who once worshipped the unity of all nature. But we came up with a strategy that I can take to Ottawa. The deputy minister will listen."

Axel's views on the sanctity of the environment inspired Kendra to write "Environmental AIDS," the title song of Survivors' last album. The press raved over the song, trumpeting the arrival of Survivors as a serious group, concerned with world survival, not mere women's issues.

Axel orders a spicy array of chutney, chili, okra, eggplant, beans, salad, chicken, fish, noodles, rice, just about everything on the menu. The waitress eyes his bony frame with a sceptical lift of her eyebrows. His jacket sleeves are too short and the heavy bones of his wrists poke out. Hairless, like the rest of him, except the two mops of brown curls.

Over French-roasted coffee, he broaches the subject. "Did your memory come back?"

She shakes her head.

"Do you want me to fill you in?"

"Not especially." She only wants to know if they really had intercourse, if he was inside her, if they both had orgasms.

"Yes to all three," he says.

"Oh, god," she buries her face in her hands. "Why can't I remember?" Her green eye fills with tears.

6

Kendra sits awake in her apartment, thinking about sex. Her story that she's never had sex before isn't quite true. She tried once. With Tim Saunders, football hero, aspiring artist, and her only friend in Eagle City Regional. She picks up her guitar, plays some songs she played then. Tim used to come to the classroom where she practised and sit on the floor, sketch, and do homework. He'd come after chess club, or student council meeting, or football practice. He was gregarious and successful, while she was a loner. She never knew why he liked her.

In their junior year, he invited her to Winter Ball, the big foofaraw that marked the end of fall and football. He was quarterback of the Eagle City Fliers that year, and they had won the league finals. The gym, decorated with green and white crepe streamers, Eagle City banners, and enormous papier-mâché eagles perched on the basketball nets, thrummed with stadium sounds. "On to victory, on to victory" – the band and cheerleaders pumped up the party crowd, which was already swaying and hollering. One by one, the entire varsity team was pushed to the platform, some of them on the shoulders of the crowd. "Touchdown sure this time rah rah rah." A cry of "Dates, too!" rose from the crowd, and Kendra, stiff with terror from the sweaty proximity of so many people, felt herself propelled towards the stage by dozens of unfamiliar hands.

Chaperones closed their collective eyes as vast quantities of liquor and beer, hidden in paper cups, swirled through the crowd. Seagram's, Johnnie Walker, Southern Comfort. Soon the whole gym smelled like Karl.

Afterwards, Tim Saunders, drunk from adulation as much as liquor, drove her to the lake and confessed undying love along with urgent longing. His eyes glazed with something – tender feeling, romance, liquor, testosterone – something that had nothing to do with her, and he tugged her towards him. When she was flush against his torso, her body slackened. He stroked her hair, her eyelids, the lifelines on her palms. Every place he touched turned numb. Instead of the kiss of life, each touch brought a little death, a dousing of awareness. When he finally kissed her mouth, she turned into an ice statue, rigid, unable to move. She was sure her lips were blue and cold.

"I'm not attracted to you," she whispered. She hoped this was a lie.

Who did attract her, she found, were cool, hip, storytelling men, who always turned out to be nasty pieces of work, woman-haters, who felt sorry for themselves and had nothing to give. Men Baker liked to go out with.

She tried twice more in Toronto, once with a man, once with a woman. Each time, she turned into an ice sculpture. The last time, she was lying on the floor with a man she really cared about, listening to Bill Evans and watching the tangerine peaks of a fire. When he moved gently onto her, she froze like a glacial lake, so thoroughly all her internal organs seemed to slow down. Her pulse weakened, her breathing faded, and a blackness crept up the back of her neck, reaching towards her consciousness. She managed to croak "no" to avoid passing out, but it took him a while to stop, and for an eternity of minutes she couldn't move any part of her rigid body.

He was the last one before Axel.

Ten years ago.

↵ ↵ ↵

A dollgirl dressed in tiers of creamy lace pirouettes in front of a mirror. Wisps from her corkscrew curls, black and glossy, snake down her neck towards a row of fragile pearls. Lace and curls whirl round her body in gyrating hoops, which coil into lassos, and thicken into wet, cylindrical bodies, cobras and rattlers and diamondheads, who slither along her nude, laceless form. The fissure of her mouth makes no sound. The only noise is the slap of flesh, reptilian against human.

The dancer awakens in her bed. Coffee grounds, twisted cans, lard drippings, scrunched-up papers, tin foil, discarded shoes litter her room. Yellowed newspaper springs from her underwear drawer. Cockroaches crawl over her jewellery and scarves. Old soda bottles. Rags. Beef swarming with maggots. Fish skeletons. Laundry. But none of her things. She opens the closet. Green garbage bags, choked at the neck, are piled one on top of the other. She cannot dress.

The aromas of coffee and frying bacon float in from the kitchen, where the radio booms morning news, sports and weather. Plates and forks clatter, slippered footsteps slap across tile. Her mother is up. She tiptoes from the bedroom, peers around each doorway, then darts across, one, two, three doorways, a flight of stairs, a corridor, until she is safe in the kitchen. Her mother glances over: Hi hon. Do you want your eggs fried or scrambled?

↵ ↵ ↵

7

The next night Axel wants to sleep over. Kendra knows it is time, but terror resounds through her interior in the sobbing cries of a little girl. Five, maybe three, she sobs as if there's nothing in the world but her tears. Her body convulses, she gasps for breath to fuel her tears but there's not enough room in her tiny lungs for the air she needs, and she chokes on the mucus and spit sliding back down her throat. Another voice, screaming. This one doesn't have a body, but if she did, she'd be lying on her back, caged in a crib, turtle-limbs waving, hands scrunched in helpless fists as the soft mush of her excrement creeps up her back toward her shoulder blades and the fine threads of her new hair.

Kendra gazes out the window. The cries sound so real she can't believe she is imagining them. In her familiar daydreams, where emotions reside in their logical sites, five-year-olds weep because Sylvie the cat doesn't come home and are rocked consolingly by Mother who murmurs in a googoo voice like she did when they were babies. What, then, are these feelings, like slabs of raw meat and bleeding amputated limbs? They have nothing to do with the frilly lace collars she wore to confess her sins of childhood: "I said damn to my mother, Father. I took the baby's bottle and drank his apple juice. Forgive me." She surveys the street but no children are playing, not in mid-October at dinner hour.

When Axel arrives, the decibel level of the screaming leaps into the red zone, where needles would flutter a warning, and pain stabs up her Eustachian tubes. *No STOP Turn it down It's okay Confess your sins NONONO It's okay, honey, calm down, be still, be still, be still.*

His face is separated into features that she sees one at a time. Thin hooked nose. Broad forehead with Neanderthal overhang. Bushy brows. Alert azure eye looking levelly at hers. Thin neck with prominent Adam's apple and ropey cords. Wide purple lips. Peaked chin with an almost-dimple. *Put it together* – a new voice, resonant and commanding.

The features coalesce into a beaming face, Axel's thankfully familiar face. He is carrying packages wrapped in brown freezer paper and Spanish champagne in a sleek black bottle. She tells herself it is silly to be afraid of Axel, a man who doesn't like to see a plant wither. He leans down and kisses her, the cool of autumn on his lips. She takes the packages to the fridge, brings out cassis and two long-stemmed glasses, thinking about the fullness of his listening, his quirky, curious questions which stretch the boundaries of her thought. A geyser of champagne explodes across the kitchen and all the crying screaming sounds uncork, spilling through her insides as she pours a finger of liquid blackberry into each glass, which he tops with pale yellow champagne. She loops her hand around the curved cool bottom of the glass, tucking the stem between two fingers. "Cheers."

"To us," he replies. "To tonight."

꒱ ꒱ ꒱

The night is deep black with a needlepoint sky and a cold crescent moon distant on the horizon. A small bird, smaller than a sparrow but bigger than a hummingbird, glides out a window into the ebony currents, which will carry her far into the civilizations of the air. At first she races up a current just to feel her power, then dips to watch the earth and its people form patterns that spin by, too quickly to grasp.

Wanting to get away from the confusion, she flies high into a grey moist patch, a low altocumulus cloud which fogs her lucid night vision temporarily. Above soar the creatures of the night: birds of many shapes and moving whorls of light in pale and rainbow hues.

One of the birds detaches itself from a small flock and flies quietly beside her.

You are troubled down there. The words appear in her head, but she knows they are his.

What do you mean? she thinks.

You have left your body. Something unbearable must be happening to you.

I don't have a human body. I have a bird body like you.

Ah. You are new here.

It is too familiar to be new. I think I used to come here as a child.

Then I weep for you, my friend.

Why? I am free here.

Because you are chained there.

And you?

I am tortured there. I am what they call a 'disappeared'.

Where have you disappeared from?

If I think about that, I will return there. I cannot do that for they have just started on me.

Started what?

Teaching me.

A suction sound pops like a plunger and then there is only a small hole, blacker then space itself, next to her where he flew.

❧ ❧ ❧

8

Baker is snoring, curled on the sofa bed in the studio. A trail of discarded clothes – jacket, shoes, socks, sweatshirt, jeans, and a crumpled heap of lacy underthings – wends to the bed. The empty indentation beside her looks like a fossil imprint: male pickup, 1990s, early North American adult, about six foot, resting posture. Kendra has come to sort the mail, handwrite a few replies to the women who send small pleas and untold anecdotes, often in the form of dreadful poems they dream Survivors will record. Kendra slaps letters into piles: bookings for Baker; bills and accounts for Angel; musical enquiries for Lena; porn, by request, to Baker; pleas to herself. Baker thinks a secretary could at least screen it, but Kendra is afraid an allusion will slip by unnoticed, and another woman slide into the zone of permanent silence and despair.

The sofa bed emits a metallic whimper as Baker stretches and hums. Kendra tosses a pile of letters onto the bed. Baker has claimed specialist status with regard to men; she says she's the only Survivor who likes them. "The only one who fucks them,"

Angel once corrected. "We all like them." Survivors make a game of the perverts, trying to identify them by handwriting, though perversion is as common as laughter, or poems, in their letters, and they defy category.

Baker squirms up, rubbing at her forehead. Naked nipple eyes stare from small mounds on her thin torso. "When did you get here?" she yawns, and slits a suspicious envelope with her finger.

"Check this!" Baker flaps the letter like she's found a lost key. " 'Your knees turn to *peanut butter* around my *pumpernickel* back as we join the accelerating rhythms of "Almost a Woman." ' " Everyone wants to do it to Survivors' rhythms. The banality of this embarrasses Kendra, but Baker thinks they should publish a book called *Porn Letters to Survivors.*

Oh lord, a letter from Hannahjean. Kendra hasn't seen Karl and Hannahjean in years. A tiny floral spray tears as she opens the flap, releasing a scent of lilacs. Hannahjean is not a letter-writer. There must be something wrong.

Baker gapes down at the fossil imprint beside her. "Where's what's-his-name?"

"Flew the coop, it looks like. What was his name?" Kendra glances at the letter.

"Guess he was afraid he might have to try again this morning. Luke, I think."

"Do I know him?" Hannahjean's handwriting is wide and loopy as if she never got past primer paper.

"Na. Don't think you will either."

"Why not?" There it is. A paragraph that starts with *The doctor.*

"He couldn't get it up. No matter what I did. It just lay there like a skin full of custard."

Found a little lump. "Maybe you scared him." Not cancer, Christ, she hoped it wasn't cancer.

"Of course I scared him. They like that. Fuck the bitch good.

Show her who's boss. Makes a great one-nighter. Energy galore."
She bounces her hips like a fast dribbler going down the court.

"Where's Gary?" It's difficult to concentrate when Baker's around. The bed is squeaking outrageously.

"Yukon, for all I know." With a grand gesture, Baker flings the blankets onto the floor. "You know what?" she asks, fumbling with yesterday's lace.

"What?" *in my left breast*

"The last three have been impotent."

"So maybe you'll cut down on the slimeballs." Kendra returns to her letter.

Hannahjean doesn't know if the lump is malignant or not. She is going back for a test with a needle next week. Hannahjean was so frightened by illness she often chose not to gather information. When she had a cold or a flu, she lingered in bed for days, left everything to Kendra, who cooked meals, watched her siblings, and nursed her mother with warm fluids, aspirin, and massages, until she was ready to face life again. Hannahjean could not manage a crisis without Kendra.

But she can't go to her now. Not after the spectre of Karl flickered in the doorway of her bedroom the last time she was there.

The second-hand stores on Queen and Spadina are havens for Baker and Quillan, as much as Isabella's Library. They speed through a pre-tour shopping spree, allay the lonely chafe of their failures in love. They boom with too-loud laughter while they don outrageous costumes. Only Baker actually buys one. When they get back to the studio, Angel is practising to their latest tape. Her square face, softened in the cantaloupe light of dusk, looks almost handsome, and the twitch in her jaw muscles is down to a flicker. She invites them home for basmati rice, jewelled with glazed vegetables, and Lena's blend of curry.

9

Angel and Lena own a shoebox of a house with a sloping front verandah that cuts off the sunlight. "Beats that Hogs Hollow ice palace I grew up in," Angel grunts. Her latest project, puttying panes into the storm windows and planing their edges for winter, is strewn all over the verandah. Over every crack in the plaster, every leak in the plumbing, every unsheathed, frazzled piece of prehistoric wiring she fixes, Angel murmurs an incantation of reproach against the glitter of her childhood mansion, the girlhood that taught her how to arrange orchids and walk with a bearing so haughty even now she can't hide it. She replaces the plane in the canvas sack, where she keeps her tools and workbooks, and slings it all over her shoulder. Baker says Angel carries tools like a scapular pregnancy.

The pungent aromas of saffron rice and curry breeze through the house, as warm as the greeting Lena calls from the kitchen. Angel pours herself a single malt and offers drinks around. With a farewell-to-Gary tie-one-on glimmer in her eyes, Baker asks for a martini. In her dangerous moods Baker plays AIDS roulette at the bars, and martinis are the drink she does it with. Kendra carries her bourbon into the kitchen.

"Have you heard from Cornelia?" The dollgirl's eviscerated guts linger like an unwanted snatch of melody.

The smile coasts down Lena's face, leaving it slushy. "She's at boarding school. She never calls during term." Her face searches for form.

"You'd hear if something happened, right?"

Lena lifts the lid on the pot of curry, dropping in shrimp with boiled baby skins. "I can't think why I wouldn't. Even Norman isn't that cruel." She spoons a curry-slick shrimp into Kendra's mouth. Lena is too sharp to let this one slide. She asks pointedly about Kendra's own well-being.

"It's not *me*. Nothing happened to me," Kendra says. "No, no. It's this dream I had." She describes the weird feeling that her dream was premonitory, the dollgirl someone she knew, even loved.

Lena's eyes rove around Kendra's face. "It wasn't Cornelia." She turns back to the stove. "If I were you, I'd give it more thought."

Baker is prancing around the living room, holding the sequined mini outfit she bought like a shield in front of her. She waves her empty glass for Angel to fill before they adjourn for dinner. Kendra pours herself another bourbon. Too many of her own worries need pickling to stay sober for Baker.

"How goes the baby search?" Baker enquires, as they arrange themselves around the long pine table. Angel and Lena glance at each other.

"*In vitro* is a world of its own," Lena says. "The technology makes intercourse, no, that's not quite it, makes love, seem *passé*. Like eating red meat, that sort of thing."

Angel gets up to pour wine.

"Too weird for you?" asks Kendra.

"Nothing is too weird when you want a baby as much as I do."

"As much as *we* do," Angel adds, leaving the wine in front of Baker.

"I think it's weird you're not talking about the doctor." Baker tops up her half-full glass. "What'd he say, what was he like?"

"A very strange set-up," Angel says. "Here's this guy, with his wife and daughter both working for him, one as a receptionist, the other as nurse. And he's, like, getting every woman under the sun pregnant. And they're all making as if we're one big family."

"Angel's mad because they wouldn't let her come in with me."

"Go on. You didn't ask." Baker thinks Angel should stay out of it until Lena sees the sperm in the tube.

"I am one of the parents in all this." Angel's motionless lips pack her statement with generations of quiet authority.

"It was unbelievable. When we got there, the waiting room was humming, buzzing with women, most of them pregnant. It sounded like a concert hall before we play. Then I said to the nurse, 'I want my partner to come in with me,' and, blam, you could hear a pin drop."

"Husbands went in," Angel says. "We saw them."

"It's no place to take a stand." Baker raises a flat hand, like a traffic cop's warning.

"I just wanted to talk to the man."

"Nobody talks to doctors," Baker says, pouring another glass. "People listen to doctors."

Lena passes around the platters. "That was true with this one. I mean, he asked a few questions, about my medical history and the relationships I've had with men, but mostly he put on a show about fertility. Starring himself. He actually projected slides and transparencies onto a screen in his office with bar graphs of the success rate of his clinic compared to other ones in Toronto, Ottawa, and Vancouver."

"Tell them about the screensaver," Angel prompts.

"A giant protozoan sperm. I could hardly take my eyes off it long enough to listen."

The curry is plump with shrimp and chicken. Floating pin-wheels of okra and florets of broccoli add to its flavour and colour.

"So did he take you?" Baker hasn't started to eat.

"He almost didn't. When he started to compare the success of his program with international contenders, like the United States and Mexico – a highly fertile part of the world, I'll have you know – I sang the praises of Italy, where that sixty-year-old grandmother got pregnant, and raved about Britain, where the first male pregnancy just occurred. He got quite frosty and informed me that the man had spontaneously aborted both the womb and the child at sixteen weeks. He only relented when he realized I'd already had a child and was only thirty-five. His best success, he said, is with women in their middle twenties to late thirties. After that fertility, and related urges, drop off, virtually plummeting around the mid-forties, when women get ornery and gross."

"He said that?" Baker asks.

"That wasn't his funniest," Lena says. "He told me, quite seriously, that fertility reaches a zenith on March fifteenth, May first, and the summer solstice, but skips April because it's the month of immaculate conception."

Baker, though a voracious eater for someone so thin, still hasn't touched her food. She had to be thinking about Ursie and Linc.

Kendra tings her fork against her wineglass. "I have an announcement." Their attention rivets immediately.

"I have found the title song we've been looking for."

The title song is the glue in a recording. Everyone wants to hear more.

"I don't want to upstage you"; Kendra draws Baker into a glance.

"But our new album will be called" – she pauses, her years on stage setting off an automatic kind of timing – "*Ghostchildren*."

Three glasses wave through the air towards Baker, whose face comes afire like a prairie sun. She chants every verse of the song, the revised version, then goes silent, her face as mauve as the feelings that hang in the air. She lets Kendra tell the others about Ursie.

No one seems to know what to say. The two kinds of creation seem to war with each other. Baker disappears into the kitchen and rattles around for a while. She returns with an extra place setting. She pours milk into a tall plastic cup and fills the plate with tiny bits of food. "This is for Ursie," she says.

Lena stares in faint horror at the empty chair. "Cornelia turns fifteen this year," she says.

Fifteen. Kendra still thinks of Cornelia as seven or eight, probably her age when Lena left Jamaica. The dollgirl is much younger than fifteen, closer to Ursie's age. She feels close all the time, ready to pop into a fantasy, dream, even a conversation, as if she could speak through Kendra's mouth. Who who who could she be? The question haunts Kendra all the time, everywhere.

Baker is chattering the nonsense grown women speak to dogs and children, while feeding Ursie the ghost. Lena, the stare swelling her face like a sting, removes the chair from under Baker's curved arm and drags it back to the corner of the dining room.

"I can't do an album called *Ghostchildren*," Lena says. "I don't even know if I can do a song."

Baker looks like she's been slapped. "Why the fuck not?"

"You won't understand."

"Try me."

There is a long silence.

"C'mon, Lena."

"I believe in ghosts. Spirits. My mother taught me about them when I was little. They are part of my culture. We call them 'duppies'. They are pure evil. They bring disaster everywhere. You see, when a person is alive, they can control their inner evil by the kindness in their hearts, the logic of their minds, but when they die, this control disappears, and the evil is released as a duppy to wander all over the earth, homeless and spiteful and mean. If they get a proper burial, and their earthly troubles are laid to rest so they actually enter their graves, maybe this won't happen, but you have to be very careful, perform many ceremonies, and you can't ever be certain. Ursie had none of this. And now we are inviting her into our homes, feeding her our food, writing songs to her. This is not right. I am sure down to the marrow of the bones, to the blood in my veins, that if we do this, if we sing this song, disaster will follow us."

"Ridiculous," Baker mutters, into the silence. "Ursie's not evil."

But she puts the plate and cup away.

"Do it anyway," Kendra whispers while Baker's away.

Angel shuffles around the table with the wine. The sound of dribbling gurgles and glugs in the vacuum as she tops everyone's glass. The food tastes heavy and sour.

Baker launches herself from her seat when the phone rings. She trips over the very chair she has slammed into the wall. "Oh," they hear, "yeah, just a minute," sunset in her voice.

Lena stays on the phone a long time, listening and asking terse serious questions like Where are you? Do you want me to come? When she comes back, her face is more yellow than when she talked about ghosts.

She has to leave. A friend is in trouble. She's going to meet her at Isabella's.

It's a quarter to eleven and Kendra's head is throbbing. Pictures of the dollgirl flash in her far mind, like a lighthouse beacon. In the kitchen, Lena asks Kendra to drive her downtown. On the way, Kendra persuades her to try about *Ghostchildren*. For Baker's sake.

Lena's friend has a stay-away aura. She sits with a spine-numbing straightness, as if she might catch something from the grime of her surroundings. Kendra could swear her elbows float a hair above the table and don't actually touch it.

"I'll leave you to it," Kendra whispers to Lena. She ducks down an aisle towards the history of music before Lena can invite her to join them.

Isabella's, or its proprietor, stocks great songbooks, dating as far back as he can get them. Kendra finds one on Screamin' Elsa McCree, an obscure jazz singer from the Mississippi delta who hollered most of her blues in Paris and Madrid. Toots Hoskin recorded some of her tunes. Rumour had it that her better ones went unrecorded, not salvaged by Folkways or the senior John Hammond, because she departed from Southern turf. Kendra is dying to have a go at her.

She winks at Lena as she drops to a corner sofa with the prized volume. Ebe, the proprietor, reads at his usual table. Two other customers, kids with their facial hair still in tufts, are arguing over something intellectual. Lena's conversation looks very intense.

Ebe looks at Kendra, and she waves. Something about him repulses her, though his kindness is legendary. He gives away books to people without money. He helps kids on the street, or through college. No one steals from him. She hopes it isn't his incredible ugliness that puts her off, though it does contribute. She feels violent around him, as if she wants to pummel the injustice from the whole world, starting with his twisted face. Ridiculous, but it happens and she blames him.

Lena is signalling Kendra to come over. She waves the McCree book through the air, trying to decline. Lena points emphatically at the empty chair beside her.

"Monique has just left her husband," Lena says. Monique has mustard-coloured blotches on her face, either a pigmentation problem or aging bruises. "She needs a ride to her friend's house, if you can take her."

In the car, Lena and Monique continue their discussion. In a musical voice, honey-silk and cooing, Lena coddles Monique towards honesty, hoping to free her. Kendra would crawl into the cradle of that voice herself if she could. She pictures Angel caressing Lena's body with that timbre vibrating through her, flowing down from her ears to her fingertips. Who could resist the lilt in that voice, the love? Monique, seated in the front, her head tilted towards Lena, who slants forward from the back, cannot. Monique's shoulders drop as her tension begins to ease. Kendra can almost hear her thoughts: Lena doesn't despise me. Lena isn't judging me. There's no contempt in Lena's voice. Maybe I am okay. Maybe it wasn't my fault.

"It wasn't the hitting that got me the most," Monique confesses. "It was how he wake me up in my *cul*."

ℐ ℐ ℐ

The toddler, running on chubby legs through a pasture, stumbles, falls, lies with her face in the earth, her rump in the air. A cloud, mucus green like the colour of fear or vomit, enmists her forehead and temples. Something moves in and out of her rump, a twig, a pencil, maybe an iron object. Her hands clutch tufts of grass, stones, bits of earth. She stuffs fistfuls of dirt into her mouth, chews her opposition to the in-and-out rhythm. The yellow cloud, swirling around her head, thickens and descends until her entire torso is shrouded by its thick vapours. A bird, smaller than a sparrow but larger than a hummingbird, flits out through the fog and disappears into the clear blue summer skies.

ℐ ℐ ℐ

The dark shadow from a car looms into Kendra's peripheral vision. Instinctively, she slams her foot on the brakes. Their car skids, halts, angled towards a motionless, parked vehicle, as if Kendra thought the street was starting to curve. But that wasn't what happened. She had faded out for Monique's story, missed everything Monique said. Christ. Joseph. But no one is hurt.

"Will Monique be okay?" Kendra asks on the way home.

"For now. She still thinks she could have been different, stopped the whole thing."

"You are so patient. I would have demanded to know why she stays with a jerk who blames her every time he hiccups."

"She wouldn't have been able to answer you. She just sees he's going off and thinks she isn't doing things right."

"I'll never understand."

"She loves him. And he loves her, probably more than she'll ever love him. He's terrified of losing her. And she senses the fear in him, knows she will never feel as sure of anyone as she is of him. After all, everything he does, no matter how mean, is designed to bind her to him. Maybe a thrashing now and then is better than being anxious all the time over some guy who hardly knows you're alive after six months."

"So why leave now?"

"I think it's because of the rape."

"What rape?"

"The one she just told us about. When he woke her up in the middle of the night by jamming himself in her rear."

God, how much did I miss? "What did she do?"

"She screamed at him. She thought he didn't know he was hurting her. He told her *qu'une putain*, a whore like her, deserved what she got."

"She thinks she provoked that?"

"She said the name of another man in her sleep."

10

Back home, strung out on rage and coffee, Kendra can't even try to sleep. Monique and the toddler swirl on the surface of her mind. The toddler's upended rump starts to glisten like a dollgirl's; the infant's wailing cries rise; a shadow rolls the toddler over and spreads her legs. Kendra's own hips are moving rhythmically. Exhausted, she stops struggling against her own mind and yields to its wilderness. She curls into her favourite armchair, closes her eyes, and lets herself descend through the blackness that divides her mind.

⁓ ⁓ ⁓

The tyke lies in her bedcrib. Alert, alone, listening for footsteps. Someone will pick her up soon. Heavy footsteps clomp towards her doorway. A large hand descends towards her head and strokes her hair gently, murmuring words that make no sense: there, there, be a good girl, don't cry, little honey, you'll like this, you will, it won't hurt. The hand rocks and pets her, until her body arches into its comforting warmth. It slides down, tickles her down there, arranges her legs into a chubby diamond. A thick finger squiggles along the crack in her flesh, wends into the tiny hole where she pees, making circles inside, then traces a line backwards to the other hole, tickling around its edges until it relaxes and opens to the pokes, and her bum wiggles and squirms. Suddenly the finger bears down into the crack line, so hard it hurts. She wants to cry, but the hand speeds swiftly up her torso and squeezes her neck until the sound drops back and her mouth drops open. One, two, three fingers push in. The other hand rubs something that looks like a bottle above her face.

A few drops squirt from the tip of the bottle and land beside her nose. A fist of fingers jams into her mouth, pushes it wide for the bottle. The bottle enters her mouth, feels warm like the fingers, but thicker. Uh oh. It's going too far, down her throat. She can't breathe, is gagging. Her mouth is stretched like an elastic. The bottle slides in and out, harder, faster. Her whole body jolts with its spasmodic rhythm. Slam: it rams the back of her throat. A volcano erupts in her mouth.

↶ ↶ ↶

Kendra is holding her knees to her chest, rocking and sobbing with sounds so primitive they seem to flow from a universal well of mourning. An invisible umbilical cord connects that hurt child to every hurt child: to napalmed children, swollen-bellied children, gassed and starving rebel children, garbage-picking urchin children, drug-numbed hooker children, children born with AIDS. They're so alone, deserted by their families, in a world without comfort. She feels compelled to write a song to the tyke, the infant in the bedcrib, to let her know other people understand what happened to her.

Exhaustion anaesthetizes Kendra's limbs. The reverie has sapped her own body. She stumbles three times on her way to her guitar, and lifting it requires a rockhard will, like Sysyphus'. But a song is there, or two lines of a chorus, *duum duum, da dum, duum duum, da dum*, in a slow rocking lilt. She plays it in a few keys until she is sure she's got it right. It's a simple song, like a lullaby. She hopes Baker can find the words.

11

Baker's face has a twisted look that means it wasn't a good night. While Kendra and Lena were tending to Monique, Baker dropped into an after-hours place. Kendra doesn't know which she dreads most with Baker, her love affairs or her one-night stands. These differ by about two weeks.

They play old favourites to remind themselves of the joy of Quillan and Baker. Baker has been studying voice and wants to sing lead when they record "Ghostchildren." Baker's voice, while passable, never quite hovers on the high edge of a note. "Ghostchildren," light on melody like a talking blues, is a good song for her. They run through it one line at a time. Kendra's rendition is heavy with melody. Baker gets tuneful as they go on. It looks like she'll be able to do it. She pops behind her drums, sings it over and over, pleading with Kendra to harmonize on the chorus. The twisted lines disappear from her face. It's a good time to approach her.

How to convey the urgency of this song? Kendra starts with Monique and the straw that broke her, the anal rape while she was sleeping. She does not mention she blanked out for that part of the story and had to hear it from Lena afterwards, or that she can't recall what distracted her from Monique's revelation. She describes to Baker the vision of the infant or toddler in the crib, enduring an experience like Monique's, harmful, yet something else Kendra can't name. The imperative need to reach this child, to sing to her a soothing, simple melody with words like shards, to bear witness to her story.

"I need that baby to know we're here. I wrote a song to her, a kind of lullaby." Kendra plays the chorus. *Bum bum, ba bum. Bum bum, ba bum.* "The music has to rock her. The words have to tell her we know."

"What happens for her?" Baker wants details, oddities, off-beat sensations.

"It's horrible." Kendra remembers the shifting of sound. "She's caught in a world with no sound. When bad things are happening to her, all sound disappears. There should be noise, but there isn't."

Kendra tries to explain the transition from acute hearing to no sound. "It's not like being deaf. Her hearing is almost hyper-extended in the beginning. Each noise, each creak, each breath, is loud, fortissimo, and broad, almost largo.

"It's like she's accustomed to it – it builds as the footsteps come towards her, then something strange happens to the tempo. It slows, gradually, almost separates from the actual sound, as if step and echo reverse. Then, suddenly, the sound snaps off. Bang, gone, right when the hand reaches down. That's where the melody shifts. *Buuum. Buum. Ba bum. Buuum, buuum. Ba bum.*" She hums the melody, exaggerating the shift.

"Sound, sound. No sound. Sound. Sound. No sound," Baker follows.

"Perfect! That's it."

They do it together: guitar, rhythm, voices. They do it many times, experimenting with the length of the notes, changing the key, adding harmony. When they finish, Baker is in motion. She grills Kendra about every aspect of her vision: infant or toddler? crib or bed? specific age or like an aggregate of ages? diaper or panties? What about her other senses? were there smells? thoughts? colours? what was dominant?

Kendra tries to describe the child's split-stream sense of the world. "Horrible things are happening to her and it's like she doesn't quite know what they are, but she does; she doesn't quite know who's doing them but she does. She knows and doesn't know, feels and doesn't feel, almost in the same way she hears then deafens. It's like the recording is too powerful for the instruments and can't be registered. She feels a volcano erupt in her body but tells herself that's silly, volcanoes aren't inside people. You know, that child's absolute sense of reality, like you're a boy or a girl, and if you're a girl you can't feel like a boy or vice versa."

"And grown-ups don't do bad things to little girls."

"Parents don't." Kendra presses her guitar into her abdomen. "Mummies and daddies."

"Which was this?"

"Her daddy."

Baker scrambles to the roll-top desk where she does her writing. She writes, paces, writes, makes coffee, crosses out everything she's written, curses, bangs on the drums, writes, makes more coffee, mutters, lies down on the sofa and stares at the ceiling, rocks in the chair, goes back to her desk. After about an hour and a half, she whoops, "I've got it. Or at least a working draft."

> Sound. Sound.
> No sound.
> Sound. Sound.
> No sound.
>
> Daddy's in me
> making me feel

like there's a jackhammer
from head to heel.

Sound. Sound.
No sound.
Sound. Sound.
No sound.

I'm out the window
I'm in a tree
I'm anywhere
but inside me.

Sound. Sound.
No sound.
Sound. Sound.
No sound.

I leave her there
on the bed
No one home
in her head.
If I stay with her
we'll both be dead.

Sound. Sound.
No sound.
Sound. Sound.
No sound.

I go to sleep
I think it's over
When I wake up
I won't remember.

Sound. Sound.
No sound.
Sound. Sound.
No sound.

Baker has done a superb job of fleshing out Kendra's vision, giving it the meat of words. Baker's mind, Kendra's heart, their partnership deeper than their separateness. Kendra feels a gratitude that brings the rocking crying wailing rippling near her surface. She tries to thank Baker, who brushes it off, prolonging their union. Together, they search for a title. "Lullaby" is too benign, "Sound for a hurt child" too general. Abuse has become a generic word and lost the punch of clarity.

There's a gap in the arc of the song, or a title would emerge. The song abandons the child, leaves her empty at the end, and the listener too. Kendra slides into her trance to comb her interior. Her eyes roll backwards into her head until only the whites show under the fluttering lids. She finds the wailing sounds, slips underneath them. There is that girl, lying in the crib, alone still. "She doesn't know we're here; we haven't reached her," she says, her voice liquid. A verse emerges as if someone else is speaking:

Little girl
Little one
Go to sleep
You're not alone.

12

Kendra is so glad to see Axel that in a burst of rare spontaneity she throws her arms around his waist and pulls his body against hers, kissing him with her wide-open eyes glued to every familiar crag on his face. The stiff crags soften in the meltdown of her eyes; the rock face turns to plasticine, and the crystalline eyes go puddly blue. He does love her, she realizes, and is amazed at this thing, more miraculous than the differentness of snowflakes and bird songs and sand grains, it's her own tiny soul print he wants pressed into his.

Yet she pulls away from his desire, and her own.

"I can't go backwards," he says.

He means to no sex, and she agrees. She doesn't know how he waited so long, though he tells her enough times. "For you, Kendie. No one else. You." But the step has been taken. She won't ask him to forbear again. Even Axel has limits, even love.

"It's stirring me up," she says, finally.

"You knew it would," he reminds her. She has stunned him. He thought she'd be mundane in bed, but her forwardness, her agility, verged on obscene. She could lie at odd angles for long spells of time. Her limbs felt like clay he could sculpt any which way. He doesn't want to understand, or be sensitive. He wants to enjoy.

"I'm having all kinds of dreams," she offers, as a probe. Does he love her enough to pull back?

"Me too," he says. "I dreamed you and Angel built a white picket fence high enough to touch the clouds. Inside was a mansion with cottage-type rooms, and an entire park and playground in the back. We lived there with our kids and their kids, in a secluded little paradise. The trouble was, the gate only opened from the outside, and you clipped the key to your belt on a big, round holder. So you could come and go, but I couldn't get out, not unless you let me."

"You made that up," she accuses, trying to laugh. That's a description of his *mother*.

"Not the feelings."

"They're from back there, your past."

"So are yours. We've honoured them."

He has been a saint, she has to admit. She slips behind him, massages his neck. It is the closest she can come to telling him he's right.

In the kitchen, he scrubs the potatoes until they are nearly bald and tells her his parents are coming in for the weekend. This is not welcome news. Axel changes when his parents are around, lapses into a state of precocious intellect, his adult being in temporary suspension. Kendra feels like she's lost him, though he's still there. She whisks the orange sauce for the salmon. She has let herself need him too much.

"I have to work most of the weekend," she says. "We have to get a tape finished before the tour."

"I realize my mother is tough," he responds. "But I'd like you to see them for one evening."

"Here?" Kendra asks. "She's better when she can't run things."

He disagrees with her analysis. He finds his mother easiest when everything goes her way. This is exactly the Axel whom Kendra doesn't like to see.

As he often does when he's preoccupied, Axel sets the table with a combination of newspapers and dishes. Unrest in the north is worsening, a Tuxtla or Oka he hopes won't erupt before his meetings in Ottawa. A coalition to preserve smoking in restaurants and commercial buildings is flooding the media with opinion editorials and letters. And now there's the visit from his parents. He thinks Friday is the best night for a dinner together. He will take them to the theatre Saturday, brunch alone with them on Sunday. The rest of the weekend, they will be with other family.

Kendra fiddles with the stereo all through dinner. She craves *sound*, big crescendos of it for her agitation. The tyke listens too, straining for a music that will calm her tense vigil. Kendra tells Axel about Monique, about Baker's one-nighters, even about Ursie, but not about the tyke, not about the near-accident. Her mistrust of men doesn't extend to all of Axel, but she doesn't give him the leeway she gives Lena or Baker either.

They are both tired. Axel, pushing to finish a brief on the hazards of inside air, is irritated with employers who want him to criticize the statistics of findings that require costly change. Kendra, the adrenalin draining from her system, is blitzed from sleeplessness, effort, and visions of violence.

Too lazy to walk an extra two blocks, they pick up a video from the corner drugstore and nestle like spoons on the sofa to watch. Before the credits are over, Axel's breathing slows into the sighing whispers of sleep. Propping herself on an elbow, Kendra watches the muscles of his face slacken, his alert, though coarse, visage fall into innocence, its rebirth occurring before her eyes. When his eyelids flutter up at her, she invites him to bed.

There, engulfed by a love unlike anything she's ever known, Kendra leans over Axel's reborn face, engages his naked crystal eyes, and sees his soul at the window, or close enough to make her extend her hand down his lean, hard body.

↵ ↵ ↵

A bird, smaller than a sparrow but larger than a humming-bird, soars quickly skyward. It is a cloudless night and the big-bellied moon is almost full, the heavens brightly lit. More creatures than before populate the sky; perhaps they gain visibil-ity on such a clear night.

No. The familiar voice appears like a thought in her head. It is because you can see more on your second visit.

Who are you? she thinks in return.

We met the last time you were here, he replies. I am Gabriel. I am your guide.

You are okay then? I worried when you left so abruptly.

I talked too much about what was happening to my earth self when I wasn't in his body. It caused me to return for a while. That is one of the things we cannot do here.

Where is here?

The half-world. It is halfway between life and death and pro-vides a home for the spirits whose earth bodies are tormented but not yet ready to die.

Who comes here?

I will show you, but first you must pick a name. It must not be the same as your earth name or you will return when someone addresses you.

Can I pick any name?

It is best if it does not overlap with your earth world – no names of friends or relatives, local streets or public buildings. That way it will not overlap with your earth thoughts. Many of us choose the names of people we admire but don't know, movie stars or characters in books. It doesn't have to be a female name; you can be male or female, young or old, black, white, yellow, green, anything you want. Except yourself.

Billie then. Billie Holiday.

Come Billie. I will tour you through the night.

Gabriel and Billie fly easily together. He is a robin-sized bird with the plumage reversed so his underbelly is dark and the rest of him red. They pass many others flying in pairs and flocks or just soloing. They look like earth birds but always something is different, either a simple change like Gabriel's plumage or something major, like a second set of wings.

What are the whorls of lights? Billie thinks. Drifting rainbows, the whorls are beautiful and small, unlike anything she has ever seen in the earth world.

They belong to the very ill, to people with AIDS and cancer, cholera, malnutrition, bubonic plague. They are different from us; they are in constant pain so they don't go back and forth very often, and have little need for any physical shape. But, look, here is Astor. Astor is a bluebird with a flamboyant streak of chartreuse down her side.

She is but a child, Billie shrieks in her head.

Calm down, my friend. Gabriel's firm thinking steels into her mind. She arrived here as a child and will remain here as a child until her earth life is through. She is one of the lucky ones. None of her older selves have returned.

ɔ ɔ ɔ

13

A fluttery kind of panic skitters around Kendra's stomach as she realizes yet another night of lovemaking has flown into darkness. Her worry about telling Axel is overshadowed by a flickering sense that she is in deep trouble, her mind has a will of its own and operates without her, blotting out some things, high-lighting others, in a pattern beyond her control. Pushing her mind towards their lovemaking, she remembers she initiated it herself, ached for it with every inch of her being, and still can remember nothing.

In panic gear, her mind skims its own lunar surfaces: Axel's parents want her to call them Sam and Ada; she can't or they'll become like Karl and Hannahjean and she wants to keep them formal and predictable – Dr. and Mrs. Berne. The informal ones slip in too close, lose the definition of proper roles; some things have to stay in their places. Axel wants to go away with her for a few days. Survivors have to prepare for their winter tour; good money can be made around Christmas if they have recordings to sell. Kendra is always grateful to be working during holidays, an easy excuse to not see her family the one time they pretend to be happy. Hannahjean may be very sick now; if so, she'll have to visit her. Kendra would never forgive herself if Hannahjean died without her; she'd die in an infantile terror and what would happen to her soul then? Not to mention her own soul, sin-stained with yellow, like tobacco fingers. Axel wants time alone with her before the tour; now it's him she abandons over the holidays. Meanwhile Baker is falling apart, drinking too much, sleeping with jerks, unable to see what bad shape she's in. Lena is worried about getting pregnant; the nurse requested a special counselling appointment and Lena thinks the program's going to give them the boot. If Kendra disappears with Axel, who will pull the group together? Kendra is terrified to be without Survivors; they are the only people she has ever relied on. Until now, until Axel. Whom she loves, but resents, because it's too hard to love when you wake up, well, birdbrained: how can you be anything but furious at a person who quakes the earth of your mind, sends everything aflutter, even if you love him more than anything else in the world?

"The Incest Lullaby," that's the title. She has no idea where it came from, but it's right, like "Ursula and the Ghostchildren." Which should be the album title instead of just *Ghostchildren*, but using Ursie's name would invade Baker's privacy. Not that Baker would mind. She welcomes any recognition that might transform her from nobody into somebody. Perhaps it might trickle down to her soul.

Baker would be better with Axel's parents than Kendra. Baker would recognize the plays and operas they saw, the politicians they lampooned, the books that have moulded their lives. She could banter her way into their three-way conversations as if she were born into them. Not Kendra. What does she know? Music and the country, and folk music at that. Kendra can appreciate Axel's mother's distaste for her. When Mrs. Berne got married, she dropped her career as a nurse, turned family into home and career with a zest that fed her energies instead of depleting them, as with Hannahjean. Axel is brilliant enough to become part of the small, intellectual elite who make an international trade of ideas. What is he doing with a rock singer who barely finished high school? Kendra doesn't think it's the Catholic-Jewish thing that makes the difference, but the disparity in wealth and culture. She is as backwoods as Karl, would rather kayak the Charlottes than fly to New York for a show at the Met. Axel, for all the folksiness of his concerns, possesses an urban arrogance that finds country values amusing yet discardable, like polyester Sunday clothes.

Axel's mother, no further inside than the foyer, and still in her coat, offers a sack of Montreal-style bagels to Kendra. Enough for a month, Kendra thinks, not unaware of being included in the attempt to "make life a little easier" that Mrs. Berne uses as an excuse to indulge Axel in the most excessive ways. Mrs. Berne's quiet, tailored appearance makes Kendra feel shopworn, as if even her best clothes are threaded with tinsel, or shiny at the knees. She mutters an excuse, or a parody of an excuse, and disappears to the bathroom for a fresh look in the mirror. Her blouse is undone one tarty button too many, and her skirt is too long. She doesn't own a skirt of ordinary length. Her hair is brassy and untamed, like a shout. She rakes it with her fingers, trying to push the curls into an orderly frame. The chaos of her just keeps popping to the surface. They'll see it, for sure. "You look fine," Axel assures her, having slipped in behind her. He makes clown faces into the mirror beside her image. "Everyone in Montreal looks like my mother," he says. He dips a finger into the smudge of mascara under her eye and draws a line of war paint along her cheekbone. "Now that's beautiful," he says. She tilts his head down, kisses his big, wine-coloured lips.

Duck was an inspired choice for dinner. The dark, succulent

meat, roasted in brown sauce and served with caramelized fruit, delights Axel's mother. She tears off strips of its crisp, forbidden skin, proclaiming how good it is to indulge oneself every now and then, while giving her husband, who is not at all tempted to overeat, portions equal to her own. The relief, the gratitude, at seeing her meal accepted surprises Kendra with its fierceness. Axel's father sneaks the skin back onto the serving platter, making her privy to a family ritual, a family whose foibles are things to enjoy. Axel doles out wine from bottles, selected just for his father, and they have a silly, erudite discussion about the relative merits of regions and vineyards in France and Quebec.

Axel's mother recalls a feast they once ate on a picnic table far behind a farmhouse in northern France. There, on a table laid with silver and linen, in a small enclave of trees with the sun setting and the birds twittering, she had savoured a juicy, tender roast. "It turned out to be horsemeat," she exclaims, "delicious, just like your duck."

Duck and horsemeat, the same? This isn't acceptance, no. This is good manners, urbane pleasure taken in something quaint and rustic. Kendra might as well have served moose or venison, the real game of her childhood feasts. She gets up to clear, nudges Axel on the shoulder when he fails to join her, watches his mother squirm with discontent. Axel in the kitchen is not her idea of a son.

Kendra meets them again at Axel's after her rehearsal and their theatre. Mrs. Berne is in an ebullient mood from an entire evening with "her two men." She slips an arm through Kendra's and steers her to the kitchen, so they can brew tea together. The warmth of this maternal gesture, the inclusion into Axel's close-knit family, enchants Kendra, seduces her by the nostalgia for what-wasn't that lodges in her heart. She forgets her annoyance at the horsemeat, and at serving two idle men in the living room, and arranges crackers and cookies and small sections of fruit on a platter. Hannahjean used to prepare platters of chips and dip with fat slices of salami, pickles, and devilled eggs and send Kendra, dolled up in a ruffled Sunday dress and ankle socks, into the living room, where Karl and his buddies were playing serious poker.

Kendra takes the platter to the coffee table where Axel and his father are thumbing through journals and drinking Scotch. Pub stench, she came to call that haze of smoke and beer and garlic. Sometimes Karl would call her his honey, his little pot of gold, hoist her onto his lap, wrap an arm around her waist and play with her dra for a few rounds. "Anyone else want some luck?" Holding her up, he always made the same joke when he won.

Axel runs his hand along the curve of her rear and thigh in an absent-minded possessive gesture that sends a bull-red rage surging through her system, rattling and shaking her hands until she nearly drops the tray and all its contents.

"You okay, Ken?" Axel glances up from a journal article he is showing his father. He doesn't say Watch it, you almost got it all over. He doesn't say What's got you in such a snit? Yet she watches, waiting for cruel things.

After his parents leave, Kendra agrees to go away with him for a few days the next weekend. Snow has fallen in the north, though it's not quite cross-country season. Being in the woods is enough for Kendra. She opts for seclusion over opulence, so they decide to try a new inn in the Upper Muskokas. At night they slumber peacefully in each other's arms, without making love.

14

Confirming Lena's intuition, the counselling appointment was to boot her from the fertility program. "Not suitable" were the words they used. Lena pressed for the explanation she already knew. What they said was they did not think Lena could provide a "gender-neutral environment."

"They called that *fair*." Lena sags against the dusty taupe cushions of Kendra's sofa. Kendra sits cross-legged beside her.

Lena took this to mean they did not trust her to raise a boy. "And I'm such a good mother," she says. "What a son I could raise."

It's too much, Kendra thinks. None of them happy. She takes Lena's hand into her own.

The nurse brushed off Lena's questions, like dirt from a wound, yet gave her some leads, a counselling centre, a copy of their sperm order sheets. The doctor did not attend. Lena was not, after all, going to be family.

"I'm going to have my baby, Kendra," Lena announces. Like: there's going to be snow tomorrow, a fact.

They talk about alternatives. She could find a feminist lawyer, sue her way back into the program, under the discrimination clause of the human rights act. She could try other programs. Or she could find her own donor. Lena's anger is neither a fit nor a tantrum, but a calmness that deepens her focus, extends her resourcefulness.

Lena does not want any relationship with the man who would father her child, not even friendship. She does not want any physical resemblance, gesture, voice tone, or talent to remind her of a genetic father. She does not want the child to know any father, except possibly Angel. A male father could change his mind, decide he wanted the child, sue for custody or access.

"You'll have to kill him then," Kendra jokes. Lena doesn't laugh. She is not going to lose another child. There's that anger again, only it's determination, seeing the exact trees in her forest, knowing which ones to clear and which ones to keep, being willing to do it, even clear-cut it. Kendra asks where she learned this kind of focus, this calm, useful anger.

"Jamaica," Lena begins, "is a land layered with trouble. Trouble between the sexes, trouble between the races, trouble between the classes, and just plain trouble. The slaveholders controlled everything: money, goods, families, even the law. Anything less than absolute loyalty to them was punished, sometimes by caning, sometimes by worse. The sound of the switch, its whistle in the air, its thud into the skin, was the rhythm of Jamaica, embedded in the memory, right down to the cells, of every male. They passed their humiliation to the women and children. Beatings were casual everyday affairs like drinking coffee or saying good morning."

Lena pauses. Kendra doesn't know if she'll continue, get personal. Lena is not in the habit of talking about the past. The stereo plays Segovia low in the background.

"My parents were a mixed marriage, you know," Lena says. "My father was East Indian, my mother a Negro with honey-coloured skin. By Jamaican standards she's white. My features are like my father's, but the honey in my skin is my mother's. My brothers and sisters span a whole range of colours and features. You'd never know we were related.

"My family was different, not violent. My father worked for the government. My mother had a degree. I had no trouble qualifying for high school, and then university, though music was my real love. I got my teacher's certificate to be respectable."

Kendra doesn't move, even to get tea or coffee. A comment could plunder this moment. She strokes the back of Lena's hand.

"I met Norman through teaching. I'd drop into his classroom – he taught history – and listen to his lectures, which were packed with statistics and stories that stood everything I knew on its head. Norman was tall and gorgeous, a deep ebony with elongated features. He was actually quite sensitive about his colour – ashamed, I came to believe. My parents opposed our marriage, but I was adamant, so eventually they gave in.

"Norman politicized me. He made black history and culture seem like the centre of the universe. I'd never heard anything like it. Black people had to know. I dropped all my other activities to go to meetings with him. At first, I wasn't accepted, but I stuffed enough envelopes to show them I wasn't expecting a leadership position." She chuckles. "They really liked me when I scrubbed out the bathrooms." The chuckle fades like the end of a song.

"For a long time, politics covered our differences. Norman knew what to read, how to behave at meetings, what strategies were going to work. Together, we analyzed new ideas, new people. Not only in politics, but religion, for the movement was trying to modernize the animist and obeah beliefs, the kind that had terrorized my mother.

"Then the day came I wanted to get back to my music.

"I expected Norman to encourage me. After all, he was an activist. He believed in independence, the right to self-development. He was full of ideals that I thought he lived.

"I was dead wrong. Liberation was for men. Personally, Norman was nowhere. An empty bag of wind, pumped up by ideas to make loud noises, like those Scottish pipes that you work with your elbow. But the basic sound, a drone."

Lena moves her hand to Kendra's crossed leg. "I don't know why I'm telling you all this."

"The baby."

"It's brought it all back. Being turned down. I thought I had finished with it."

Kendra squeezes the long fingers, quiescent on her thigh.

"Norman questioned everything I did without him. Why did I need more classes? Why give concerts that benefited no one but the elite? I should give free lessons to the *pickneys* – he'd affect dialect when he was trying to emphasize the gulf between us."

Pickney children. Like the tyke in the crib, or the urchins. Lena and Kendra are still holding hands.

"Then I got pregnant. It was an accident, of course. The last thing I needed then was a child. I didn't tell Norman. I knew he'd want to have it, but for the wrong reasons. A child would make it hard for me to do anything on my own."

Lena's hand feels as smooth as a lucky stone washed on the Lake Huron shores. Her face is pleated with pain.

"I decided to have an abortion. Every doctor refused me. They gave various reasons, but they all asked my husband's opinion. I had forgotten the allegiances of medical people were first to the father and then to the baby. Even when I lied and said I was single, the doctor asked who the father was and what he thought."

"You forgot again."

"I don't know why I thought this would be different."

"Different country. New era." Kendra presses the hand, warmer than a lucky stone heated by the sun. If she could slip it in her pocket, she could imprint its luck, which is courage, into her thigh.

"Then one doctor decided Norman had a right to know what I was up to, and called him. Norman was waiting for me when I got home, and lost control. He told me it was his baby and I was going to have it. He told me he'd had enough of my airs, my white skin, my rich family, all my selfishness. He told me it was time I thought about him for a change, time I learned to be good to him and to his child."

Oh Lena, not you.

"He never got violent. Not even a threat. But he said I wasn't fit to be a mother, that any baby we had belonged solely to him. I tried to prove he was wrong by all the things women do. Like Monique. I quit doing music, kept the house perfect. I smiled at babies I saw on the street. I smiled at his friends. Though not too much. I even made my eyes smile. I'd picture the dance of the sunlight on the sea, the smell of the port on the day I would board a ship with my baby to leave Jamaica forever."

And I'd smell the pine forests, listen to the night birds.

"His politics were a substitute for personal liberation. He wanted my spirit to shore up his own.

"But my spirit was all I had left. There was no way he was going to have it, though I'd almost let him break it. I found a book called *The Wild White Goose* by the first woman in a Japanese monastery. I discovered that monks learned to transcend their bodies by being slapped while they meditated, so I practised, then used it when Norman was being a fool. My calm seemed to tranquillize him in some odd way and he'd wander off and leave me alone.

"But my pregnant body revolted him. Or he was afraid of me still. He began having sex with sad little political groupies who idolized his charisma. But once in a while . . ."

"Tea? A drink?" Kendra really should serve the tea from the kitchen.

Lena's mouth is still forming words. Kendra hears some of

them: "better after Cornelia ... freedom ... transcend barrages ... four more years ..." The tea is dark and cold.

Lulled by the tranquillity of surfaces, Norman had no idea how much Lena hated him, was shocked when she left. He hired a political lawyer, a radical who went after her in court as if she were the mother of racism. He brought in affidavits from the doctors, a schedule of her concerts. Norman won complete custody. Lena got one weekend a month, the week of Christmas or Easter, a week during the summer. She applied for her visa the next day.

"You know the oddest thing?" Lena slants her head at Kendra, her eyes glinting as if she were picturing that dance of the sunlight.

"Sometimes, I miss him."

15

On the drive north with Axel, watching his bony wrist drape over the steering wheel and noticing the casual way he whistles, Kendra catches herself wondering if Lena had started off loving Norman the way she loves Axel or even (her mind stumbles) if Hannahjean had once loved Karl. Could Axel change then? Could he fade into a shadowy figure, drained of his humanity, avenging each humiliation of his day with a monstrous conviction in his own rightness, as if inflicting pain could salve his wounds, ancient and recent? Jove and Allah (calling to one god never seems to be enough), could anyone become evil then? If so, where were their horns? Where is their tail? How can she judge?

Axel reaches across the console and squeezes her hand. "Look." A *V* flies across the blue November sky in late migration.

"Do you know Billie Holiday's 'Strange Fruit'?" she enquires, not exactly sure why birds and Billie are related.

"Lillian Smith wrote a book by that name."

"The book was named after the song, or for the original poem by Lewis Allan. Strange fruit is bodies dangling from trees after lynchings. Billie started singing it after her father died. He caught pneumonia when he was playing in Dallas, and white hospitals didn't treat blacks then. But he had been in the army when he ruined his lungs, so finally a veterans' hospital with a separate-but-equal ward took him, but it was too late, he hemorrhaged and died. She was a star by then, so she could sing her rage.

> Southern trees
> bear a strange fruit
> blood on the leaves
> and blood at the root
> Black body swinging
> in the Southern breeze
> strange fruit hanging
> from poplar trees.

"Her father was only fifteen years old when Billie was born. Her mother was thirteen. He was a musician too, a trumpet player. He left them both to play music, had two more families on the road, one of them white. Billie adored him right to the end. Her mother did too.

> Pastoral scene
> of the gallant South
> the bulging eyes
> and the twisted mouth
> Scent of magnolia
> sweet and fresh
> and the sudden smell
> of burning flesh.

Here is a fruit
for the crows to pluck
for the rain to gather
for the wind to suck
for the sun to rot
for a tree to drop
Here is a strange
and bitter crop.

Billie used to puke every time she sang that song."

The countryside is starting to hump into shapely hills as they drive up from Toronto towards Muskoka County. Kendra can't wait to get onto the backroads where she feels embraced by the towering trees, so much like the shaded pine-scented clearings of the U.P. where she could hide from Karl for hours until slowly slowly the good-helpful-girl persona that infected her mind dissolved, and she could get a tiny dose of her true thoughts. They came in little murmurs like *Karl is a weakman*; then the blasphemous thought would quickly fade to be replaced once again by the gospel-according-to-Karl as told by Hannahjean: Karlsays, Karlthinks, Karllikes, Karltoldmethat. But one dose was enough, it was addictive, this thinking-for-yourself business. Kendra developed a taste for it and began stealing often into the woods, the very peculiarity that made Karl believe she was having hormonal spasms with dozens of adolescent penises younger and more agile than his own (how one's own thinking propels itself into the behaviour of others), but she was indulging a taste far more dangerous to the security of her future (and his) than fucking, she was eating from the apple of dictatorless thinking, a time bomb for sure. One fall day, much like this fall day but twenty years earlier, lying on her back under a big spruce, this thought appeared: *Tell Ellen*. Well, there's a thought that makes no sense, Kendra automatically responded; *tell Ellen*, what does that mean? Tell Ellen what? *Tell Ellen about Karl*. With that thought the flip-flopping of her fourteen-year-old heart got so loud that it drowned out all independent thinking for three months. Thinking itself was hard enough. She could only do it in absolute solitude. The presence of a rabbit, a skittering squirrel, even a butterfly could interrupt this fragile filament to her own self. Talking about what she thought was out-of-the-question, why her tongue would go numb, her lips would refuse to open, she might never be able to sing again.

Two Loon Inn is a big, white clapboard house with green shutters and a two-storey screened verandah on one side. The lapping sound of lake water reminds Kendra of the thousand moods of the Great Lakes, Superior and Michigan, and the peaceful rocking oblivion they always offered. She jumps out of the car before it stops, flashes an impish, six-year-old grin at Axel, whose mouth freezes in fish-like warning. Racing around the house while he parks and locks up, she almost reaches the dock before he catches up to her, his long-legged, sneakered lope soft and silent on the fall grass. They wrap their arms around each other and stroll to the end of the long dock to gaze into the teal water and inhale the moist, crisp, rejuvenating air, exhaling blue-grey fumes from Toronto in little puffs. "Exhaust-ed air," Axel exclaims. "I didn't think it had hit the north yet." Except for the sound of a distant outboard the lake is quiet, off-season.

The inn, spacious and cool, is furnished in Canadian pine and flowered muslin. A large Mennonite quilt with a star pattern hangs on the dining-room wall. "I'll be right with you," a woman's voice calls from the depths of the house.

Adele introduces herself by extending a well-groomed, floury hand. A slight, fiftyish woman with a permed blond ponytail and an open-necked shirt, Adele seems comfortable, confident. Unlike the rough-skinned, ammonia-soaked hands of the wood-chopping, floor-washing, chicken-gutting women of the U.P., Adele's hand is coddled, baby-soft, with a firm grip.

She smiles with her whole face, not the narrow, cautious

crack Kendra has come to expect from Ontarians. "Your room has a balcony overlooking the lake, and a private bath. I think you'll like it." She wipes her hand on her shirttail.

"When did you leave?" They are climbing a wide, oak-banistered staircase. "My husband is driving in this morning, and I don't expect him for another hour."

"We were pretty eager to get out of the city," Kendra says.

"What does your husband do?" Axel asks the question they debated in the car.

"Teaches political science."

And finds the promise of a good skirmish. "He's here a lot?"

Adele says Tom is usually around for five months during the summer. They just renovated and opened last July.

"How was your first season?" Kendra asks.

Adele opens a pine door with a wreath of dried flowers encircling the number seven. "There are a lot of new inns and bed and breakfasts in the area," she says.

The centrepiece of the room is a four-postered pine bed covered by another Mennonite quilt. European cushions rest against the headboard, and French doors with curtains of Provençal lace open onto a tiny balcony. The silhouette of a jade plant shades onto the glass.

Kendra slides open drawers, liberating scents of lilac and rose from potpourris of dried stems and petals.

Adele motions to an entertainment centre the size of a wardrobe, colonial-style, with a large Sony TV and a VCR, says tapes are available in the downstairs library or from the local grocer. The rest of the inn is equally well equipped. She shows them exercise equipment, a sauna, whirlpool, canoes, sailboard, cards, board games, the library, and, finally, a renovated, country-style kitchen, where everyone prefers to eat. Several long picnic tables are arranged in an eating alcove with a lake view. Outside, the water froths up into minuscule peaks. They have missed breakfast, but there are muffins and coffee till noon. Axel devours three muffins, two corn and a blueberry, while Adele finishes explaining arrangements for lunch and dinner.

They unload the car and decide to go for a long walk, Kendra to familiarize herself with new territory, Axel to scout hiking and skiing trails. By the time they return, Tom and the other guests have already lunched, so they microwave potato-leek soup and warm up fresh, multi-grain bread. Vetoing an afternoon nap – "There'll be nothing to do but sleep at night" – Kendra suggests they bundle up, pack snacks, and take out a canoe.

Two Loon Lake is a vast, deep lake, its shoreline convoluting into unexpected coves and peninsulas, its isolated cottages closed for the winter. Kendra wants to veer into each nook or clearing, while Axel prefers to skim the whole shoreline, to see The Big Picture. "We won't even get halfway around before dark," Kendra protests. Compromising with ease, they decide to explore and make maps. Axel devises a visual code for coves, beaches, clearings, cottages, docks, and possible trails, which he marks in meticulous detail, as they paddle energetically around the lake in alternating fore and aft shifts.

Towards the late afternoon a wind blows up, which whips Kendra's locks across her face in stinging lashes and makes the work of paddling engrossing and strenuous. It's a challenge Kendra enjoys, this testing her strength against the elements. Her keen awareness that every sleek sweep of her paddle eases the strain on Axel, who is steering, adds love-lustre to this exhilarating, backbreaking, muscle-building task. Axel says they should head back in the straightest possible course, before the shifting, strengthening wind gusts into a force beyond their limits, a danger of late-autumn canoeing in deserted lake country. Now their partnership ripples through every straining, bowing muscle as they lean to and fro, back and forth in the absolute physical harmony of a true team, inspired not by competition, nor by the desire to win, but by love's compelling need for the life of the other, which allows them to paddle safely through the frothing, troubled waters in record time.

Sweating from exertion, they haul canoe, paddles and life-jackets into the boatshed and stumble back to the inn, where aftershock turns their soaked bodies into weak, trembling blobs. Grey storm clouds race over the water, cutting off the twilight, like a great black door closing over the heavens, damping out the sparkle on its rippling, earthbound twin. Suddenly cold and life-less, the two vacationers drag themselves up the now-endless stairway, leaning their torsos heavily on the curved oak of the banister and pausing to rest after each step. In their room, stripped down to clammy, weary nakedness, Kendra draws a hot bath and they both slide into the oily, bubbly soothing waters, two weary paddlers in identical positions, Kendra sitting between Axel's outstretched legs, her opal-skinned back leaning against his melanin-toned chest, the back-and-forth of their canoeing partnership extended into absolutely synchronized bathing.

Enmeshed, entwined, and enfeebled, they sleep in this strange new unity, each one turning or tossing at exactly the same moment as the other, as if their neurons were firing across the skinwall into the other's system. The storm passes; the night passes; and who knows what the skin of each partner passes into the other during the night, for traffic goes unseen at border cross-ings at midnight and beyond, but in this new light, in the deli-cate tendrils of a dawning morning, having successfully traversed the troubled waters to togetherness, it is impossible to tell who initiates their lovemaking, so great is their synchronicity, so strong their union.

❧ ❧ ❧

Gabriel, I am puzzled why I keep coming here.

Your earth self is in torment, my friend. It is so for all of us in flight.

No, Gabriel. I have arrived here during a happy time in my earth life and I am missing it.

Tell me, Billie, but be careful with language; you must be so vague that no one on earth will know what you mean. There is something wrong about your happy time and you must not return. Think of political speeches you have heard or self-help books you have read; we have found them to be the best models for this type of communication.

Like: it is a peak time in my life?

In the life of our nation, Gabriel intones, then apologizes for digressing to his own interests. What kind of peak?

A pinnacle of great love and understanding has at long last been reached between two separate and distinct people. It is now time to give expression to this great love, to unite without rancour or rage, to merge without submerging, to speak in the common language beneath all language. At this moment, the finest hour in the long divided history of two separate people, this bird has flown, split, you know, Gabe, taken a powder.

Couldn't keep it up, eh? Billie can hear Gabe's warbling laughter in her head. You caught on so quickly, I thought you were a politician or a priest. NO, don't tell me. His sharp warning ejects the songwriter thought that has almost formed.

Can you help me? she thinks. I don't know what to do.

We must seek the advice of the One Who Knows, if she will talk to us. I don't know what she is calling herself these days. I will try to find out.

♪ ♪ ♪

At breakfast, Axel and Kendra meet Lynne and Greg, Tom and Adele's friends from Toronto, and a couple from Barrie. Tom, slender and bearded, in baggy green cords and a sloppy turtleneck, helps Adele serve plates heaped with pancakes and sliced fruit. Willow, their fifteen-year-old daughter, recognizes Kendra.

"You're a Survivor!" she yelps, so the whole room can hear. "Mom, Dad, do you know Who This Is? Why didn't you tell me She was here?" Ignoring the hushhush gestures of her parents, she plunks herself across from Kendra, who, light streaming from her face like a Renaissance angel, is unflappable this morning.

Willow is a blue-streak talker. A few-sentences spurt of familiarity with any subject seems to satisfy her curiosity. "I've been a Survivor follower since *Almost a Woman*," she confides. "Most of my friends didn't even know you existed until *Environmental AIDS*. Airheads. They dunno what's good until it's like number one, or some guy says it's okay," she giggles. "And the guys didn't exactly like 'Almost a Woman.' But I played it for everyone, especially my mom." Her voice drops to a whisper. "Did you bring your guitar? Will you play for us?"

"After dinner," Kendra promises.

"But just a few songs," Axel adds.

Kendra snuggles into Axel, taking his hand, while Willow chatters on about her boyfriend, Ahmed, whom her parents don't like because he's Arab and dark even though he's Christian just like them and about her girlfriends who don't want to do anything-except-get-married while she plans to go to law school and help immigrants living in Canada.

Willow directs her talk only to Kendra, her idol, so each new paragraph inserts a tiny invisible wedge between Kendra and Axel. Kendra reaches for coffee and drops Axel's hand. Axel disentwines his arm to refill his plate with fruit. Their physical closeness has become awkward, and they inch apart into a small separation.

Stirred by a light breeze, the post-storm air is laden with moist, earthy smells. Axel wants to canoe the opposite way from yesterday's adventure, a delight to Kendra, who can canoe for weeks at a stretch. Adele is outside the boathouse, rigging a small windsurfer. "It might be the last good day of the season," she smiles, holding the boom with her feet as she threads the outhaul. Adele thinks the water's too cold for beginners, even suited up like herself. "Beginners fall so much, it's better if the water's warm and they're not afraid to try things that might tip the board." She pulls on a pair of black booties, grinning as if slaking some secret joy. "I hate to see anyone ruin such a good sport with a bad start." One hand on the daggerboard, she tucks the board under her arm and trots down to the beach. "Come back in the summer," she calls, tossing the board onto the rippling water, "when we teach."

Adele pops the mast into the board and whisks across the lake, until she's just a tiny pastel dot on the horizon. "She looks like she's flying," Kendra says.

In the canoe, she tells Axel that, in her bird dreams, air feels just like water, flowing or still, filled with winds in currents, dense or thin, and teeming with invisible life.

"You're still going there, then?"

"Often."

"Every time we make love?"

His face sags with hurt as she nods.

⌐ ⌐ ⌐

A long melanin-skinned pencil disappearing into a charcoal hole. Two popping eyeballs, seagreen, skyblue, stare across an inch. A flattened porcelain breast with a bony thumb revolving around its shiny crimson nipple. A tubular thigh.

⌐ ⌐ ⌐

"I remember last night!" She doesn't tell him it's in shards and fragments. To her this shattered-china memory is a glint of gold, the start of a vein, the fork in an unmarked road. I know; I know; I know; I know, her heart sings, her mind sings. She has a new song to write.

Axel looks as if a mountain has been lifted off his back. With a great surge of energy, he paddles them halfway across the lake towards the island Adele told them to explore. Approachable only by boat and deserted in late October, thick-forested Magic Isle is lined with beaches of grey sand, like the old fishing port of Grand Marais near Pictured Rocks, where the Quillan family used to vacation during the summers. So a four-levelled day unfolds as Kendra-now and Kendra-at-six-eleven-fourteen wanders through these woods and those woods, lies on this beach with Axel, plays on that beach with a plastic scoop and two baby sisters, wades with rolled-up jeans and laughter in this freezing water, swims so far out into that warm summer water that the family and Karl shrink into dots on the beach, Lilliputians on a shore not yet distant enough, but she cannot lift her arms one more stroke.

Has she made it now? Is this the other shore she is on with Axel? Not quite. She still drags her six-eleven-fourteen-year-old selves with her, and while Kendra-now wades and laughs with Axel, Kendra-then gazes into the depths of the teal water and wonders if she can get her water-heavy limbs to relax long enough so the rocking swells will carry her down under, to the great wet womb, which has brought peace to many a mariner and – but she doesn't know this yet – to Virginia Woolf, who subdued that contrary will-to-live that pops out of the will-to-die by weighting the death-side of the scale with a rock before wading into the river. But Kendra is rock-less against the will-to-live when it rises like bile from her innards, so she swims back to shore, back to Karl, and back to now where her skin and perhaps a few muscles, a single chamber of her heart, a few inches of intestine, are sufficiently available to laugh with Axel and have what she thinks of as a wonderful day.

During dinner Willow squirms excitement. She has brought both *Environmental AIDS* and *Almost a Woman* and propped them on the window ledge. Everyone likes the idea of a concert after dinner, though only Willow has heard of Survivors. Kendra, who estimates at least one closet performer in every group of five, discovers that Greg Grayme is a fiddler and Adele is a mime.

The two of them take turns entertaining until Willow slips beside Kendra. "Please please do 'Almost a Woman,'" she begs, "my abso-very favourite."

Kendra tunes up the guitar. "Song for Willow," she announces, her arm wound around the girl beside her.

> Endless nights of parties
> Admirers flock around
> Nouvelle cuisine and roses
> Gaiety, shimmer, gowns.
>
> I'm doin' fine without you.
> I'm on freedom's run.
> If I stop a moment
> You'll come and black the sun.
> Tender memories tumble
> Unbidden in my mind
> An internal lifescape
> Oedipus couldn't blind.
>
> It's still like I told you
> When you nested in my heart.
> "I'll never try to hold you
> If you choose to part."
> A woman's love starts dying
> When she cages up her dreams.
> Her soul dims, she's lying
> While she coils inside his arms.
>
> So, alone
> I'll face the world
> Almost a woman
> I'm a big girl.

So many people are admiring Kendra-now, encircling her with their impersonal love. Willow-Tom-Greg-Adele-Willow's boyfriend-fiddling-mime all wedge innocently between the synchronized Axel and Kendra, blithely severing their rare two-as-one unity which, had they recognized it when it happened, they might have called Bliss.

In bed, unaware that their bliss of unity has dwindled into the mere happiness of individuality, they make the unsynchronized love of ordinary mortals, and since unsynchronization leaves space in between, and into in-between spaces seeps the unbeckoned stuff of individuality, a kaleidoscope of the myriad flesh and fantasy lovers of past and future marches into Axel's fingers, making them squeeze this breast too soon too hard, as the flashbulb picture of a stiffened nipple under teenaged-Willow's teeshirt gets mistaken for the go-ahead signal from this protruding nipple, which cringes then remembers *do not resist*, until the body breaks apart into movable objects to be pushed apart and around and in between.

♪ ♪ ♪

It seems like forever until she finds Gabriel. Meanwhile Billie drifts aimlessly through this black starless night. Birds, deep in thoughttalk, wing past in flocks and pairs, but she can hear nothing, can link to no soul. Talk to me, Gabriel, she implores, come and find me here.

I have found the name of the One Who Knows, the deep familiar voice resonates in her head, and the bird world fills with sound. The One Who Knows calls herself Glinda.

Glinda-the-Good? From Quodling Country, Oz? Billie can't believe her luck. Oh, Gabriel, how I loved Glinda when I was a child. I used to imagine travelling with Dorothy and Ozma to her palace where she kept the Great Book of Records, an account of all events that happened anywhere in Oz. If she deemed you worthy, she would unlock the book, and you could learn anything you needed to know.

Let us hope she finds you worthy then, Billie. It is said that she turns away many a tired traveller.

Glinda's queendom is a pinpoint of light in a far galaxy, so distant that Billie and Gabriel fly for a very long time. The atmosphere thins into a vacuum and blackens into a void, so they fly sightlessly and thoughtlessly, completely incommunicado. All false plumage drops away during this journey to Truth, called Quodling, where Glinda presides. No avian travellers know at the outset how much of their epidermal outgrowth is the weak barbs and discontinuous vanes of false feathering. Periodically, a feather from Billie or Gabriel drops into the void, reminding them that even tortured souls have no corner on truth.

They are scruffy little birds when they reach Quodling. Gabriel has lost all his red feathers and is only a dark underbelly, while Billie's neck and crown have been deplumed, leaving her face a feathered mask in the midst of raw and bleeding flesh.

Glinda, in a gown that shifts through more shades of grey than stars on their journey, greets them. You wore white in Oz, Billie thinks.

Oz and white truth belong to children.

White children, Gabriel amends.

There is no need for such primitive politics in Quodling Queendom, Glinda thinks to Gabriel. They are givens. We are working on more complex truths.

A strip of red feathers re-appears along Gabriel's side as he considers without rage that white men have burdens.

You have journeyed too far and too long for idle chatter, my children. What truth do you seek?

I have told Gabriel that I come to the bird world even though my earth self is not tormented. He said I must ask the One Who Knows how this could be so.

Are you sure you want this knowledge?

I am missing the best part of my life. I must know.

There is no guarantee your life will improve. Truth can be an agonizing vision.

I must know.

Then I will consult the Great Book of Records, which contains all events that have escaped from earth. But I must warn you: some do not survive a face-to-face encounter with even a tiny facet of escaped truth. Are you quite sure you want this?

I am sure.

A thin spiral notebook appears in Glinda's mind.

I thought the Book of Records was a big fat book like the *Complete Oxford*, Billie cries.

Your truth is not the same as all truth, my child.

Pages are turning in the spiral notebook.

Ah, here it is. Dreadful, just dreadful. Last chance to run, my dear. I can keep the truth safe just as long as you want.

Billie hesitates.

⌐ ⌐ ⌐

Someone is shaking her arms and face, calling the other name, "Kendra, Kendra, wake up, where are you." The voice is saying words into the air, which muffles them, makes them lose the resonance and fullness of thoughttalk. Thoughttalk reverberates far into distant corners of the mind where thin-timbred earth voices cannot reach. Bye billie, bye gabriel, bye glinda, bye Quodling. She has to reply with some words and her lips won't move, her limbs either, they are limp, dolly limbs, a rag doll flung across the bed. *How to get back? how to get back?* She is panicking. "Are you okay?" the airvoice is asking. *Count backwards, say your ZYX's, repeat nursery rhymes*, Gabriel's fading thoughts instruct helpfully. *Marymaryquitecontrary.* "Let me sleep" – an inaudible mumbly, drugged voice. *Howdoesyourgardengrow.* "I must sleep." It's her voice. *Jackbenimble.*

Two days later, in zipped-together down sleeping bags under

the green-needled spruces and bare-branched maples of Magic Isle, lying in the dappled sunlight of the distant fading October sun, their crumpled clothes for pillows, Axel and Kendra culminate a dream they share.

⌐ ⌐ ⌐

Wait, Gabriel cautions. I am worried.

Glinda closes the spiral notebook.

If you speak the truth, Billie will return to whatever it is she cannot live through.

That is why Quodling is so distant from earth and its ozone suburbs. We can think anything here, even banned thoughts. Do not be afraid, Gabriel; there is no overlap between here and there, no danger of thought-crossing. Her problem will be different; she will not retain her Quodling thoughts easily. Billie?

I am ready.

STAY near her, Gabriel. This will not be easy.

Billie draws a breath.

⌐ ⌐ ⌐

Axel and Kendra drag their sleeping bags down to the beach where the water slips in and out of the shore, making small lapping, gurgling sounds. Oh, if her audiences could see their feminist heroine now, this Kendra of the forest and of the beach, all body and no mind, as pliant and fluid as a maid of the mist, a nymph, a sylph, transformed as Axel watches, by love and an isle of Magic.

⌐ ⌐ ⌐

The one you have asked about arrived in the half-world as a yellow-rumped warbler with outsized wings, due to acts committed on her body in the year of her birth. These acts have no names in earth language and are therefore inconceivable and unspeakable. Since then she has returned one thousand, eight hundred and seventy-seven times as twenty-nine different birds.

Stunned, Billie squawks: In the year of her birth!

Who? Gabriel asks.

Kendra.

God.

She has no memories of anything like that when she was an infant.

Of course not. She was here.

She'll never believe it. How can she believe what she doesn't remember?

You'll have to find her memories. If they have flown, they are here, my friend. Like Astor.

ↄ ↄ ↄ

Driving back to the city, nothing seems right. Where are those blissful two-as-one feelings? Axel-the-stranger lolls in the passenger seat, whistling off-key opera and stroking her gear-shifting arm as if it's a piece of driftwood. Rivulets of blood appear along the trail of his fingers, does he not see them? A gleaming red Cherokee guns past her on the right, then cuts deftly in front of her little silver Prelude. Too close, the sleazy slimy tattooed cock-brained son of a pervert, big metal hulk blocking her vision, probably masturbates every time he cuts off a woman driver. Horn squawking, she rides his tail, shaking a small fist out the window. Axel's hand tightens over the blood-trailed arm in a calming gesture that sends its opposite message, and she snaps, "Stop that damn whistling. It's driving me crazy."

"You liked it on the way up."

"That wasn't opera."

"Operetta."

"Pardon me. Ain't no opry but the Grand Ole in the U.P."

"Kendie? This isn't about whistling opera."

"Music's mine. Why're you stealing it?"

"Music's everybody's. I learned that from a songwriting friend of mine."

"Between you and me, it's mine." What in the name of Mary is she picking on Axel for? "And you're horning in."

"Explication time." His singsong tone feels like one last whistle.

"It goes back to male privilege," she pronounces. "Mozart, Beethoven, Vivaldi, Haydn, Bach, Telemann, Holtz, Bruchner, Chopin, Berlioz – where are the women? Classical music was all composed by men for men. It's all about male passions, male emotions. That's why you know it and I don't." Even to herself, she sounds ridiculous. "Every time you whistle opera, I think about how men have controlled the great music of the world. Men's versions of love and death in big melodramas. I can't listen to any of it without my blood boiling."

That last part is edging towards Quodling, where truth is.

Axel removes the offensive stroking hand. "I'm sorry if I upset you." The hand drops onto his lap, where it belongs. "But what's that got to do with us? Am I responsible for all male sin?"

"Yes."

He hunches against the passenger window, as far away as he can get.

♪ ♪ ♪

Hah.

Fuck and whistle.

♪ ♪ ♪

"I'll tell you what it's got to do with us if you really want to know."

"I'm not sure."

"Make up your mind. I don't want to force anything on you."

"Tell me."

"Take music. Look at all the male singers who can't sing worth diddleysquat. Leonard Cohen, Bob Dylan, John Prine. But women, we have to be able to sing. More than three notes. We have to strip to our souls every time we're out there. We have to sing so good it makes us sick. Like Billie.

"Well, you can't sing, buster. You're always off-key, and it don't stop you. That's male.

"You just step right into my territory without even knowing.

"Singing's mine, man. Keep your hands off what don't belong to you."

16

Sweetie, I miss you so much, and you've only been gone an hour." Baker is the first voice on Kendra's answering machine. Kendra flips up the volume as she unpacks. "Last night I dreamed we were in Beijing and got arrested for saving girl babies." (Baker). "I'm gonna have to call a *therapist* if you don't get back soon." (Baker). Kendra crams her underwear in the laundry. "Hello Kendra. Remember Monique? She went back to Gilles, and he beat her right into a two-day stay in hospital. She is at our place for a few days." (Lena). Why in the world did she sling those cheap, feminist cracks at Axel on the way home? "And you know what *therapists* did to Anne Sexton." (Baker). Cracks like that make her cringe when someone else says them. "P. blues. P. blues. P. blues. Help. Call me." (Baker). She sounded like a petulant twelve-year-old who had just noticed that prime ministers and Blue Jays were all guys. "My daddy can do anything in this town. He'll run that sperm hoarder all the way to Baffin Island, if I ask him." (Angel). Kendra slides into a scalding bath, watches the dough of her skin turn red and blotchy. "I put an end to that. I'll find my own way." (Lena). The oily, bubbling water loosens and soothes her. "Suspect was described as a white male, about five foot ten, wearing brown pants and a tan ski jacket. We are reminding people to please lock their doors anytime they go out, even to shovel the walk or put out the garbage, as he is armed and may be dangerous." (Police). Axel puts up with so much from her. "I'm in love. I'm in love. I'm in love. Call me right away, toot-sweet. Cloud Nine." (Baker). Of course, she was right, but Karl used to use that kind of rightness on Hannahjean, word bludgeons, assaults on thought: think like me, bitch.

Kendra's skin feels buttery-soft from all those days with Axel. She actually touches it as she dries. The concentration creases between her eyes have slackened, her laugh folds deepened. Too bad it will reverse itself during the tour.

Baker answers the phone on the first ring. "You're back!" she screeches. "Did you notice I never called you once while you were away?"

"I didn't give you my number."

"You would've. If I'd insisted."

"I would've taken you along if you'd insisted."

Baker harrumphs. "Have fun?"

"More than I can handle. What's the P. blues about?"

"One night when you were away I got into one of those moods. So low, I had to look up to see the mud. I decided to go watch the hookers play the johns, down at Sherbourne and Parliament. Suddenly, I couldn't figure out the difference between them and me. Near the old Selby, where Hemingway once stayed, there's this leather bar. A guy comes waltzing out in a pair of leather pants with the whole rear cut out. His tight little butt was gleaming in the streetlight, and all his pals would pat it as they went by. He could just bend over and do it, behind a tree or in a washroom, boomboomboomboom, done. He was a walking invitation to be used. And I thought, Am I like that? A sexual joke? That's when I phoned."

"Better now?"

"Tell you later. Now I'm in love."

Kendra wants to call her old music teacher, Ellen Tremayne. Ellen reached into Kendra's soul with music, and Kendra belted back the blues. She could tell Ellen about the bliss of unity and the shattered-china memory, about the bird world and the collapse of time. She wants to tell Baker too, but Baker reacts before Kendra even articulates a problem. Kendra's mind drifts backwards across Two Loon Lake and Magic Isle, floral wallpaper and four-postered pine, scented sachets and russet sheets, and Axel in the canoe, Axel at the table, Axel in the bath.

꜒ ꜒ ꜒

If we think Astor's name enough times in synchrony, she will appear if she can, Gabriel instructs.

Why Astor? What can she tell me?

Astor has flown from her childhood. Perhaps she can tell us what happens to the children. Have faith, my friend.

Gabriel's bass voice enters Billie's head calling Astor, Astor. Billie harmonizes automatically. The bluebird with the chartreuse streak down her side appears.

Let me do the thinking, Gabriel cautions. Astor, when did you arrive here?

When I was eleven, a child's high wavering voice replies. In 1941.

Have you been here ever since?

I have never gone back.

Why not?

My earth self would die of shame.

From what? Billie breaks in.

From even an inkling of the four years of memory that I have brought here.

Is your earth self okay?

She has nightmares and fits, which her friends and family think are epilepsy. It is better than her memories.

How can it be better?

Otherwise she is happy. She is married, has children, a career in the arts. She works in California, sees the best doctors. They give her many medicines to help her sleep. Some days she is not even sure she was ever in Auschwitz.

Ah. Then you can tell us what happened to her without endangering you both? Gabriel enquires.

Yes, but it will bring her a new episode of seizures, and I will have to sequester myself on a cloudtop for a while. I need a good reason to offer such help to you.

You don't speak like a child, Billie reflects.

Nobody who comes here can stay a child, my friend; the moments we bring are lifetimes in themselves. Let me explain your problem to Astor before she disappears.

I am still here, Gabriel, the squeaky, wise voice responds.

Billie tells me she flies from a happy earth self.

Don't be ridiculous, a sharp voice intrudes. Astor and Gabriel fly at the intruder, chasing him away.

The One Who Knows has explained that she has many childselves here, Gabriel continues. We thought you might know what that means.

Then I must show you my story. Fly with me, my friends. I will take you into the hills of Yugoslavia in 1941.

They follow Astor through a tunnel of eddying, echoing winds, a short, tumultuous flight, and arrive at a cottage, deep in the woods.

In the cottage is an adolescent girl, half-guiding, half-clutching a younger girl with brown curling hair and pale skin. The young one is gorgeous, though no older than seven. That is me and my sister, Astor thinks, where we were kept by the soldiers for most of the war.

A second picture forms in Billie's mind: a stack of shelves lining the inside wall of a building called a Block. On each shelf lie emaciated, bald women, clothed in stinking rags and covered by filthy blankets. The bunks are so closely stacked that no one can fully sit up. Diarrhoea from an upper bunk drips onto the two girls huddled on a shelf underneath. That was the night before my sister left me there, by myself.

But which was it? thinks Billie. The Block or the cottage?

Astor's voice fades as the picture dims.

Go, Gabriel intercedes, before your earth self hears you.

≀ ≀ ≀

The Holocaust is Axel's obsession, yet Kendra carries its images, or pale fragments of them, in her mind. Did their consciousnesses mingle in that two-as-one union? Does Axel now remember the slashed crimson of her first guitar case? The sheltering dimness of the quarter moon the night she ran? After the Holocaust, Axel's father helped treat the rampant tuberculosis, dysentery, and other diseases that kept killing its survivors. "The body we could fix," he told Axel, "but the spirit we knew nothing about." It was the aspirituality of medicine that had discouraged Dr. Berne from becoming a psychiatrist, though word about him as a general practitioner had leaked through the Montreal grapevine, and survivors with their escalating ailments and infirmities kept arriving in his consulting room. He tried to talk with them about the past, but they would shrug, refuse, dissemble. "Something happens to the memory when the soul is wounded," Axel quoted his father as saying. "And the only people who know disremember."

Disremember. Such a wilful word. Kendra wants to pump Axel's father about memory. How could people not remember the most vivid experiences of their lives? Dissembling and shrugging aren't powerful enough to will anything away. What did people do to keep memory at bay?

She uncrumples Hannahjean's letter from the bottom of her bag. *Kelley, Kimmy, and Kiki are coming in for Christmas. We would like it so much if you would come too.* Survivors' tour arrives in the heart of the U.P. just before Christmas. Kendra could see her sisters for the first time in years. The paragraph on breast cancer whispers: I might not be alive next year.

She dials nine-o-six and her old number: *nine-seven-two, eight, three, eight, three.* Hannahjean is on the line before she hears a ring. "Ma?" A word she hasn't even thought in twenty-five years.

"Kendralah."

A term she hasn't heard in even longer. The tender syllables always made her expect huge parent arms to swoop around her. She explains about the concert in Marquette, that she'll be able to come for Christmas, but Hannahjean has put the phone down and is hollering for Karl.

"It's your One and Only." Her words are an offering. "She's gonna come!"

Now they both gibber into one receiver.

"Get upstairs," Karl blazes.

Hannahjean's footsteps scuffle off.

"Y'aren't planning to bring any of those girlie friends of yours now, are you?"

"The band members?" Kendra is intending to bring Baker. "Nope."

"We'll pick the tree when you get here. I'll start scouting now."

"A twee so tall it go over the wall." That jingle is from when she was five. *Fly, Billie.*

Hannahjean is back on the phone, bubbling plans. Karl and Jerry will eviscerate the turkey. Kiki wants to do appetizers. Kimmy is bringing California wines. Kelley, the vegetarian, will prepare salads, vegetables. Hannahjean will bake. Everything that Karl loves: butter cookies, shortbreads, almond crescents, berry pies, chocolate layer cake, breads. She'll exhaust herself with all that Christmas baking, Kendra protests, weakly, her taste buds in a swirl of memory. They never talk about the little lump.

Did you understand what Astor was trying to show you? Gabriel asks.

I understand that some horrors are irreconcilable with life. That she showed us only a glimpse.

Wounds like hers reopen with each visit. She invited you into her nightmare for you, my friend.

They are flying through endless stretches of brilliant blue. It is Billie's first daytime flight. She just wants to fly, she doesn't want to think. She can hear Glinda: I can hold the truth just as long as you want. Gabriel: Your earth self is in torment, my friend. Astor: She would die from the four years of childhood that I brought here.

It dawns on her: My childhood selves are here. They know. We can visit them like we visited the Block or the cottage in the hills.

They have already been visiting you, my friend.

↵ ↵ ↵

She has a blinding headache, almost a migraine. Big mistake to agree to go to Eagle City, damn and damn. Maybe some coffee will blast away the headache, coffee and aspirin. The cup clatters into the sink. How did she let it happen? She fills the cup with water and opens the medicine cabinet. How did she forget years of resolve so completely? Cup and water slide onto the floor. She's lost her grip. She squeezes her hand and finds she can't make a fist. As she walks towards the kitchen, her ankle turns. Rubbing it, with her head down, she cracks her temple against the doorframe. When she was a kid, everyone teased her about being clumsy. She was always bruising herself and never knew why.

A moist filter of old coffee is still in the plastic cone. She tosses it toward the garbage, misses. Karl's speech decelerates, every syllable a separate word. "We will pick a tree when you get here. I will start scouting." She responded like it was a command, she always had. *Kill him.* Her knees buckle. She will never get this coffee made. Grains of coffee are spilling on the counter, the sink, the floor.

♪ ♪ ♪

The boy climbs onto the kitchen counter. His parents are both sleeping, or should be. He counted the wind of their breath, each puff as it gusted into the dark. Twice he counted to a thousand, then he timed his footsteps to match the rhythms of their wind. He tussles with a cabinet door, guides it open with only a whisper of sound. Right in front is his new cup, robin's-egg blue with a looped handle, his name blocked in big letters on the plastic surface: Miles. The cup is not what he wants. On the second shelf are the cookies and crackers he eats with milk from his Miles cup. Snacks are not what he wants.

He spreads his bare feet in a wide stance on the countertop. By gripping the shelf's edge and stretching to the top of his toes, he manages to balance and peer into the third shelf. There sits the object of his stealth, the black oblong box with the fuzzy insides. He taps and pushes, pushes and taps until a black triangle protrudes from the edge of the shelf. He grasps the triangle and yanks. The box gongs against the counter.

No one stirs.

Miles traces the narrow sides with his fingertips, exploring for the bump of hinges, or a clasp. He finds a metal island with a round shape in its centre, and presses, certain it's a clasp. Nothing happens. He knobs the button to the right, to the left; still nothing. Maybe the box is locked. Maybe he won't get what he needs. He twists and presses, presses and turns, nothing, nothing. Rubbing his thumb around the clasp, he feels a tongue no bigger than the wing of a mosquito. He hooks it with his fingernail, gives a sharp tug. The clasp springs open. He pushes the lid until it is flat open, a book with a broken spine. Nestled in the dark, plush folds is what he has been searching for, the knife set his father sharpens when company comes. He removes a slender, gleaming knife, cradling it in both hands. That'll do, he thinks, that's long enough to reach his heart.

↶ ↶ ↶

17

When she tries to apologize for her feminist seizure, Axel shrugs. He thought she was right.

"Still love me?" he asks.

"I'm not sure I'm capable of love."

"Don't let that stop you," he teases. "Be a man about it."

Whaddya mean glints from her eyes.

"Calm down," he laughs. "I mean that doesn't stop me from singing."

She doesn't want to laugh. She wants to hit him. She laughs, punches him on the shoulder. It's different, dammit, not being able to sing, not being able to love. "You absolute cur," she says.

He does a dramatic backwards fall, holding his shoulder, ouch, ouch. "You feminists are all the same." She punches him again, and he grabs her wrists, pulls her onto him, laughing, laughing. She's falling on top of him onto the bed.

⁐ ⁐ ⁐

I want to find a childhood self, Billie thinks. How can I do it?

We do it together, my friend.

I'm not sure I want you to know what I find.

It is the only way. One outside person must bear witness to every truth or the truth will not consolidate. Where do you want to start?

At the beginning, when she first came.

Concentrate, Billie. She will come to us.

They enter a moonless patch and fly deep into the navy-black night.

Nothing happens.

They fly and fly. Through the dense navy, Billie can hardly see Gabriel, though she can hear the air rustling through his wings.

Where is she? Billie demands. Why doesn't she come?

Shhhh, Gabriel cautions. She flew because she was hurt, my friend. And we are coming to find her. She doesn't know if we are friend or foe. They are identical to her.

A yellow-rumped warbler jets past them.

Stop! stop! Billie races after her.

Whoa! Gabriel's thought is iron in her head.

The warbler circles them in a wide arc. They flap their wings passively, treading air. The yellow bird darts in, out, in again, then hangs in midair, staring into their beaked faces, which have acquired the stripped look they had in Quodling.

Do you know who we are? Gabriel asks.

I know *her*. The warbler's voice is tinier than Astor's, a faint thought, easy to miss.

I want to know why you are here, Billie blurts.

You want to coax me back, make me do what I left to a-void. I know how you think, Billie. I have been waiting for you for years. A squall of sobbing eddies through the air, a thousand infant wails melded into one rolling thunderclap of sound. When it's over, the warbler has disappeared.

ᶜ ᶜ ᶜ

"I hurt you, oh god." Axel brushes Kendra's filmed cheek.

She can't get her tongue around the floating words, shrugs instead of explaining. I don't feel hurt, she thinks. Tears flood her face, pooling warmth and salt into her mouth. She has to attribute them to something. She grabs a word. "Orgasm!" Axel nods, yes, orgasm. Facets of light bounce from his eyes, a million smiles. She remembers a thunderclap. "Oh uh wow uh?" She doesn't know if the cannonade of sound was his or hers. Her pores are a skin of crying eyes.

He extracts the finest meaning from her words, grins with a boy's shiny pride, believing he has made her happy. This is the last night before her tour. Their air is dense with sentiment.

"You going to Montreal for Christmas?" She cradles herself into his contours.

"I told my mother I was going to Eagle City with you."

"I can't do that, I told you."

"I think you need me there."

"I do. God, I do."

"So. If you change your mind, I can come."

WORK

18

They open in Halifax. A hard-driving zydeco band called Acadiana kicks off, eggs the audience into a fervour. It's a tough, resistant audience, overpopulated with beer-bellied men, not an easy, woman-dominated crowd that suckles milk from their music. Not the right place to launch an incest lullaby.

"Hit 'em with 'kiss of Life, kiss of Death,'" Baker hisses. It's the song Kendra met Axel with, running into the swell of silence that had followed his speech to hand him a bouquet of mauve daisies, sharing the mike with him for their encore numbers. How the audience had stomped and cheered. Kendra was their precious Ice Woman, known for her indifference to men.

> He came awake when he kissed me
> His skin from green to flush
> The fairy-tale frog prince
> Who feeds on youth and trust.

Broad green
reptilian lips
he wants me to kiss
he wants me to kiss
the kiss of life
he calls it

The zydeco-primed audience claps and sways to the chorus. Baker taps drum jokes: loosen up Kendra, frolic with me. Each instrument in the band separates into its own personality: Lena's melodic tinkling laughs up and down the keys; Baker patters frisky rhythms on top of a steady oceanic pounding; Angel weaves webs of understated bass beneath them all. Now Kendra hears her own voice outside herself, full and mournful, resonant with sweetness and rage. Miraculously, they finish together: *your kiss of life is my kiss of death; your kiss of life is my kiss of death.* The audience is clapping hard. A man leans over the balcony, throws posies onto the stage. The brew of audience and band fizzes and bubbles, a heady mix.

A basket of mauve wicker and beige macramé arrives backstage. Two bonsai twine from a bed of loamy earth in a miniature garden of swirled sand. Baker snatches a small buff envelope from between jagged rocks in the sand. She passes the envelope to Kendra, her look as black as the rocks. Axel? He knows how strung Kendra is for this tour. The flap tatters as she glides her finger under its thick linen. Embossed in greenish-gold, the colour of bog water, a miniature frog leers at her from a lily pad. The frog has a crown and a sceptre. Not Axel, that's for sure. A cramped signature inked by a thick-nibbed pen reads "Frank."

"Know any Frank?" Baker is hanging over her shoulder.

"Nope." Gifts from strangers are not unusual any more. Kendra traces a swirl in the soft sand. "Does anyone?"

"No way," Baker says.

"The man's a ringer for Hog's Hollow." Angel rubs the linen

between her thumb and forefinger. "Wedding invitation weight."

Lena contemplates the two bonsai with unswerving eyes.

"Kiss of life? Kiss of death?" Baker fans the air with the buff card. "I'm taking bets."

Lena watches the bonsai from the antennae of her eyes.

"They're lovers," she announces.

Kendra moves to Lena's side.

"I was trying to figure if the bonsai were friends or twins, enemies or brothers, but they're lovers. Definitely arranged as lovers. I'd be very careful of that Frank, Kendra."

The sky over the harbour is black and thin and pricked with starlight, the dark water pinching into slivers of white, like hundreds of priests' collars. Reflected lights from Dartmouth elongate into pale yellow cathedral windows floating on the bay. Survivors are on the second storey of a restaurant, surrounded by platters of fish and a fleet of drafts, foam pooling around their tops like beached surf. Schools of bubbles swim up the amber, trying to surface.

Baker ties a bib around her neck. It has a sketch of a lighthouse and a cove above two homey-looking lobster traps, a bit like pet carriers. "Whadja think?" she asks. Her mouth is full of clawmeat and butter.

"A choice of single malts" – Angel swirls her Scotch – "is a great place by me."

"Of the gig, asshole."

Kendra watches a rivulet of butter drool down Baker's chin. She knows what's coming.

"Why didn't we do our new stuff? We were hot."

Everyone looks at Kendra. A beacon flashes on the harbour, like a searchlight.

"Too many men." Kendra fakes a shrug. The harbour looks ebony after the flash.

"Back home, we have a saying for times like this," Lena says. "When you don't try your hardest, spirits slip in through the gaps."

Angel is scribbling figures on a napkin. No matter how she calculates their sales, she says, Survivors won't make money from old stuff alone. *Ghostchildren* sold fewer copies tonight than *Almost a Woman* or *Environmental AIDS*. They have to launch their new songs.

"This tour took months to book." Baker is spooning green innards from her lobster into a small dune at the side of her plate. "I don't want to waste it."

"I know," Kendra mutters. It seems a long gap before the beacon flashes again.

"What's *wrong* with me?" Baker asks, when they are back in the room. She is standing in front of the mirror in bikini underwear. "I'm not ugly. Not sexy, maybe." She runs her hand along her abdomen, which is flat as an iron. "But fit, athletic." She presses the jut of her hipbones, then flips into a backbend. "I do weights, yoga." Tumbling backwards onto the floor, she extends her legs in a wide split. "I was a cheerleader in high school. How 'bout that for a Jew?"

She somersaults to the coffee table, perches cross-legged in front of the bonsai, tipping her head to examine the gnarled trees as she rotates the basket into various positions.

"And you don't do a thing."

She picks up a hand mirror. "Look at me. I'm getting wrinkles around my eyes and my pores are huge. My breasts are getting smaller and my chin is pointy."

"Ugly women get married."

"Are you saying I'm ugly?"

"Are you trying to pick a fight? I'm only saying looks don't make a relationship."

"Easy for you to talk, you're so beautiful."

"You're beautiful too, Baker."

"I am?" Baker holds the trunk of the bonsai, her palm below the tines of its branches.

"More beautiful than a slimeball will ever notice." Kendra points at the buff envelope, back in the grip of the rocks. "And Frank is a slimebucket. Count on it."

Later, Kendra hears muffled sounds across the room. Baker is a small hump under the covers. Every snuffle is voluminous in the dark, like a footstep, or the whoosh of a trapped insect. When the snuffling releases her, Kendra floats along a watchful sleep, part of her awake and listening.

19

A box of hand-dipped chocolates is waiting at the hotel in Wolfville. Survivors gobble the chocolates. Nothing is open late in Wolfville.

In Charlottetown, the gift is a silk scarf, a smear of pond-scapes and luminescent frogs. Tiny emerald eyes glitter from carved gold frogs, dangling by their long legs from earwires curved like daggers, in St. John's. A frog of jade, brush-stroked with fragile petals, stares from a bed of slivered paper in Fredericton.

Survivors are tiring of the whirl. Baker has booked back-to-back gigs throughout the Maritimes. Some days, when the travel time is long, they don't have time to eat before the sound check. Kendra is a perfectionist about the monitors, and adjusts the treble and bass back and forth, as if her own auditory register were calibrated in steps finer than milliseconds, beyond the point anyone else can hear a whisper of a difference. Baker, knowing nothing can stop Kendra until she hears perfectly balanced sound, has written a dinner snack into the rider of every contract, so they get at least a platter of fruit and cheese before the gig. They are always exhausted at gig time.

Frank is almost a refreshing diversion. Baker takes book on what he looks like, when he'll appear. They scan the audience for repeating faces. *Your kiss of life is my kiss of death* is not a benign image. Lena thinks Kendra needs protection. Baker, though convinced that Frank is the great, fleshless lover, develops a schedule to ensure Kendra is always accompanied by another Survivor, never alone. In Angel's estimation, Frank is out to get what he can't buy, the unattainable Ice Woman. Lena gives Kendra a taliswoman carved in rose quartz on a keychain with a whistle and a small flashlight. Kendra is getting strung: jumping at small noises, seeing shadowy shapes on benches and in doorways, being churlish to strangers. Every night, she peers into the audience for oddballs, creeps, loners, gawkers, as if she could tell by their faces. He'll dress in buff clothes, she predicts, he thinks he's unique. Her face grows more out of alignment with each passing day.

The second part of their tour jets them through western Ontario, the Prairie Provinces and the American Midwest, into the Upper Peninsula. North Bay produces an audience of corpses, and no gift. In Sudbury, the organizers foul up: nothing is ready for the sound check; Baker says her drum kit plays like wet shoe-leather; the stage monitors have constant feedback. They never do hear each other properly, but the audience is a gas, noisy with appreciation after every big number. Survivors are stoked when they return to the hotel, and no gift douses their spirits. In Thunder Bay, the audience is enraptured by "Ghostchildren." They cheer long enough to let Kendra call Baker out for special bows, and a replay with Baker singing lead. By the end of intermission, the CD and tape have trebled their sales, and Baker is firing off verbatim imitations of the compliments she overheard in the lobby. The snuffles she calls allergies disappear.

In the Sioux and Kenora, Survivors try works in progress: a

raunchy blues tribute to Screamin' Elsa McCree, a country heart-break parody called "White Whine," and a talking blues, "No Votin' Here," about families. Still, Kendra doesn't launch the incest lullaby. She can never remember the words.

There is no better audience for their music, or any music, than a Winnipeg audience. Every Winnipeg concert is crammed with savvy musicians and feminists whose horizons are as vast as the prairie skies. Kendra has been toying with the idea of just recording "The Incest Lullaby," hoping a never-performed song will attract a mystique, like an unrecorded Beatles tune. Winnipeg is the last chance to break her muteness, her mutiny. It's Winnipeg or never for "The Incest Lullaby."

She dresses in a suede suit the colour of terra cotta and a cobalt green blouse, cowgirl-cut and fringed like the suit. For luck, she takes the green-black cowboy hat Axel bought her. She puts it on, feels stupid, fraudulent, takes it off, imagines Baker urging her – c'mon Kendra, you look dynamite – puts it back on, feels like a donkey about to bray, removes it, and places it on top of her guitar case. She can decide later. Green Navajo earrings dangle down her neck, earthier than the frog earrings she hasn't given away.

She catches the end of the opening act, a lesbian feminist blues singer with a Dylanesque style, charismatic more than rous-ing. The singer's vocal range is as limited as Baker's, but the sheer force of her musicality drives her songs into the mysterious netherworld of inspired art. A loyal following of women mouth her lyrics, which are complex and sad. Baker has already invited her to join them later in the show.

Onstage, a woman in a flowing dress is making announce-ments, while a technician tinkers with the sound system. One of the organizers corners Survivors and invites them to a hotel party. Baker, in her role as manager, accepts with glee. The woman in the floating dress elevates her voice: "Back in Winnipeg by popular demand, bringing their new recording *Ghostchildren*, Canada's number one feminist band, four gutsy gifted women from Toronto, won't you please welcome – Survivors!" Survivors run onto the stage to solid applause that swells for Quillan and Baker.

It's a women's night, and they play to it, starting with a lesbian love lilt called "Home" and running through a range of songs about women's lives: "Almost a Woman (I'm a Big Girl)," "Triathlon with Cradle," and "Valentina Was an Astronaut" – Baker's historical song about the first woman in space. "Ghostchildren" ignites a wave of enthusiasm, long enough for them to run off the stage. In the second set, they intersperse new songs with old favourites, rendering "kiss of Life, kiss of Death" at a feverish pitch for the finale. A couple rows of women in the front link arms and sway in a unity they used to see often, in their days as Quillan and Baker, and as Mauve Survivors, before Angel joined. They have time for one more song. Kendra's pace is slow, and dreamy.

> Daddy's in me
> making me feel
> like there's a jackhammer
> from head to heel.

Her voice drifts in from another universe.

> Sound. Sound.
> No sound.
> Sound. Sound.
> No sound.

There is no sound. All music from the monitors, all buzz from the audience, has ceased.

> I'm out the window
> I'm in a tree

I'm anywhere
But inside me.

Billie is singing. It's a Quodling voice.
Sing, Gabriel urges.

Little girl
Little one
Go to sleep
You're not alone.

The audience is still. There is no motion, no roar, not a clap,
not a cough. People have crossed their arms over their abdomens.
They are folding into hunched, isolated figures.

Kendra averts her eyes. This is the worst failure of any song
she's written. Cords and wires could make good nooses.

A woman jumps to her feet in the back of the hall. Kendra
cringes in anticipation of the heckling and derision. "Aaaaaa-
aaaahh," the woman shrieks, a tortured voice, "Aaaaaaah." The
whole audience loosens. Some scream, or weep, and there is clapping, in frail, uneven bursts. But many of the women sit in stony,
frozen postures. Every time Survivors try to leave the stage, a new
swell stops them, and the tense sounds continue for quite a while.
How many of us were abused, Kendra wonders, how many feminists, how many lesbians, how many writers, how many college
professors? She can't stay onstage for the encore; there isn't an
ounce of strength in her body. While the other Survivors play a
joint encore with the lesbian songwriter, Kendra doubles over the
toilet bowl in a ratty washroom behind the stage, puking her guts
out. I've finally made it, she thinks, just like Billie.

Kendra has no energy for the party. Packing their gear, she
and Baker have a big row. Baker insists Kendra will recover when
she eats something, and Kendra flies off the handle, picking at
every fault she can find: you commit us to parties when you

know I hate them; you don't think of anyone but yourself; you're just like your father; you're gonna get cheap and slutty. Baker stomps off the stage. Even Lena chides Kendra for unnecessary cruelty. As penance, Kendra (though she'd rather say ten Hail Marys and go home) drags herself to the party, but the damage is not easily fixed. Baker tosses down drinks like a naïve date, and Kendra can't get near her.

"Are you an incest survivor?" A tall woman in an African vest steps in front of Kendra. She should have insisted on home and Hail Marys.

"I am," the woman continues. "Great song."

"Do you mind if I ask you something?" an eavesdropper asks. "Why call it a lullaby?"

"Amen," says a third voice. "I haven't slept through one night since it happened to me."

More and more women gather. A few men. They are telling their stories to each other. "Mine started when I was seven and my mom remarried." "Mine was with my grandfather on summer vacations." "My stepbrother used to bring his buddy and they'd take turns." Kendra stands on tiptoe, trying to spot Baker. "My daddy" "My sister" "He stopped when I" "My mom was in the hospital" The sound is dizzying. "A teacher asked me if" "I never told" "I caught him with my little" She spots a gap in the crowd, wedges herself through: "Excuse, excuse please." What has she unleashed here? She wanted to comfort the little girls, not to hear all their stories. Excuse please, excuse me.

Kendra spots Baker in the centre of a throng of men, writhing and dancing, pounding imaginary drums. A man with a pierced nose sidles up to her and grinds his hips at hers. Baker doesn't withdraw an inch. That show is for me, Kendra thinks. Baker doesn't throw a glance her way. Kendra hurries past more compliments. "Thanks, thanks."

Lena's voice arcs out of the crowd: "The child *does* know from the outset." The couple Lena is talking to must have concocted a story to tell their *in vitro* child. Kendra whirls around. Angel is swirling Scotch around her mouth the way she does when she's concentrating, saying she thinks fatherhood is a psychological state, that she could be as good a father as any partner. "In my country," Lena says, "lies of the heart are called God's whispers. But that story of yours will have to be shouted."

Kendra ducks through a hole in the crowd, towards the coatroom. An organizer follows her, catching her arm. "These arrived at the Festival office," he says, thrusting a brown paper sack at her.

"Who delivered this?" Kendra snaps, rapping the buff gift with her finger. The fellow shrugs. He wasn't in the office when it arrived.

"Who was?"

Maybe Marcie, the administrative assistant who runs everything. Marcie is never at parties. Kendra moves towards the door.

A Quodling voice eddies through her head. *Get Baker.* She glances at the throng in the corner. A few women have joined the outskirts, and men are pairing with them, in between taking turns with Baker in the centre. Baker won't leave with me, no way. Kendra reaches for her coat. *Don't leave her. She is helpless.*

Hands grab as Kendra weaves through the spinning bodies. An excited murmur welcomes her. A stocky white boy jumps into her path and she shoves him away, clasping Baker around the shoulders. "I'm sorry," she murmurs. "Come home."

"Fuck you." Baker unbuttons her blouse to the waist.

"Please. I need to talk to you."

"Leave me alone."

A crowd from the party is gathered at the elevator, so Kendra trots up the service stairs. She hurls the sack across the room and herself into a slash across the bed. Though it's very late in Toronto, she dials Axel's number.

His slurred voice is the best music she's heard in weeks, and she tells him, letting his answering murmur warm her from the inside out, melt the Ice Woman, dissolve her politics into contentment. She'd rather crawl into the cradle of his arms than talk, but talk is all there is, so she chats about the odd reception to the incest song, the fight with Baker, but omits the buff parcel. "Your audience was too moved to respond," he says, "stirred past their limits. Baker was jealous." I really have to talk to her, Kendra thinks, while Axel analyzes his trip to Washington. "In some neighbourhoods," he says, "the only difference between the United States and the Third World is that the bums are more confident." He laughs. "They think they have rights." The women in Kendra's audience with their arms creased over their stomachs didn't think they had rights; they have less confidence than beggars in America. Axel was scared by what he saw, she can hear it in his voice. "The great American middle class, world custodians of rebel democracy, is shrinking," he says, "squeezed by corporate politics, free trade and the national debt, by homelessness, street violence and a dearth of serious jobs." She was scared too by all those raw women exposing their pain. Axel rails at the callousness of leaders, a helplessness in his ranting that she has not noticed before. The same helplessness she felt when she heard those women. 'Scuse please, excuse me.

Axel's love is like an antidote to the nightmare of their stories, dissolving their army of faces into will-o'-the-wisps. His voice reaches the private galaxy where she has crouched in a prenatal curl for all these lonely years. Arousal soars like weakness from her knees to her throat.

ε ε ε

Do you have a name? Gabriel asks the yellow-rumped warbler as they fly in an amputated *V* towards childhood.

Not exactly, says the tiny voice, almost inaudible in Billie's head.

What then? Gabriel booms.

Gabriel, Billie decides, has an obnoxious, overconfident streak, as if guide is not too distant from god.

A chuckle resonates in her head. Of course, my friend. My earth self is a reversed politician, an insurgent.

Politicians and revolutionaries look the same from Quodling perspective. What's a not-exactly name? she asks.

A group of words that has a meaning, the warbler explains. They reveal something about the memory behind them, like the age of the escapee, or the job she performed for her earth self, or even the locale where she'll be stuck if she goes back.

So you are?

The Little One.

♪ ♪ ♪

20

"Goddamn, father fuck, *tabarnac.*" Baker's leg has cracked against a corner of the night table. "So eager for me to come home, you don't even wait up for me." She kicks the walnut leg back, hard, several times. "What a friend."

Kendra couldn't answer if she wanted to. Billie has her tongue. The Little One peers through her eyes, gaping at Baker's rage, her dishevelled appearance. Baker's sequined pants yawn open, her shirt is a garden of stains. Jockey shorts hang from her belt, like trophies. She tosses a pair onto Kendra's bed, stirring the air into a breeze of urine and beer, like the toilet stall backstage. "Wanna hear about my adventures?"

Nonononononononono rebounds around Kendra's skull in high wavering tones. She shakes her head.

Baker weaves vaguely towards the bathroom, miscalculates the angles, and bounces into the doorframe, teeters slowly around and flips on the light switch, oopsing as if every misstep were a little joke she made on purpose. Framed by the fluorescent light behind her, she peels down the rest of her clothes and remains swaying in the doorway. "The firzt wasz . . ."

         ♪ ♪ ♪

Where are you taking us, Little One? The warbler is flying from the sunlit skies towards a patch of storm clouds.

We are going to Eagle City in Michigan. There I will show you the event that made me leave for good.

A shroud of silence drapes Billie's mind. They pass through a tunnel, the turbulent, black air whirling around them.

Eagle City enters Billie's mind like a photograph: the main street with Berry's Hardware, the old five-and-dime, Luigi's pizza, chicken, steak, Tiny's ice cream, and the Copper Country Pharmacy that sold pink greeting cards and gifts no one liked. The rifle shop with army surplus, a laundromat, a variety food store to hang out in when Tiny closed shop for the winter.

On the outskirts of town, in another shot, appears the Quillan farmhouse before it ran down and got ramshackle. A rambling, three-storey white clapboard with green shutters and old polyester curtains, mail-ordered from the Sears catalogue, in lemon yellows and chocolate browns, draped gaily across the windows and tied back with ruffled sashes. There's the brown plaid sofa, when the stuffing and springs were still inside and its polished walnut veneer gleamed proudly. And the black rocker with the eagle decal painted on its headrest. Two-tiered end tables still flank the sofa, holding lamps with winged cherub bases and sloping cream shades. The Westinghouse console TV positioned exactly eight feet away from the brown plaid armchair where Karl sat.

Where Karl sits, for there he slouches, a big man with a broad, flat face and sandy hair, sipping beer, no, sipping yellowish liquid from a squat glass. A smile plays at the corner of his lips, set like a razor cut across his square, clenched jaw. On the rug, a toddler with a mop of red curls sits splay-legged, concentrating on a few jagged puzzle pieces spread out around her.

Billie looks at the flimsy skirt with the yellow bud print. It doesn't reach the toddler's knees. The patch of white cotton is a beacon between her splayed legs.

He thought she was seductive when she sat like that, the warbler says.

A three-year old? Gabriel sputters.

Very, very seductive. He told her she was coming on to him, that she was a temptress, a little Eve who cast a spell on him and made him do what he did.

Ridiculous! Billie thinks.

Maybe. She believed him.

You were going to show us the event itself, Gabriel prods. Are you by any chance procrastinating?

᷍ ᷍ ᷍

Baker is still talking. Mother Mary, I haven't heard a word she's said. Maybe no one ever listens to her, maybe that's why she overplays everything. Kendra doesn't even have audio recall. Her mind is as blank as an erased tape. Baker stumbles off into the bathroom. Tomorrow, Kendra promises herself, her mind sore like it's done a hundred pushups, tomorrow I'll talk to her. A wall of pressure drums against her eyelids and she pitches into sleep.

21

Brandon, Regina, Saskatoon, Medicine Hat, Lethbridge. Soon the Canadian Prairies are finished, and they drop down for the U.S. part of the tour. The U.P. is only days away. It's been seventeen years since Kendra spent Christmas on the farm, nearly ten since she's visited at all. She asks Baker to come with her. Axel would be threatening for Karl, but Baker can provide a shield invisible to Karl, female. Baker teases, asks if she really wants to bring a coked-up slut home for Christmas. "In Eagle City," Kendra says, "sluts are so commonplace they have a special pew at church. It's Jewish sluts who are outsiders."

Even seventeen years away from Eagle City, thoughts like these are hard to think. A familiar pressure drums behind her eyes, etching midnight and shooting stars onto the lids. *Little girl. Little one. Go to sleep. You're not alone* repeats obsessively in her head. *Fly Billie, fly Billie, fly Billie* sounds faintly underneath. *We will go to Eagle City in Michigan.* I can't find you, I can't get there. *Are you procrastinating?*

In less than two hours they have to be at the airport to catch their flight to Fargo. Six concerts to Marquette, eight days to Eagle City.

Fargo, Rochester, Minneapolis, Milwaukee. Life is a blur of silver wings, hot lights, big bland hotel rooms. Even Baker can't find much to amuse herself in the endless trail of oversized lobbies and three-machine fitness centres. In Ann Arbor, she finds a bookstore and buys a stack of poetry and psychology, and it's like old times, Baker ablaze with ideas and passages, Kendra, in headphones, fingering arrangements on her acoustic guitar.

"God," Baker says. "This man says the degradation of Jews in the *lagers* was done with intent, as a policy." She holds up a book called *The Survivor* by Terence Des Pres. "He says the humiliation, the defilement, the making them stinky and filthy and slimed in their own excrement, made it easy to murder them. They looked like animals. They stank like animals. They even behaved like animals. You sure you want to go home?" Baker glances at Kendra, expecting the exhilaration of discovery to unite them, but the owner of Kendra's eyes has gone on vacation.

ᶜ ᶜ ᶜ

I can't show you. The warbler's thin, yellow voice quavers.

Why not, my Little One? The whisper of a thousand summer breezes could not match the soothing in Gabriel's voice.

I am too close to her here. Too close, tooclose, tooclose tooooclose We will merge and explode. Explode,explode,explode, explode

Quodling can only be borne from a great distance, Little One. Is that what you mean?

Yesyesyesyesyesyesyesyesyesyesyes The string of shrilled words is an incantation against explosive thoughts.

Can anyone else show us, now that we're here? Gabriel asks.

I CAN. A gigantic, four-taloned hawk blocks the sun with broad, flapping wings. The warbler vanishes, although Billie hears Gabriel speculate that she has not flown far.

Who are you? Gabriel intones in his most impressive voice.

I go by the name The Four-Taloned Hawk. I'm the one like him. The hawk nods at Karl sitting in the brown plaid armchair.

Billie's stomach lurches.

I'm the only one who can tell you what really happened, the Hawk proclaims.

Not the right version, Billie thinks, but Gabriel's acceptance speech drowns her out.

Come, the Hawk beckons, watch the little flirt.

The white patch between the toddler's legs enlarges. Her red curls and serious face disappear.

See how she entices him, the Four-Taloned Hawk narrates. He can't take his eyes off her. He is weak and helpless, completely controlled by a patch of material and an orchid. Poor man. He succumbs to her wishes. Pulls aside the petal and touches her little soft stigma with all his restrained love and passion. Watch her smile up at him.

Billie sees two faces, a smiling, luminescent angel, an enraged, contorted demon.

That's mine, the shrill voice of the Little One confides about the second face. That's the face in Glinda's album.

↜ ↜ ↜

Kendra begins the second set in Detroit with "The Incest Lullaby," under its new name, "The Incest Song." This time, she tumbles through the wake of silence, like a pitch-black tunnel of viscous fluid, to find herself heaved by teal waves rippling out of her diaphragm, and races offstage before any clapping starts. Stumbling into a turnip-coloured bathroom, she leans over the small toilet. Years of urine waft from the stained, cracked bowl, and a crescent-shaped smear of unflushed faeces hangs from the inner rim. Drool runs from her open mouth; she can't seem to swallow any more.

❧ ❧ ❧

You can get used to any smell, Astor tells the Little One.

I can't, I can't, she howls, though faintly. I'd rather eat spinach slime, raw eggs, nose mucus, used chewing gum, but not that sour pickle covered with grit and hairs, and dipped in a toilet someone forgot to flush.

I learned to sleep with diarrhoea on my face, Astor says.

But you were with family. Your sister's arms were around you. I had to swallow my own vomit, and the white stuff.

Astor flies closer to the warbler, to be sure no thought slips by.

Those cloudbursts of white goo, the warbler continues. I didn't know where it went. I thought it was going to fill up all the space from down there to my heart until there was no more room inside me and I'd blow up. Or it would ooze into my brain and I wouldn't be able to think normal any more.

❧ ❧ ❧

The spasms of nausea are slowing now. Kendra hauls herself away from the bowl. Was I quiet enough? Did anyone hear? Can I flush yet? She strains to hear the rumbling sound of snoring that signals respite. There it is. She pushes the handle and watches the surge of water cleanse the walls of the bowl. I want to sleep now, lie down right here and sleep. The snoring is getting louder. It's got whistles and hoots in it. She glances in the mirror, but the wrong face stares out, and she splashes icy water over her own until the contortions disappear. The snoring is clapping.

Onstage, Baker is chanting her way through "Ghostchildren" with Lena playing lead on the keyboards. Kendra slides in on harmony but her spirit is depleted, and she leans heavily on the group for the rest of the concert. "The Incest Song" will have to be last or unsung after this. Their next gig is in the U.P., where she would like to belt it from the heavens.

The Iron Mountain Men open the Marquette concert. Six white boys in flannel shirts twanging a lament about some churchgoin' man bein' whupped by a money-grubbin' mama. Kendra's home all right. Six Karls in a semicircle setting the tone for her act.

"Isis and Ishtar," Baker chokes. "Look at those women."

"Don't underestimate the women here," Kendra hisses. "Look at their hands, not at their clothes."

"Look at their eyes. Way past cowed. Dead and gone."

"Hiding, Baker. Biding their time. Same as I did."

Baker wants to punch out with "The Incest Song," but Kendra won't, not here, not yet. Anyone might be in that audience, people who watched her yield to Karl's will the last time she performed in the U.P., even Karl. She is going to savour this show, song by song.

The Iron Men finish their set with a medley of favourites. The big one with the peppery beard does a virtuoso "Duelling Banjos" on his mandolin, and the audience hollers for "Foggy Mountain Breakdown." Baker has underestimated this audience, a restive, spicy lot, out for a binge on rollicking music, unimpressed by cleverness in song. Some are fans of the Iron Mountain group, but most want to hear this uprooted home talent with their own ears, see if she's any good.

The stagehands rearrange the amplifiers and instruments for Survivors' set. Kendra can hear the emcee spin a legend from her Eagle City roots. The ovation that greets them is lackadaisical and sparse. Kendra will have to earn their approval. Kendra runs out last, as planned, takes her place at the centre mike, looks out.

In the front row sit Kiki, Kimmy, Hannahjean. Next to them, their neighbours, the Dorseys. And the St. Jameses, the Greens, Mrs. Esfakis, the Johnsons, the Bells. The entire Rogers clan is seated behind them, along with the Harrisons, the Jordans, the Koulacks, the Ipps. Sharon Bajer is there, with her daughter Ameena, and her son George, and Brenda Willcox has brought Silas and Eli, Ginny and Greg. There are at least three rows of people from Eagle City. Seventeen years from Kendra's life evaporate as she tunes. There is no empty seat for Karl beside Hannahjean.

Every song seems too risky. The contingent of political women is small, and the college kids look like engineering majors. The audience is shuffling and coughing. She has to decide. Baker does an extra sound check with her snares and toms to take the heat off. Kendra can still hear that low, reverberating growl from her graduation night. She had been about to sing the Billy Taylor song, "I Wish I Knew How It Would Feel to Be Free," that she learned from Nina Simone's *Silk and Soul* album. She has never played it. *Play it now.* A tiny voice. *I've never heard it.*

She signals with an opening riff. Lena has to lead. They nod, no questions. It's her night, her town, she can call whatever she wants.

> I wish I knew how it would feel to be free
> I wish I could break all these chains holding me
> I wish I could say all the things that I should say
> Say 'em loud, say 'em clear
> So the whole round world could hear.

Smile, Kimmy. Smile, Kiki. Her sisters' faces are lit by the stage lights, so she can sing to them with her eyes. Harmonize with me, Hannahjean.

> I wish I could share all the love that's in my heart
> Remove all the bonds that keep us apart
> I wish you could know what it means to be me
> Then you'd see and agree
> That everyone should be free.

A chorus of tones and undertones cascades back from the monitors. Her voice has a resonance she has never heard before.

> I wish I could give all I'm longing to give
> I wish I could live like I'm longing to live
> I wish I could do all the things that I can do
> Though I'm way overdue
> I'd be starting anew.

Billie and Glinda and Astor and Gabriel and the Little One and Miles and the Four-Taloned Hawk are singing away like a Greek chorus. No wonder her voice sounds so full.

> I wish I could be like a bird in the sky
> How sweet it would be if I found I could fly
> I'd soar to the sun and look down at the sea
> Then I'd sing 'cause I'd know
> Yes I'd sing 'cause I'd know
> I'd know how it feeeeels
> Yeah, I'd know how it feeeels
> to be free. Lord lord lord
> > how it feels, how it feels, how it feels
> > to be free.

She could sing that chorus a hundred times. Especially with all the new tones and timbres she is finding tonight.

> Oh shoobe doo, to be free freeee free.

She remembers longing the most. Other people had love, she had longing: longing to be seen, longing to be held, longing to be touched, longing for laughter and love, longing to be free. Democracy, that bright shining ideal of men's etiquette towards men, that sweet notion of inalienable rights, and tolerance for contrary, even hateful, ideas, was never meant for the interior of families in which men like Karl would not tolerate dissent from their own wishes. (Will Hannahjean hug her after the concert? or rush off, afraid to act without Karl?) The applause is lukewarm, unsympathetic still. She woos them with country rock, Jean Ritchie's "Sorrow in the Wind," the McGarrigles' "As Fast As My Feet Can Carry Me," and wins them with fifties tunes, the Miracles' "You've Really Got a Hold on Me," Buddy Holly's "Rave On." Kiki and Kimmy love that one; their faces beam, their feet tap. After Chuck Berry and some Aretha Franklin, the whole stony lot of them are eating out of her hands. She withholds her own numbers. She would never have written them if she hadn't run away.

Baker is throwing questioning glances at her. Lena looks as if she's uttering prayers, or messages. Baker taps a riff from "Almost a Woman." Kendra whips her head back and forth in the no of a child, and introduces another fifties favourite. By break time, the audience is swimming in other people's sound. Baker grabs Kendra's sleeve and hisses, "What are you doing?" Lena asks if anything is wrong. Kendra, frozen at seventeen, fourteen, and who knows what other ages, gazes out of agonized eyes and can't find words. These words do not belong to her. *Billie, Gabriel,* she calls, and she can hear them, but it's cacophony, white truth: *Only tell what they can know. Hide, Billie. Hide. Open your mouth and close your eyes. Tell and die, tell and die. Sing and die, sing and lie. Lie and live, lie to live.*

"I know this audience," she announces. "Half my home town is out there and I'm going to give them what they want. If I call 'Jesus Loves Me' for our finale, you'd all better be with me."

"We have fans out there," Baker squawks.

"They'll live."

"We need the sales," Angel says. "The Christmas rush."

"I don't care. Not tonight."

"What's wrong?" Lena's warmth arrows into her heart.

"I can't give those people my songs." *Sing and die.* "None of them helped."

"These are the people you've been writing for," Baker says. "Don't let them off the hook now."

"Come out to them," Angel exhorts.

Kendra shakes her head, nonono. *Live and lie.*

"So blow you old winds of time." Back onstage, safe in the music of Connie Kaldor, Kendra moans "Grandmother's Song." "You've wrinkled my heart with your blowin'." Her blue voice electrifies, purples the air. By the end of the set, Kendra-now is so distant she can even do a song of their own. With an elaborate bow to Baker, she strikes the chords of "Almost a Woman (I'm a Big Girl)," and Billie Holiday is singing, not Kendra Quillan. In the back of Ellen Tremayne's classroom, in her high school days, she used to say to herself NotKendra, NotKendra, notKendra, notkendra, an incantation to make herself disappear. She could make her skin so numb that if she pinched or scratched or bit herself, she wouldn't feel a thing. Sometimes, it wouldn't even leave marks. If it did, she could will them away, then will them back two hours later, or two days, just by thinking about the injury. Of course, it was notKendra who could do those things, so Kendra never told anyone about her abilities. *Tell and die, tell and die.*

22

Kendra and Baker rent a four-wheel-drive, all-weather, sport utility vehicle to cruise to Eagle City. Along the way, Kendra regales Baker with local lore, points out landmarks, pauses at vista points. God, she loves this country, this Upper Peninsula. She loves every bend in the road, every white pine, arrowing up towards a circling hawk or a daytime moon. If it were summer, she would feed Baker fresh trout, pan-fried over an outdoor fire, or coho salmon, so fresh a buttery texture would ooze from its natural oils. She insists Baker order a fisherman's breakfast of eggs, home fries, cinnamon toast, and chunks of pan-fried white-fish.

"'Take a trip with me in 1913. To Calumet, Michigan and the copper country,'" Kendra sings, as they head into the heart of old copper country. "Calumet is just north and west of here," she explains, singing on.

"'I'll take you to a place called I-tal-i-an Hall. Where the miners are havin' a big Christmas Ball.'"

"What song is that?" Baker asks.

"Woody Guthrie's '1913 Massacre.'"

You ask about work and you ask about pay.
They tell you they're making less'n a dollar a day
Workin' those copper mines, riskin' their lives . . .

"Looks like tourist country to me," Baker says.

"'So it's fun to have a party with children and wives.' It is now," Kendra explains. "The copper's been mined out for years, though there's iron ore near Marquette.

"It's a funny thing about the U.P. Michigan and Ohio fought over the border area, where Toledo is, for years, until Michigan got statehood from Congress by giving it up. The U.P. was a consolation prize, and it turned out to be full of resources."

"I don't remember any war between Michigan and Ohio."

"No? It was called the Toledo war. There was one casualty. A deputy sheriff in Michigan was killed by Two Stickney, the second son of some fanatic Ohioan. The first son was named — guess."

"One?"

"You got it."

Glimpses of Superior glint through the trees as they drive up the Keweenaw Peninsula.

"It wasn't really a war, Baker. Just a lot of arguing in Congress."

Near the northern reaches of the Keweenaw, the main streets of the old boom towns from the 1840s and '50s have degenerated into tourist attractions, lined with shops that sell copper knickknacks and tours of the upper shafts of played-out mines. In the old days, the spurs reached far under Superior, miles from sunlight and safety, though copper wasn't prone to the gaseous fumes that tripped the deadly explosions in the coal mines.

The U.P. character had been formed by its rugged industries: mining, fur trading, fishing, logging. Once the copper and lumber played out, there wasn't much left, especially in the Keweenaw. The U.P. emptied, making room for people like Karl to scratch out a living in a frozen wilderness of parks and forests. Karl, dreaming of enough space to set his spirit free, moved north against the tide, onto land that a century earlier had been sold by the government at $1.25 an acre, including mineral rights. He wanted a hundred acres between himself and his nearest neighbour. Back then, he could have afforded it.

"The way you talk I thought he was planted like a tree here," Baker says.

"Transplanted like a tree. He was a cop in Flint before he moved up here."

Live and lie. Why Karl gave up policing ran like a polluted stream under her childhood, roiling to the surface in accusatory whispers late at night, conversations Kendra would strain to hear yet be unable to recall the next morning, as she lay under the crumple of her bedcovers and breathed the faint, lingering reek of Karl's beery tongue. On those mornings, Karl awoke in a stunning good mood and insisted on a special outing, fishing at sunrise, or tobogganing down the flank of a nearby hill, all the while whistling like he had a prize lottery ticket up his sleeve. If it were summer, Kendra would ferry Baker up to the rocky wilderness of Isle Royale to search for fossilized footprints from her childhood under the web of her favourite trees. If there was one thing Kendra could love without reserve, it was the land.

They enter the hamlet of Eagle City. The houses, built like Quonsets, look small and sparse, straggling into the air like winter saplings. Baker's home town, ten thousand people in central New Jersey, surrounded by highways that speed off to New York or Philadelphia, is bustling in comparison. The two-lane highway out of Eagle City leads nowhere for a very long time.

The snow blanket is thin for December, though storm clouds are gathering in the distance. The farm is a mile or more outside town. Kendra spots a black-lettered sign for Karl's new venture. The farm used to be dairy – U.P. soil is too poor to support grazing – but Karl has converted much of it to Christmas trees. Through a break in the triangulated trees, the lake sparkles.

The house looks gay and freshly painted, unlike her memories. Hannahjean poses in the doorway and waves. As they clear the top step, she extends her arms and stumbles, clutches onto Kendra's body to steady herself out of a backwards fall. Kendra wraps her arms around Hannahjean, who drops her head against Kendra's shoulder and weeps. Streams of tears from this child-woman, who is her mother, freeze into stilettos of ice that pierce Kendra's heart and fill it with the anguish of Hannahjean, which is the anguish of all women who live their lives as the ribs of men. For Hannahjean's sake, and for the sake of Kendra's own unrelenting love for her mother, this Christmas can be no different from any other.

Kiki and Kimmy materialize out of the kitchen. Even in a chef's apron, Kimmy looks as lithe and neat as a *Vogue* cover. Kiki, in huge, nubby sweat pants, is covered with splatters of oil and flour. The spatula in her hand is globbed in dough, and she is threatening to rub it across Kimmy's cheek. Kimmy opens her jaw like an oven, tilting her head backwards to receive the offering. Kiki tiptoes over to Kendra and Baker, deposits the sweet dough in their two mouths. They muffle their laughter, to see how long Kimmy will stand with her jaw unhinged. The kitchen is the only room anyone ever laughed in.

Hannahjean settles Baker in Jerry's old room and Kendra into her childhood bedroom at the end of the hall. The others are sharing a clearing in the unfinished clutter of the attic, on the third floor. Kendra's old room has turned into a strange mélange of Karl's gear and the remnants of her girlhood. A rainbow trout carved from white pine, like the pulpit of the Holy Redeemer Church, is nailed to a wooden pedestal. Next to it are a fox, a fawn, the horns of a moose. Karl has turned whittling into an art form. The closet is filled with flannel shirts, overalls, and jeans.

Shoving his clothes aside to make room for her own, Kendra sees all the clothes she left behind on graduation night. Her entire high school wardrobe is hanging on hooks in the back.

Karl is booming hellos downstairs. The loud wait of his pacing summons Kendra for their ritual Christmas outing. She scoots downstairs, only now noticing the plaid sofa has been replaced by Naugahyde, brown like the moist bed of a creek. Karl's down-stuffed clothing makes him look square and powerful, though his sandy hair has thinned and silvered. Kendra starts to run to him, arms outstretched to hug him like she used to. *Freeze*, she hears, *freeze now*, in multi-voices, and her arms drop to her sides. Soberly, she pumps his hand, dry and sandpapery against her own. One of her eyes is cobalt blue like his two, which penetrate her, searching for his Kendra-girl, who is her notKendra. Together, they start out the door.

"Can I come?" Baker calls into the wind. Neither of them turns around.

Karl talks to his Kendra-girl. He tells her about improvements he has made on the farm, about Jerry's gas station and repair shop in Hancock, about newly paved roads and lodges that have opened. In almost the same tone, he tells her about the hunting and fishing expeditions he is leading with Jerry. He opens the glove compartment and slides out a brochure, folded into thirds on blue copy paper. On the cover is a black-and-white picture of Jerry and Karl in mukluks and parkas, sawing a hole in the winter ice. A box of lures and a teepee of sturdy fishing poles lie on the ice beside them. The brochure is called Quillan Adventure Expeditions. Quotations from satisfied customers attest to the value of the experience, the daring. Karl has devised another inventive way to eke money from a brutal land.

They drive along two frozen ruts to the rear of the tree acreage, the truck in four-wheel drive. Cones of light from the top of the cab thread through the sloping arms of the trees. Baker calls these spotlights "leer lights" for the way they trap women in their glare. The heat in the truck is blasting, and Kendra feels suffocatingly warm. Karl parks under a thatch of branches, the truck idling in a low snarl. He takes out other versions of the wilderness brochure printed on yellow and mint green paper and dumps them on Kendra's lap, reaching behind him for the axe. He angles the axe, its head sheathed in hide, against the console. The wool of his black-and-white plaid shirt balloons out from the quilted puff of his vest. "You don't need that down coat, Kendra-girl," he says, sliding next to her, tugging at the tongue of the two-way zipper. NotKendra, notkendra. She removes her coat, and frost numbs her torso from the inside as she watches him play with her nipples, which are no longer nipples, but metal coat fasteners. He flicks and twirls the nubs of metal with his skating tongue. Tongues should get stuck on cold metal, but his doesn't. "It's good to have you home, kendra-girl, kendra-girl," he mutters in his voice-that-blurs-all-words-into-mush. Then he says something that makes no sense at all, like "latermykendra girlmysweetestlittlehoneychildlaterlaterlater."

"Zip up that coat, girl. Let's go pick us the best tree in the U.P."

A new snow is falling in big flat flakes, hiding the treacherous patches of the trail under a layer of twinkling white. Their steps echo into the gaps between the trees as they pick their way to the trees Karl has selected for her to consider. Of the three he has chosen, one is marked with a tinsel ribbon. "That's the one," she says, tapping it through the wool of her glove. He chops for her with wide, arcing swings. Chips of timber fly like flaxen snowflakes. A strange impulse to chop with him seizes her, though this wasn't part of their ritual. *Grab the axe. Off with his head. Off with his* The tree falls into the snow with a muffled thud, and Karl, axe tucked back in his belt, drags it to the pickup.

They drive in silence as the late afternoon sun bleeds across the horizon. The flurry has ended. Long, dark fingers of a cloud squeeze the carmine sky at its neck, while high above a mixture of pale blues and grey-bellied whites lingers, two lives that can never come together.

Kendra strips off boots, socks, gloves, scarf, coat, and tiptoes into the living room. A lattice of birch logs roars in the fireplace. The corner of the room has been cleared for the tree. The air is oiled with the fragrances of Christmas, the shortbreads, the holly, the mustard-coated ham, rum in chocolate, in eggnog, in punch. A single red candle with a flame-shaped light glows from every window ledge. Amidst the hubbub of voices from the kitchen, Kendra can hear her sister Kelley. Kelley and Baker are arguing over the future of the *Roe versus Wade*. Kelley, louder since she started law school, is telling Baker she should read the bills that don't pass the House if she wants to know what the boys are really up to. Hannahjean darts cowed eyes at Kendra as she enters. "He's parking the truck," Kendra replies. "Why don't you get out the decorations?"

Hannahjean fetches a terra-cotta pot from the pantry for the tree. A porcelain inlay of sleighs and reindeer circles the upper rim. "Is this big enough?" she asks Kendra. Karl always grouses that the pot is too small, too flimsy, improperly prepared. "Perfect," Kendra says, and winks.

Hannahjean fills the pot with earth and pebbles, careful to aerate each layer. The way Karl carries on, you'd think a family with Hannahjean at the helm would just flounder from one disaster to another. Kendra pours herself a tumbler of rum and eggnog. Hard to believe when you watched her knit, crotchet, sew, darn, preserve, can, freeze, cook, refinish tables, wallpaper, paint. A Hannahjean family would be built on cooperation, would be a democracy of the heart.

"Where the hell is the undermat?" Karl shouts from the living room.

"Coming, dear," Hannahjean singsongs.

Kendra hurries into the living room to clear anything that might obstruct the spreading of the undermat. Karl is propping the tree against the wall, trying to fiddle with a piece of green felt.

"She can't get anything right," he mutters. "No matter how many times I tell her, she never remembers. Every year she forgets the undermat. Every year she puts down the green felt without the undermat."

Kendra rolls up the felt mat.

"What the fuck is taking so long?" Karl yells.

"Let me take this end," Kendra says.

"Same old story. Every year, same damn story." He lets Kendra absorb a bit of the tree's weight.

Hannahjean scuttles into the room with a foam undermat. She unrolls it, patting out rancid dust in little clouds.

"Christ, woman, lay it flush," Karl snaps.

"It looks good on the diagonal," Kendra says.

Karl glares at her but holds the tree in the air while Hannahjean crawls underneath with the pot.

The tree fits easily, as it always does when Karl lets anyone help him with it. Everyone oohs at its splendour until his bad humour yields to the adulation that makes him feel less of a failure. From his slum childhood in Detroit onward, Karl's life has been full of errors, missed opportunities, bad bets, nasty breaks, humiliations, and slights. The whole festering pile can be ignited by the most minor criticism, like "isn't that tree listing slightly to the right?" (which it is) or "let's clip the sagging end of that second branch" (which Kendra does). Here, in the U.P., no one can witness his errors (and he makes so many fewer when he is completely on his own), although, when he does make one, the ridiculing eyes of all the people who have ever wished him ill or gloated in his failures reappear, laughing and jeering, until he can no longer stem the rage and explodes at the nearest witness, whether dog or tree or that cringing, sexless, girl-birthing wife of his. Only his Kendra-girl understands him. She has been his solace since she was a baby and now she is home again, by his side, more beautiful and wilful than ever. She is the one who is just like him.

23

Baker lifts her glass and calls for a toast. The festive table sags with appetizers, salads, wines, breads. Kendra tries to glare Baker into silence. Last summer, at the celebration of Survivors' tenth anniversary, Baker had raised her flute of bubbly "To womankind, who will save the earth. To goddess-rule of our universe." Gary aimed his glass at Baker's face, but at the last moment jerked his arm upward so it sailed above her head, spilling a rainbow of water through the air until the glass finally shattered against the wall. Kendra makes a lobbing gesture at Baker with her wineglass to remind her. Baker clinks her glass against Karl's. "To a great leader of a great family."

"Did your family celebrate Christmas?" Hannahjean asks, after they drink.

"Only when my father turned up," Baker says. "About once every three years."

"What did your father do?" asks Kelley.

Baker stabs an artichoke. "He was a journalist," she says.

"The kind of guy you'd see now on CNN with a lamb's-wool hat and the Kremlin behind him."

Karl waves a doughy triangle of spanikopita in front of Baker's face. "Can you tell me what the hell this is?" he says.

"Didn't you celebrate Chanukah?" Hannahjean asks.

Baker takes a nip out of the waving dough. "Spinach, olive oil, pine nuts, feta, phyllo pastry," she says, and pushes the triangle right into Karl's mouth. "Chanukah is a holiday made up by New Testament rabbis, my mother used to say. We never observed it." Karl gobbles the entire triangle and suctions Baker's two fingers into the purse of his lips, flicking his tongue around them. Baker tilts her wineglass at Kendra, who stares in awe, thinking, My god, she's a genius, she has him eating right out of her hand.

Kiki raises the delicate subject of midnight Mass. She wants to go to the Holy Redeemer Church, where they went as children on the nights Hannahjean wheedled the truck keys from Karl. Once Kendra had loved the rituals of the Church, especially the organ music, and the Latin intoned by the priests, sounds that crested high above the congregation as if God himself were speaking. She adored the gloriously carved altar, and the sculpture of Christ crucified, his head lolling to one side, tortured but pure, staring far into a vision his tormentors could never see, just as they could not anticipate his transmutation into a force stronger than their fists and lashes and thorns, his return as an idea so sacred and compelling it would destroy the very authority they had used to limit his life on earth: an idea like feminism, through which all the starved, choked, swollen, bruised, pummelled, knifed, gagged, whipped women would rise up, in their slimy, filthy, sperm-greased skins, every stretched, torn, and bleeding orifice visible to the world, instead of the fawning, loving, brilliant smiles they pour like honey into the faces of their tormentors – rise up and say in the unified scream of the silenced, NO MORE.

Christ was the first victim to become God.

Karl has rolled a white napkin into a neat cloth strip, which he flattens and ties around his neck. Leaning towards Baker, he invites her, and everyone, to attend his midnight sermon and save themselves the trip. Baker actually tweaks his chin. "I'll bet you're great," she says. "Great." Her smile is radiant. Kiki says she's been going to a religion class where they study the wisdom of the saints and apply it to their lives. Kimmy almost leaps over the table. Her lama in California has been advising her the true path is often found through the religion of birth. Karl does not seem to hear any of this.

Kendra particularly liked the story of how Joseph believed it was a virgin birth and didn't barrage Mary and her unborn child with fists and words: whore, slut, tart, you expect me to believe your lies about God's child, probably spread your thighs for that fat merchant sniffing round these parts last week. God's child, God's child, she tells me, and is God going to feed it? Is God going to clothe it? Will God provide a crib for it to sleep in? Later, Kendra realized this wasn't what virgin birth really meant, but she liked this Joseph-father idea so much, she preserved it, a life-raft thought, an earth father who listened and believed a woman's words about her own life. Joseph, this child just sprang into my womb, it must be God's will, God's child. Don't be angry with me, Joseph, let us love this little seedling as a gift from the heavens, and he does, this listening Joseph, this Joseph without walls. And so Kendra recognized Axel as a good man, a listening man, when she met him, although he was unlike anyone she had known before.

The wind's song has changed to a growl, as if siding with Karl about Mass. Hannahjean swings open the back door, where the gale is knocking, to show Baker a force too strong for midnight travelling. Midnight Mass was a society event in Baker's home town, so Kendra promises to take her to Mass in a cathedral back in Toronto. Baker says God doesn't dwell in cities. In the living room, she starts carolling when they decorate the tree. Everyone joins in, even Kendra. The Christmas honour of placing the final decoration on the top of the tree is given to Baker.

Cold, travel, and the strain of families tire everyone early. One by one, they traipse up to their rooms, leaving Karl watching television and whittling by the dwindling fire. Kendra is as exhausted as a spent mine, so many selves is she dragging with her as she climbs into the bed of her childhood, where part of her will sleep and part will watch for any of the myriad possibilities of this Christmas Eve night.

ↄ ↄ ↄ

Someone is calling: Fly Billie fly. Fly fast. Fly hard. Fly far. Over and over like a chant: fly Billie, fly fast, fly hard, fly far. Billie flies frantically. Senseless snatches of thoughttalk, like subway blather, drift by, in phrases. The urging, insistent voice sounds beneficent, helpful, nearly wise, but not familiar. In her haste, Billie flies directly into a cluster of light whorls, who are so insubstantial she can fly right through them. Their voices wheeze indignantly at her rude intrusion, yet the urger advises her not to stop, even though she has erred, and offended them.

Fly Billie. Fly fast. Fly hard. Fly far.

I have a message for you.

Gabriel, Gabriel. I'm so glad to hear you.

Glinda has asked to speak to you.

About what?

I don't know.

Will you come with me?

She wants to see you alone.

Gabriel, how can I get to Quodling without you? I don't know the way.

You do, Billie. You showed me.

Fly Billie.

Did you hear that, Gabriel?

141

Hear what?

The voice saying Fly Billie.

No.

We don't hear the same things?

Not unless they're directed to us both.

Someone's been talking to me ever since I arrived.

Ask who it is.

Billie thinks the question.

I am Glinda's assistant from Quodling, Crystal. Fly Billie. I will keep calling to you. Follow the trail of my voice past the friendly clamour of half-truths, who will sing to you along the way. Follow my quavering, thin, reedy vocal thread, which is all I can offer you so far from Quodling. But remember, dear Billie, the skies are laced with the sweet music of poignant, unambiguous, simple truths, each convinced of the power of their own beauty, each spinning their severed facet as the entire diamond, each looking for believers to disguise the surrounding void. Fly Billie. Fly fast. Fly hard. Fly far.

Bye, Gabriel, wish me luck.

I wish you more than luck. I wish your truth to dawn on earth so you can go home, my friend.

What about you, Gabriel? When will you go home?

You will be an envoy for me too, my friend, for truths are cousins to each other, like tortures. Go now, Billie. We will meet again before you are done.

The half-world is frightening without Gabriel. Only the tiny ovum of trust, sprung to life at her first meeting with Glinda, fuels her journey. Voices she knows and loves call to her: Miles, the Little One, the Four-Taloned Hawk, Astor. They offer fabulous tales and fables, but that ovum of life shimmers, brighter than courage, stronger than will, more fascinating than stories. Not now Miles, not now Astor. She conjures the voice of Gabriel to reassure herself until she hears Glinda's assistant. Fly Billie, fly fast, fly hard, fly far. The reedy voice shifts into a steady, confident call, and the sweet, friendly melodies fade into a cacophony of onrushing sounds. She is near Quodling. On the descent, she remembers: Glinda has news.

She touches down in a sandy paradise of palms and bougainvillea. Lonely for Gabriel, she nestles into the warmth of the sand, and the tropics drain from the skies, now sepia, now charcoal, now black. The sand crystallizes, and moistens, cold on her skin. Icebergs float along the sea. Dunes freeze into drifts of Arctic snow. She has forgotten about Quodling. Here, objects reconfigure, colours shift, flowers bloom or wither, seasons, even landscapes, alter in accord with interior states. Heights, weights, genders, even species shift in an endless combining and recombining of fragments of thought, mood. If truth is Quodling, thinks Billie, it is neither lawful nor beautiful, not science nor art.

Glinda's approval sends a fine love, aged across centuries and galaxies, through her being. The snowdrifts melt. Gardens bloom. The skies fill with birds. Lovers twine in the grasses. Billie aches to understand the ingredients of such blood-warming love, but Glinda declines. Understanding, she explains, can only come to pass when all banned truths, even those of the poor, the ugly, the enraged, the contaminated, the maimed, the contagious, the marked, the perverted, return fully to earth. And understanding, she cautions, is a fragment of love.

Let me introduce you to our new arrival, Glinda invites, and they are in a city square. Strutting along a patch of grass, head bobbing as if on a loose coil, roams a rock dove, a common pigeon, the urban nuisance. Two squab wings are tucked along its head like stunted metal wings. For a recent arrival, Woodrow's plumage is remarkably intact.

A cold sorrow drenches Billie's mind like a slab of wet marble. What kind of feeling is this? she sputters.

Come with me. Woodrow's thoughts are a queer mixture of bass and soprano. They enter a conduit of flat, suffocating air, its moist, feculent pockets perfumed with sludge and scented with roaches and rodents. When they emerge they are in Center City, Philadelphia, a block from Rittenhouse Square.

A soiled, tattered blanket of a coat reminds Billie of Astor. The blanket's inhabitant hails everyone who passes. "How ya doin' today how's the world treatin' ya have a good day." A gentleman in an overcoat hurries by, his head bent to avoid the wind. As he passes, his hands swell fat and pink with the cold. By the time he reaches the corner, his boots have cleaved, and hornified. A small scarf of pink curls through the slit at the rear of his coat.

A woman with a watch that glitters like diamonds, and a bald patch at the crown of her tinted, apricot hair, leans over the tattered cocoon.

She always gives him money, Woodrow says. And she never tells him to get on with it.

Part of her flies here with us, a familiar voice explains.

Gabriel, Gabriel. I miss you so much.

Meanwhile, Gabriel continues, some poor bird is flying in frantic circles, trying to protect her from remembering why she gives.

What might happen?

A tiny bit of truth could flash across her mind. If he spots the glint, he'll snatch it like prey.

What could she see?

A Quodling picture.

Like?

Depends on her truth.

Like?

A belt strap the size of a horsewhip. A nose scattering raindrops of blood.

Are Quodlings always pictures? Woodrow asks.

A blank wall covers Gabriel's thoughts. He doesn't know who Woodrow is.

Woodrow and I met in Quodling, Billie explains, and pictures the park.

Gabriel reopens his mind. No. Loneliness can be a Quodling. Or a tear sliding up a duct. Anything.

Can you tolerate another scene? Woodrow asks.

Can Gabriel come?

Gabriel is welcome.

The putrescence of this tunnel is unrelieved, the air so viscous it contains no space and can hardly buoy up their weight. It is a rough flight.

Walnut Street is thronged with beggars. Well-dressed people pick their way from limousines to store entrances. At each door stands a uniformed guard, open holster and patent leather boots mirrors to the sun.

Army? Police? asks Gabriel.

Private, says Woodrow. Capitalist.

The guard bars the entrance to someone without identification.

It takes two valid credit cards with pictures to get into a store, Woodrow says. Money is carried only by thieves and beggars. There is no way left to give.

How do they live? Billie cries.

In a camp, a tent city. I'd show you, says Woodrow, but we must get back to Quodling. Glinda is waiting.

Space is empty and black, not a star, not a cloud, no friendly calling voices. Some of Billie's wing plumage flutters off, so she must flap harder and faster to get anywhere. The cold marble of sorrow tells her Woodrow is near.

On Quodling, Billie collapses. Maybe I can die here, she thinks, beside this changeling called truth. Maybe truth was the wrong quest, after all, a middling idea, like communism, not fully imagined. She stumbles along the ridge between death and sleep, without dreams to guide her way. A trailhead angles down the side of the cliff. It looks inviting, easy. She lets herself slide. But Billie is no longer alone. She has let Gabriel in, and Glinda. Glinda enters her Quodling sleep and inserts a few drops of aged love, enough for Billie. The love rainbows her out from her sleep.

Am I dead?

Glinda shakes her head.

What is this peace then?

When the homeless feelings go away.

Is that why you sent me with Woodrow?

Woodrow is from your childhood.

Wine and marble fight for Billie's mind.

You choose, Glinda smiles.

The marble is rose, like a rainbow. It is all one, in Quodling.

Now I can give you my news, Glinda says.

What?

Another bird is flying from the farm tonight.

♪ ♪ ♪

Karl is whistling up a storm this morning. Its strains sound like distant pipers in a dream parade, *ah dee doo ah dee doo dah day*, one of Karl's favourites. Kendra and Karl are in a field. It's summer. He's whistling "Someone's in the kitchen with Dinah," swinging her onto his shoulders. How her legs hurt when he pulls them around his neck. "Fish and whistle, whistle and fish" – he *would* like John Prine. She can't remember that tune from the old days. Funny how she never whistles in any of her songs, hates to hear Pete Seeger whistle. She must have eaten or drunk too much last night. Her body feels blimpy and swollen, like a water-logged stump.

Baker bounces into the room, wearing a flannel nightgown with a sweatshirt over it. "Happy Christmas, gorgeous," she bubbles, sitting on the edge of the narrow bed. She sounds as distant as the pipers.

"Wake up, wake up. This house is a music box. Open any door and it whistles."

I'm awake.

"C'mon, lazybones. It's Christmas morning in your fabulous U.P. and I want to see the dawn with my best friend."

Stop yammering. I'm awake.

"Kendra. Answer me."

Uhoh. I thought I was answering.

Baker leans over, her face hanging like a bloated moon in front of Kendra's slitted eyes. "Open your eyes."

I can see you.

Pores like craters.

Baker jostles Kendra by the shoulders. Kendra's sinewy, rubber limbs wave back and forth pliantly.

Stop shaking me, you bitch. Can't you see I'm right here?

Baker shakes her harder, rattles and jounces her, calling, "Kendra, wake up. Dammit, Kendra, are you okay? Talk to me. Tell me what's wrong. Dammit."

Silly airwords don't penetrate, just float. Face screwed up like a mask. Shifting mask. Furrows ploughed between her eyes. Shifting. Old, young, old, young.

I wish she'd stop pushing my body around. It's gonna hurt when the novosthetic wears off. She can't hear me think, can she Gabriel?

No, Billie. You'll have to signal her that you're there.

Opening an eyelid is like lifting a truck. What's gravity for, if not to keep eyelids at rest? *I will pit myself against the force of gravity. I will raise the cover from one eye.*

After all that effort, Baker doesn't even notice.

These human bodies are clunkers, Gabriel. So awkward and hard to move.

You are lucky to have a body to go home to, my friend. One that doesn't die when you enter it.

She tries to signal Baker with her hand and the eyelid crashes shut. Moving two body parts at one time is gargantuan to coordinate. Whistling sounds pass through the walls.

I hear terrible sobbing, Gabriel.

It's the Little One. I think the whistling scared her.

The hand moves. *Got it.* It flaps up and down, flops back on the bed like a dead weight.

147

Feels a bit like a plucked wing.

Baker is not reassured. "What the eff is wrong with you, Kendie?"

Everything.

On the air side, the word translates "Nothing."

I'm all numb and limp, can't move my body, and I don't know what's wrong.

"Just tired." The voice comes out whispery, laryngitic.

"Do you need help?"

Yes, yes, yes, yes. Help me. Help me.

"I'll be okay."

Baker cradles Kendra by the shoulders, like a wounded kitten.

From the movable hand, Kendra makes a finger-gun, pokes it into Baker's chest, jabs, jabs. A membrane coats over the chocolaty softness of Baker's eyes.

We all love you. "Go away."

Baker lowers the limp body to the pillow and kisses Kendra on the forehead. From the doorway, the sign of the cross as a crease between her eyes, Baker blows a kiss full from her fingertips, then scoots. When she leaves, Kendra lets the kiss land on her cheek, and yowls from the pain of so much love.

But only her cheek has returned. She tries the nursery-rhyme trick Gabriel has taught her. No Kendra thoughts appear. She counts backwards from ten, then a hundred. No Kendra.

How am I going to move this body? I've never done it.

Of course you have, Glinda's messenger replies in her reedy voice.

What are you talking about?

You used to control this body for days at a time. We looked it up.

I did?

It is written.

I've never heard her *think that.*

She doesn't know.

NotKendra moves her body. It's numb, like it used to be for a stretch of hours, or days. She slides a leg over the edge of the bed, knows the toes are touching the floor, but can't feel them. She has to look down to see if they're wriggling. They are. The other leg won't budge, so she pushes and shoves it with her hands until it drops over the edge. She hauls up her torso, but it slumps forward, neck bobbing.

This will never do. Every part of her is operating separately. If she listens – she hears whistling – she can't see, or smell. If she breathes – coffee is brewing – she can't hear. Feeling is totally absent from her skin. She pinches herself and no weal appears.

She must will her body to function, get downstairs for Christmas breakfast. She pushes with her hands, inches her torso high enough to roll to her knees, inserts one foot at a time between the hands, then lurches upwards into a stand.

There, she's done it. With fingers like cucumbers, she goes to take off her nightgown, but it's already gone. Under the warmth of the comforter, she must have torn off her socks and underpants during the night, though the thin, ribbed undershirt remains. She hoists on yesterday's clothes. Her running shoes are hard to tie with the bloat in her fingers. In the bathroom, balancing against the wall, an old subterfuge to hide the fact that she isn't there, a marionetteer from above splashes water on her face, brushes out her mouth, and moves her body jerkily down the stairs towards Karl, towards Baker, towards Christmas.

24

NotKendra lurches into the kitchen and slips into a place beside Baker, at the foot of the table. The room coalesces as a still: Karl bent over his plate, jaw hanging open like a front-loader; a stream of black liquid arcing through air, the handle extending from Hannahjean's floral-coated arm; a knoll of eggs trembling on the spatula in Kiki's hand; Kelley staring into coffee steam. Baker gets up and pours Kendra a cup of coffee, loading it with sugar and cream.

"Same old lazybones, I see." Karl's voice, as ringing as his whistle.

"Nothing's as snug as a childhood bed," says Hannahjean.

The juice glass slides out of Kendra's hand and spills an orange puddle on her plate, near the eggs.

"Egg à l'orange." Baker soaks up the puddle with her napkin.

No one knows, Gabriel.
Knows what, Billie?
That she isn't there.

"When do we do presents?" Kelley asks. Kiki says they should wait for Jerry and his family.

Baker lifts Kendra's coffee mug to her lips. Karl gapes at the gesture. On his way to the living room, he pokes his head between them and drapes his mouth open. Baker tips her own mug into his lips, and slurping sounds lap through the air between them.

The tree looks bleached in the cold morning light, its tinsel reflecting the washed-out colours of December. A winking gaiety from the multicoloured lights flickers over the dull winter tones. One batch of presents is wrapped in Oriental newsprint.

Jerry and Suzanne arrive with Mariette, their five-year-old. Suzanne unloads shopping bags of cheaply wrapped presents. A triad of globes protrude from Suzanne's body, yet she moves lightly for a woman that pregnant. Jerry pops a beer can in the kitchen, brings one for Karl.

Mariette hangs over the presents but doesn't touch or ask, watches Jerry for a sign. Kendra recognizes that stilted look from the inside. Hannahjean asks Jerry if Mariette can be Santa and give out the presents.

Opening presents weighed on the love side of the Quillan household when Kendra classified events, like plucked petals. Karl put iodine on her knee, love; Hannahjean potted a flower, love; Jerry buried Kiki's teddy near the barn, hate; Kendra let Kimmy sob all night, hate. The presents don't look like love today. Suzanne has wrapped every plastic toy from the dime store where she works.

The big hit is Baker's gift for Mariette. Baker brought a Swiss doll from Ursie's collection, blond with a perfect china face. Suzanne complains that their skin is too brittle for kids' play, but Jerry knows expensive when he sees it, and joshes with Baker. Baker is a genius with people. Karl is still whistling.

151

❧ ❧ ❧

I want to smash his skull with one of those logs. Bam.
Wham. Make pulp ooze out of his body.

Miles, where have you been?

How do you know who I am?

I hear you think sometimes, angry thoughts, plans to maim
and kill.

He's a bastard. Listen to him, whistling away. I want to throw
every gift in his face. Lies, I'd yell. Lies lies lies lies.

Before or after you beat him with the log? Billie asks seriously.

Fiery log. So he could feel the terrible burning that never
goes away.

❧ ❧ ❧

"Will you stop that damned whistling?"

"What's the matter with you?" Karl snaps. "It's Christmas."

"Here we go," says Jerry.

"Everyone is trying to talk and you're whistling. You don't
listen to anybody."

"You're the one blowing your lid. Christ almighty, girl, show
some respect."

"Earn some."

"Don't start with me. Not in my own house."

"Kendra, honey, he hasn't done anything wrong. He always
whistles when he's happy. It doesn't mean he isn't listening. He's
just happy to see you."

"Yeah, like the rest of us. Seeing you pick on him for fuck-
all brings back great memories," Jerry drawls.

"Let's get out of here," Kendra mutters to Baker. "I can't take
any more."

Baker squeezes Kendra's forearm. "As soon as possible." Karl
walks towards them. "What're you muttering over there? I can't
hear you."

"Kendra, honey, tell us about your band. Where'd you get a name like Survivors?"

Baker starts to explain that survivors are veterans of domestic wars, that they used to be Mauve Survivors, because mauve . . .

"Is the colour of survivors' faces," Kendra inserts. "Humiliated." The last is a whisper.

"You a girl band or a dyke band?" Jerry interrupts.

Suzanne asks if they burn their bras on stage. Baker tells her girdles and pantyhose.

"Lena and Angel are in a relationship," Kendra says.

"The pretty dark one and the big blonde?" Hannahjean asks.

"No one ever burned bras," Baker explains. Suzanne is leaning into the dyke conversation.

"But the dark one is gorgeous. She could get any man she wanted."

"She doesn't want, Ma. She's been married. She prefers Angel. They have the most loving relationship I've ever seen."

"It's not natural," Hannahjean says. Suzanne sends Mariette upstairs.

"At least they don't hurt anybody," Kimmy says.

"What the hell do they do together?" asks Karl.

Jerry says he has some pictures he can bring over.

"The media invented the whole shebang," Baker says to Kelley, who is interested in the bra story. "When the New York radical feminists disrupted the beauty pageant in Atlantic City, they refused to give interviews to male reporters. Some asshole made up the bra thing."

"That big one should make herself more attractive," Hannahjean says. "Then maybe men would like her."

"We better see about dinner," Kiki nudges Hannahjean.

Jerry asks about money, what kind of bucks they get for a concert like Marquette. Karl invites Kendra to look at a horse he is thinking of buying.

୵ ୵ ୵

Don't go, don't go.

She can't hear you, Billie.

What do you mean?

We can hear her, but she can't hear us. She has a pitifully limited range of thoughts.

Oh, hang the bloody teaching, Gabriel, and help me stop her.

There is one thing we can try.

What? What?

Filibuster. If we all gabble nonstop, we can leach her energy. She'll be a wad of wet newspaper.

C'mon everybody, c'mon.

Fuck, no. The little Jezebel's been goading the poor bugger, the Four-Taloned Hawk cries.

Shut up, you buzzard. I'll rip your feathers off. Everyone laughs. Miles is no bigger than a hummingbird, despite his fluty mockingbird's voice.

They have all gathered to help. Billie and Gabriel. Astor and Miles. Woodrow. The Little One hovers at a distance, too frightened to participate. Glinda, herself, never leaves Quodling unguarded. She has sent her assistant, to lend a hand and answer any queries.

Where's the new one? Billie asks. Can we talk to her?

She wants to die so badly Glinda quarantined her.

Without her story, I'll fly forever. I'll never return for the joy.

You know her story. It's your own.

୵ ୵ ୵

"I'm too tired to ride," Kendra says. Karl keeps at her: she hasn't been home for years, when else will she have the chance, who but his Kendra-girl can appreciate how far he has come? Poor Karl, no one to talk to all these years, no one to appreciate the kid who scrabbled his way up from the Detroit slums, who can give savings bonds to his kids during the recession of the nineties. Kendra's eyes water for him.

But she can't get up. A wave of exhaustion knocks her flat into her chair. Her body will not do what her mind orders. Finally, she just says no. It takes until he reaches the door before he squares his slumping shoulders.

↗ ↗ ↗

WE DID IT.
Yay, hooray.
Teamwork, that's the ticket.
Don't stop now. She's not out of danger.

↗ ↗ ↗

The phone rings, a harsh, unexpected clanging. Everyone hopes it's Katie from India, but it's for Kendra. "Some man," Kiki says. Kendra hasn't told them about Axel. Axel, Axel, Axel, Axel.

Axel notices the flat, hoarse quality of her voice and asks what's wrong. She can't think how to answer. His visit with his parents was great. Good. They went to a bistro in the Plateau Mont Royal area. Terrific. Montreal is in an ugly, separatist mood. Mmmhmm. The gulf between the two heritages looks unbridgeable. Absolutely. Kendra volunteers nothing, even when he says he misses her all the time, every day. Finally, he asks to talk to Baker. "I can't either," Baker whispers. "She's like a duppy."

Packing, once again, to escape her family, Kendra thinks about the hate she carries. It marks her as surely as Cain. She has to break up with Axel before she poisons him too. No more shilly-shallying. She glances into the mirror, to see her ghost. Her face is out of alignment, a Picasso painting, mirror looking at woman. Bi-coloured eyes, that is her mark. And red hair, just like

Cain's. Sooner or later, everyone notices. One blue eye and one green, they ask. Was your grandfather a husky, ho ho? or a unicorn? All those jokes, because they are uneasy. She is different and it shows in her eyes. One for hate, one for love, she quips, which one will you look into?

Hannahjean is rustling around the bathroom down the hall. Kendra rushes out to speak to her alone, to ask about the breast lump. It was benign, a cyst, Hannahjean tells her. They taught her how to examine her breasts every month by making spiralling circles out from her nipple, then mapping any hard or ropey areas on a xeroxed picture of a breast, but she is too scared to do this or to ask Karl for help. Kendra offers to demonstrate on her own breasts. She, Baker, Lena and Angel practised together for months. Hannahjean flushes and shakes her head. Bodies are not a source of pleasure for her, neither her own nor her children's. Kendra wraps her arms around her mother. Hannahjean's vertebrae feel like small, hard tumours. "It was a fine Christmas, Mummy." Mummy is a Canadian word.

As they load their bags into the sport utility rental, the family gathers on the stoop. Kimmy says she flew in from California just to see Kendra, the one sister she never got to know. Kelley makes Baker promise to stay in touch. Kiki carries out a bag she is still stuffing with cookies and aluminum-wrapped packages. Hannahjean says nothing, just looks with soft, sad eyes, and stands with no artifice in her posture. Karl has stopped whistling. He goes to put his arm around Hannahjean, and she brushes him away, lifts both hands free, and waves. Jerry is so happy to see Kendra go, he stays inside with Suzanne and Mariette. Karl hands Kendra a new map of the U.P. An edge of blue copy paper sticks out along the fold. There's our happy family photograph, Kendra thinks, climbing into the driver's seat. She wonders whose funeral will bring them together for the next family gathering.

25

All Kendra wants to do is feel that vehicle hum at the press of her hand. Every crank of the shift or twist of the wheel attests to the precise command she can exert over this rhino of a car. She zips along Highway 41, roaring past hidden junctions and blinking signals, through tiny towns, forcing the landscape of her two-lane escape route into a blur as she races from a past that is leaking into her present. Driving is control over chaos. If only she can keep driving, she might never have to think.

Baker is attuned enough to her mood to be quiet. After a couple of hours, Kendra begins to slow her pace. "Fuck," Baker says. "That was one long Christmas." She is twisting her spine into yoga poses. "Let's watch shit reruns until four in the morning."

"Not till we're past Marquette," Kendra says. "Then we can decide what to do." Their flight from the Sioux to Vancouver is two days away.

They stop at a motel east of Marquette and sleep by the flickering light of the television. For breakfast, they eat cookies and pastries from the leftovers Kiki packed.

It's an easy drive from Marquette to Munising. If it were summer, Kendra would rent a boat in Munising, glide past the towering sandstone cliffs of Pictured Rocks, and laugh as Baker moaned her delight at the sight of their sunset hues. When Karl was flush, they vacationed here in a small cabin deep in the woods. The dunes along this part of Superior formed a backdrop behind her on the days when she gazed into the waters and dreamed her earliest dreams of escape. If she swam long enough, she could become a mermaid girl, her fins a flash of silver in the grey, churning waters, guiding her like a rudder, until she emerged, free and untroubled, on the far side of childhood, the Canadian side, somewhere, she now knew, between Thunder Bay and the Sioux. She wants to explain to Baker, and to Axel, how the glistening beauty of a landscape could inspire a belief in a different life in the same way as books, but it is the wrong season, and the wrong time, and maybe landscape is a cheap excuse for beauty, the substitution by a gnarled, inferior mind.

It doesn't seem possible to tour and escape at the same time. Kendra says they're going to take 28 through Newberry and skip Pictured Rocks and Grand Marais entirely. Baker turns serious and asks if Kendra's really okay. Kendra's talked up these places for so long. "I just want to get out of here," Kendra says. "Then I'll be fine." They sip coffee from huge plastic travellers' mugs that they buy at a souvenir shop in a gas station. Baker's mug has a U.P. logo on it, but Kendra gets a plain one. As they bypass the swamplands and the Tahquamenon Falls, and skim down the fastest route to the Canadian Sioux, Baker asks again if Kendra's okay. Kendra points at a shop with a sign for freshly baked pasties. "You never did try one," she says, implying Baker lacks a sense of adventure, laughing when she rises to the bait. Baker would call them fake knishes anyway, so Kendra just lets her yowl while they pass stand after stand. They speed by bait 'n' tackle stores, last-stop gas stations and tourist shops until they come to the bridge and cross over to the tawdry, rugged Canadian side, where Kendra gulps deep, cleansing breaths of Canadian air, as if she can inhale freedom. When they find a motel, she drops into bed and sleeps a full twenty hours, until Baker wakes her to get ready for their flight to Vancouver.

26

Kendra has forgotten the breathtaking beauty of coastal British Columbia. Mountains that split the sky, flowers to placate the goddesses, Indians whose totems rise tall like the mountains, a coastline of jagged inlets, spray and surf bouncing from rocks and cliffs, greenness and the scent of pines and cedars, gorges, winding roads, the shimmer of glacial lakes. As the plane banks into its final descent, she cranes at the window, ravenous for sights that can open her heart's mind. A winter's breath of clouds reaches down to the ground, forming a mist of rain and fog, typical pale grey Vancouver weather. A spatter of droplets smears across her window as they taxi to the gate. Someone will soon ask if she has webbed feet.

The airport is on a flat delta in suburban Richmond, a short drive from the city. Baker scoots off and wheels back two carts. Their instruments are huge and clumsy in their flight cases, hard to manage. Both carts wobble. At the rental counter, they discover the car booked by the venue is too small, so they have to renegotiate to get a van. Manoeuvring around airports, lugging instruments and tour baggage, always takes forever, but travelling west puts time on their side. It's early when they leave the airport. They are booked at the Sylvia Hotel in a small room overlooking English Bay, a few blocks from the south entrance to Stanley Park. Across the street, on the seawall, rollerbladers in helmets and black kneepads weave in and out among people strolling and biking. The arms of the skaters slope like the branches of a Christmas tree.

"Let's go. Let's go." Baker is dying to walk the entire seawall around Stanley Park, but the mist is changing to big drops of rain, splattering upwards from sidewalks like oil from overheated frying pans. Kendra, cranky from a flight that jounced her throbbing head through air pockets the size of gorges, slides her Martin out of its case and begins to play an old English ballad. Soon she is playing "The Incest Song," her cheeks as wet as the sidewalks. She plays the chorus over and over. Baker disappears into the bathroom to draw herself a bath.

Sound, sound, no sound. Sound, sound, no sound.

♪ ♪ ♪

What a beautiful lullaby. Billie is floating more than flying.

I gave it to her, the Little One says, proudly. That's why she got it right.

Did you give her your memories too?

Just the one in the crib.

Does she know it's her own? I think she's ready.

Nobody's ever ready, Billie. I gave her a tiny dose of my feelings, and look at her cry.

♪ ♪ ♪

Survivors' gig is in East Vancouver at the Cultural Centre. Surprisingly, the sound check starts on time and goes smoothly. They even have time for dinner at a local trattoria. When they return, people are queuing up for the last seats. Even the singles are selling. Baker grins and hauls an extra box of tapes and CDs in from the van. Angel asks if she needs some extra muscle. The theatre is large, but intimate enough for interchange between performers and audience, and the buzzing audience is almost all women. It's good to see vests, and faces without makeup. The house is jammed to the last row in the balconies.

The fog around Kendra begins to dissipate. She can sing anything here. One after another, she calls their feminist songs, their new songs, the old favourites. When she strikes up the chords to a song, someone in the audience breaks into a smile, or nods with the vigour of a seabird's wing. Sometimes, a flutter of clapping rises to meet the first line and lifts her spirits on the gentleness of its swell. Their tie feels basic, umbilical. At the break, a vibes player invites them to jam after the gig, at a party, and they accept.

The gig speeds towards a finish. There is a lull in the sound as they retune and glance at each other. From the left balcony, loud enough to be heard, a voice complains, "I wish they'd do 'The Incest Song.'" Kendra and Baker freeze. No one knows that song yet. On purpose now, the voice rings through the hall: "The Incest Song!" From an orchestra seat, someone takes up the cry. "The Incest Song!" A third voice bellows, a fourth. Soon the entire audience has taken up the chant: "The Incest Song! The Incest Song!" Baker looks at Kendra and shrugs in disavowal: I don't know how. Kendra nods, let's do it. She walks to the edge of the stage and motions for the crowd to be quiet. A ripe stillness, the sound of a wilderness midnight, settles over the crowd.

> Daddy's in me
> making me feel
> like there's a jackhammer
> from head to heel

The intake of breaths is audible. The audience had not known the song.

What birds can only whisper

In me in me in me in me

Kendra improvises

I'm in a tree a tree a tree a tree

in a blue voice that's half child

alone alone alone alone

and half Quodling. Tears strip her painted adult face, streaking her with runnels of mascara and powder. She is sure a puddle of rouge and lipstick and eye makeup is creaming around her feet, in the colour of earth tones.

"Again! Again! Again!" The audience, a patchwork of seated and standing people, is calling, not "more" or "encore," but to hear "The Incest Song" one more time. This never happens. Nausea burbles up Kendra's throat and she swallows heavily. She doesn't know if she can do it again. The audience resettles, having made its wish known. Kendra swallows a mound in her throat. Survivors are waiting for her signal. She isn't going to make it.

Heaving, she bolts off the stage. She doesn't make it. A couple feet shy of the exit, she vomits. Her legs buckle, and she crashes to her knees, puking her insides out in public. What little dignity she possessed is finished. She is crying uncontrollably between spasms. She is huddled in a knot. Someone is leaning over her, stroking her hair. Baker. Angel's there too, grabbing an arm, trying to pull her off the stage. The audience has gone still. Or the sound has snapped off. No. She can hear Lena, improvising on the keyboards, distracting the crowd with her radiance, her talent. No sound no sound no sound. Thank you, Lena. Thank you, Baker. Thank you, Angel.

27

Baker's hands are soft as summer grasses as she helps remove Kendra's vomit-soaked clothing. A scent of lilac perfumes the air as the bath fills the hotel tub and steams the mirrors. Kendra sinks gratefully into the solitude of bathing and tries to remember what happened around the moment of collapse, but Baker yammers nonstop, as if she knows the pull of the water. Other voices chatter inside Kendra's head, but she can't quite hear them with the distraction of Baker's voice. The voices hold the key, know why she collapsed. She dresses in a soft chamois shirt, vest, and buckskin skirt.

The party is in the Kitsilano district, near the university. Kendra, riding shotgun, fixates on the snails of light in the water, reflections of streetlamps in the dark currents of Burrard Inlet. Lena and Angel discuss a new method to screen donors. They have decided the only way to prevent a paternity suit is to blend the sperm from several donors into each batch. Baker asks if they plan to pull donors from the sky. "Men'll dump their sperm any-where," she says, "but ask if you can keep some, and they get real possessive." Kendra just hopes they have started. It would be nice to have a baby in the family.

They pull up in front of a renovated house. A balcony, like a widow's walk, circles beneath the Cyclopean bulge of a skylight. Inside, the house has been gutted into a cathedral of space under a peaked roof, high over walls of slanted cedar. No one is jamming, though people mill everywhere. They come up to Kendra, praise the concert, her singing, the courage of "Ghostchildren" and "The Incest Song." No one mentions the vomit. It's that nightmare where you forgot to dress, and no one tells you. It's walking out of the ladies' room with a tail of toilet paper. It's the whispers as you step away from your friends. Kendra keeps dabbing her face as if it's still sticky. Someone presses a drink into her hand, and she gulps it down. She's surprised that it's bourbon. She rarely sees bourbon north of the border. She threads her way to the refreshment table and notices a soldierly row of Kentucky bourbons. A fleshy B.C. salmon smells of lemon and the churning sea. Survivors' music booms from loudspeakers mounted in every corner: *Broad green reptilian lips.* Sometimes she hates her own music. She decides to compare bourbons. The Wild Turkey honeys down her throat. *He wants me to kiss, he wants me to kiss.* Smoother than the Jim Beam.

At her elbow, Baker jabbers something about the host of the party. "Guess who it is. Guess, guess." She doesn't wait for a guess. *Your kiss of life* She beckons across the crowd. *is my kiss of death.* Kendra pours herself a third sample of bourbon. *Your kiss of life*

A tall man with a thatch of Ivy League hair glides up beside them. He is a man who knows he makes heads turn.

"Prince, huh? Huh?" Baker whispers.

Frank presses Kendra's hand between his, a flower between pages. "Let me show you around." He has hypnotic eyes.

Time warps into a tunnel where there is only Him and Her.

The party stills. The twilight of the lamps fades. Faces look skeletal in the shadows. Eyes skate like airplane lights across a dark sky. Kendra can focus only on Frank's quivering face: petals of white teeth, plush black eyes, nose a millimetre short of classical, nostrils flared with breath, a cluster of papules under the left eye, sepia skin as smooth as a farm egg, a delicate, charming face, unshadowed by blueness despite the enamel gleam of his black hair.

She imprints to him, follows without another thought in her mind. She has no mind, only a black hole where his mind can enter. She thinks his thoughts, feels his feelings, sees his view of her, of himself, of all of life. She walks where he steps, pauses when he stops, and gazes through the trajectory of his eyes, waiting for the words he will utter to know if she should like or dislike what she sees. She knows this feeling from somewhere, this total enthralment of her being, this post-colonial re-enactment of master and slave, this drama between the willed and the willing, this dream of original Conquest, this insane, incredible, maniacal Love-at-First-Sight, described and descried by artists and murderers and poets, by the gods of all mythologies, this Passion that makes a man into a man and a woman into a girl.

Frank escorts her through the upper levels of his home, into rooms angled for a view of the bay, up to the loft where he works. In a folding frame on his desk is a picture of Kendra with Survivors. Two boys around seven and nine stare from sombre eyes in the other frame. Frank motions her to sit on a window-seat beneath the dome of the skylight, and sits next to her. Small speakers pipe a Mozart rondo from a separate sound system. The widow's-walk balcony is just outside.

Frank teaches economics at the University of British Columbia. His eyes keep quivering, like limbs afflicted with palsy. He was born and raised in Bombay in the forties and fifties, educated in India and England. His hand is steady enough, when it drops from her shoulder to her breast. He received his D.Phil. from Cambridge, emigrated to teach in

Canada, has lived in Vancouver since the late sixties. His accent is hybrid, musical, yet exact, small. His first wife was English and hated Canada. They were divorced three years after they moved. He rubs Kendra's breast through layers of vest and blouse. The children in the picture are from his second marriage. He unbuttons the front of her blouse, inserts cold fingers under her bra. His second marriage was to one of his colleagues. The fingers settle on her nipple. She wasn't a colleague to start. The other hand, a rock compared to his eyes, drops onto her lap. His second wife was one of his graduate students. He tugs at her hips, dragging them closer like a hill of books. "You'd like her," he says. "She's a brilliant economist." A woman who gets involved with a divorced man should interview their ex-wives, according to Baker. "She introduced me to your music." He slips off her vest, and blouse, and bra, and the thought disappears.

"God, you're gorgeous." He stares at her. She hops into his eyes to see what he appreciates. Yeah, pretty nice, that narrow torso with the orchid-skin breasts.

A stripe of light falls across his black hair as he bends forward and licks her nipples. He leans back to gaze some more. "You're incredible," he says. She slithers her eyes up and down with his, admiring the contrast of her short buckskin skirt against her rice-paper skin.

ɾ ɾ ɾ

Gabriel, I have to return. She is ruining her life.

No, Billie. If you go now, everything will crash on her all at once. She wouldn't survive.

How do you know?

It's happened before. Someone like you decides to – what's that silly phrase they use down there? – get on with it, ignores all warnings, and hastens down to save their earth self. Wham, bam, blast. Every banned memory returns in full force, as if it's happening now, today, all at one point in time, the big bang. Of course, it's too much. The person offs themselves, and anyone left flying up here explodes. Don't do it, Billie.

What do you suggest I do then? What? What?

Flash an old scene, quick as lightning.

Hey, guys, no problem. I'm helping her, the Four-Taloned Hawk boasts. Every time she has a feeling, I show it to her through his eyes. She doesn't feel a thing.

Some help. Billie flies at him angrily.

Fly, Billie. Fly to Quodling. We will explain.

The memory, first the memory. We won't be able to send one from Quodling, the Little One shrills.

ɾ ɾ ɾ

A sepia hand with shining black down on slender fingers rotates the rust medallion at the heart of her breast, yet she doesn't have breasts, she's nine, seven, six, five, her chest as flat as the page of a colouring book, but a hand, a broad freckled hand with yellow, hard nails, clumps of ear hair on the fingers, orange tobacco stains, tweaks a dime-sized nipple on her chest, in a pincer-like grip, twisting, pulling: *I'll make it big.*

ɾ ɾ ɾ

One of Glinda's assistants, Emerald, pipes up. Oh great, a little maelstrom in the present. That'll wipe the Noël time right out, save us a lot of work.

That's no solution, Billie storms. She's got a love thing going, something worth saving. I've got to stop her.

NO. Glinda is in imperious form.

WHY?

I will convene a meeting to answer that question.

A dense, canopied mass of twining trunks, vines and branches materializes. At its edge, slender branches arch into rows of seats. Birds fly in and seat themselves along the branches:

the Little One, Astor, Woodrow, others who seem familiar. When Gabriel arrives, the count is twenty-nine.

Okay, Glinda announces. The only one who is missing is too weak to travel.

She invites the group to help Billie.

Billie's body electrifies into a grid. Shock after shock jolts each organ.

A bonfire tongues up her pudendum.

A thousand razor blades finger her skin.

Rage makes her an assassin, and also a poet.

Doors close. Windows shutter. The sun chars.

I want to die. Help me die.

Say aunt, Glinda's Emerald advises.

Aunt. Aunt. Aunt, Billie shrieks. Okay, all right, you've convinced me.

♪ ♪ ♪

Kendra has no idea where she is. Drab grey light seeps through a skylight. Her buckskin skirt is crumpled to her waist. Thick freckled hands with yellow fingernails and thickets of ear hair are what she remembers. She is very thirsty.

The sheets around her are navy and soft. The room is painted in strong colours, taupe and blue, like sky and the bark of trees, or bruises. Frank opens the door. His penis swings like a wilted mushroom on a short rope. He is carrying a cardboard tray with two Styrofoam cups and a bag of pastries. His pubic hair is peppered with grey.

"You proved something to me" – he hands her coffee – "that no one else could."

She can't imagine teaching him anything.

"Every part of me is a touchable."

He sits on the side of the bed. She guides his coffee cup under her nose. It has a pungent scent.

"Cardamom," he says. "I didn't put any in yours."

He pulls the sheets down so he can look at her. She draws them back up, props the pillows, sags into them, eggshell against navy.

"Those gifts," she says. "Weirded me out."

"You didn't like them?"

"Did you, like, have a reason to choose them?" She edges down until the sheets turtleneck around her.

"I dreamed them up." He slides a hand under the side of the sheets. "Someone else shopped for them."

His hand spiders over her hip. She slides it away. "You're high and mighty this morning," he says.

"Different feelings," she says.

He puts the hand back. "Mine are the same."

"Hey," she says. "Stop it. No." She is starting to understand why Baker never stays the night.

As an answer, he tightens his grip on her pubic area. He removes the coffee cup from her hand, steers her head towards the mushroom. "Suck every inch of me, Princess Bibi." He yanks a fistful of her hair in warning. "Do like you did last night."

The discoloured mushroom ivories, the peppered hair turns flaxen, the sepia thighs grow pink and stumpy. A cloud of stale Scotch and smoke descends around her head, clogging her nostrils. She remembers how to choke back the gag reflex, how to silence the screams. But the cardamom is new. With a jolt of her abdomen, she pukes all over the mushroom, all over the salt and pepper and sepia. During the moment his hands relax, she bolts up and out of the room.

28

"What the fuck happened to you?" Baker is folded into an armchair, reading the *New York Times*, with a pot of room-service coffee on the table.

Kendra unbuttons her trenchcoat, revealing skin and a rumpled buckskin skirt. She turns to Baker and parts the flaps of her coat, holding them out like wings. The coat slides from her shoulders, crumples into a rag. She walks to the bureau, unzips the pocket on her overnight bag, slips out her Swiss Army knife. Its blades are folded, like still wings. She unsheathes a blade, a large silver wing.

She slices the coat to ribbons. Then the bag. Then one of the pillows on her bed. She looks around.

"Talk, dammit," Baker says. "Don't do this."

Kendra takes her favourite silk blouse from the closet. "It's the clothes or me." She draws the knife along her thigh. "Filthy slut. I'm gonna call Axel and tell him what a little pigwhore I am."

"Don't be stupid." Baker blockades the phone. "Now's not

the time to talk to Axel." She extends her arms in the wings of a mama-hug.

"DONTTOUCHME." Kendra rests the knife tip against her own throat.

"OK OK. Do what you want."

Kendra hangs the mauve blouse from a hook outside the closet. Amputates the eagle insignia from the breast pocket. Excises the other breast in an exact circle. Brings her jeans. Cuts out the crotch. Black cords. The crotch. Green cords, tan cords. Crotch, crotch. Black leather pants. Can't get the crotch out. Can't. Spreads the leather legs into dark wings. Stab. Stab. "Now everyone can see what I am." Hurls the pants over. Honeycombs the rear until there is a long serrated tear.

"Now this skirt." Scissoring herself across the bed, she hacks at the edges of the crumpled buckskin. "Filthy filthy filthy skirt. Bad skirt. Whore's skirt." A rip whispers down the seam.

"I'm a whore a tart a slut no good no good bad bad bad girl bad bad bad girl." She stabs her dra. Hacks it like the skirt. "Badgirl badgirl" stab stab "he put it in your mouth" twist push "swallow now, good girl good girl" gouge "ear hair goo me sick sick" cut bleed

29

♪ ♪ ♪

Stay close. She's trying to fly up here with us.

Billie and Astor and Miles, Glinda's two messengers, and the Four-Taloned Hawk hover above people in masks and gowns.

What will happen if she does? Miles has discovered curiosity.

Her body will be empty.

A waxwing in camouflage feathers pops next to Billie.

Who are you? Billie shrieks, terrified that the one in surgery has slipped out.

Do not worry, my new friend. I am a protégé of Gabriel. He sent me to take you on a journey.

I can't go anywhere. She needs me.

They share a picture of tubular limbs in metal stirrups, steel instruments, laughter and bad jokes.

Yes, I see. But you can still come. Just send someone into the one on the gurney. To help her stay.

Woodrow appears, and two others. No one volunteers to enter the flesh.

In the end Glinda's messengers, Crystal and Emerald, slip down together.

The waxwing calls herself Amelia. Billie follows her to the edge of the sky into a creamy, searing light. They soar over jungle, village, through endless miles of rain, across swathes and craters of denuded land.

They arrive at a hospital on a peninsula. There I am. Amelia's in fatigues, a nurse's insignia on her helmet, hair shorn underneath, humping packs. The boys taught me everything, she explains. I begged. I insisted. I had to do what they did, to face what they faced.

She carried an M-16 and knew how to use it. She carried grenades, and knew when to lob them. She learned when she was yellow – all the time – and when she was courageous – for friends, without thinking. She forgot she had a cunt. The daily slog for everyone was shitwork. Grunts were the army's women.

Wiggins, a big Southern boy from Biloxi, Mississippi, who stopped cursing and said Ma'am to anyone in a skirt, took her on. Amelia would have hated him instantly if they had to be male and female with each other but they were in a neuter zone. One scorching day, Wiggins was the guy who couldn't take any more. Amelia volunteered to take his place in a body-count mission. The field was booby-trapped. A lanky kid from Idaho tripped the wire. His nose somersaulted from his face. The body count for the other side increased by one.

Wiggins and Amelia were inseparable after that. It was one of those inexplicable friendships that should never come to pass. When Wiggins was machine-gunned to pieces in an NVA ambush, Amelia lay with her arms, her body, staunching his wounds, until they came to pick up the dead.

Never again, she vowed, I'll never get close to anyone again.

᷍ ᷍ ᷍

Axel cocoons Kendra's hand between both of his. Everything aches between her legs, and she is having crampy spasms. She can hear the murmur of Baker, senses Lena and Angel too. The room smells like a mixture of yesterday's clothes and vitamin pills, sour and stale. She keeps her eyes closed, her face slack, aware of the long whisper of her breathing. Two voices talk back and forth in her head. They are discussing whether or not they can exit now that she's survived. One is thin, and vibrates like a reed. When she probes who they are, they disappear.

"Shit," she mutters.

"Some greeting," Axel says, and kisses her.

She starts to cry uncontrollably.

She doesn't want anyone near her (but she can't get them close enough). She wants to pulp their brains, skewer their lungs.

Karl lies on top of her, knifing into her like an auger into the earth, fitting like a mallet into a keyhole. She is seven.

With this memory, clarity rises like a sun on the prairies, no obstruction all the way to the horizon, too distant to see.

The doctors don't know how well she will heal. Her vagina was punctured in several places. Her cervix is damaged, and she managed to cut the tough, muscular walls of her uterus. They put several stitches in her rectum.

They notice scars inflicted at earlier dates and think she has been wounding herself for years. They imply she gets a masochistic thrill from pain. They try not to show their revulsion. One of them suggests she see a psychiatrist when she gets back to Toronto. He thinks this is kindness, an act of deep humanity, beyond what she deserves. They don't like her much.

Axel wants to know if she'll be able to have kids. A Jewish doctor takes him aside. "Physically," he says, "maybe, but emotionally?" He tries to steer Axel away from Kendra; damaged goods, he implies, unfit mother, he implies. "Come back to the fold," he entreats this *landsman's* son. "You've had your *shiksa* fling." Baker is furious when she hears this story. She buys red nail polish and heavy gold jewellery for Kendra to flaunt during the next doctors' visit, scatters copies of the *Canadian Jewish News* around the room. Axel just laughs. His father taught him about this genre of physician years ago, when Holocaust survivors were coming to all the Montreal offices with ailments as recalcitrant to treatment as the SS to pleas for mercy. "It was mercy they needed," Axel's father told him, "but medicine was what they got. It's all you can expect from most doctors," he explained. "The spirit left the body when the discipline was formed." Axel squeezes Baker's hand when he says this.

Kendra agrees with the doctors. She thinks Axel should leave her for someone worthwhile, someone who is capable of love. They have had this discussion many times, but now Kendra's mutilated body floats through their minds. It is not a loving image.

A deep peace has settled into her being since her mutilation, her liberation. I am a fucked-up, useless, cow flop of a person, she thinks, but not shamming any more, not empty.

She refuses to complete the tour. As manager, Baker is hardly empathic, or flexible. Self-inflicted health problems are poor grounds for the medical release clause in their contracts, and Survivors may forfeit a lot of money. Despite the skill of her manoeuvring to keep the story out of the media, underground rumours abound.

Baker encourages Kendra to try one or two concerts, if only to quell the rumours. "Go without me," Kendra says. "Nothing in our contracts specifies me." But Kendra is Survivors. They cannot hire a replacement for her, like they can for the others. It took enough moxie to alter the dates.

Finally, Kendra tells them the truth. "I can't sing," she says. "I open my mouth, and no sound comes out."

They book seats on the next flight to Toronto.

SOLITUDE

30

Kendra feels like a bird who has migrated north when the leaves turn gold, her path the choice of poor radar, tuned by the wounds in her dra. Her own melody, her themes, her lyrics have not been composed or orchestrated, authored or authorized, by her. She has never heard the sound of her own music. Her trust in herself is broken.

A longing to know herself seizes her heart with a fierceness that can only come from the unheard voices, chattering inside. They are speaking to her, strengthening her resolve towards solitude. She decides to nest among trees and birds for six months, a year, as long as it takes to come face to face with the multitude of voices from her fractured soul. She will move up north, find a cottage in Haliburton or the Muskokas.

Her impulse is to pare to essentials. No phone, no TV, no radio, no CDs or tapes; maybe she will even leave her guitars. She sits down with her bankbooks and begins to figure. Her budget is minimal; a year if she can rent her condo, if their recording does well. She could always find work as a handywoman. Karl trained her well. She can fix just about anything.

Angel will think her bullheaded, which she is, and unhinged by her injuries, which she is not. Lena will spin tales from "back home" about mythic, wandering women and their strange and radiant powers. Axel can grasp a myriad of visions with his incredible mind, yet will see this one as flawed. The flaw he won't mention is the absence of him. But Baker will feel as if an eye has been blinded, a leg severed, an ear deafened, as if half her self has been carried away. Baker will help as much as she can.

Toronto is still a word-of-mouth town. Angel passes Kendra the name of a real estate agent with a line on rentals up north. The agent isn't hopeful for much on Kendra's budget. Lakefront, isolation, and a long lease are hard to get when spring is drawing near.

Kendra needs refuge until she arranges everything, perhaps to talk to someone who will just listen. Neither Baker nor Axel can provide the tranquil ear she requires, and Lena would send her to a spirit guide. Still, the idea of a therapist makes her think of the doctors in Vancouver.

She begins to teach herself to meditate. She consumes books from the library and from tiny, jumbled shops that smell of incense, and learns that meditation techniques span the sensory modalities, especially sound and vision. She practises mantras from books and invents her own. She concentrates on pinpoints of light, single snow drops, petals of flowers. She experiments with the remembered hiss and lap of waves from Lake Superior, the call of loons. She calls to mind the chirp of crickets, the hum of bees. She finds kinesthetic focusing effective, and meditates on granules of warm sand against her feet, or the tap of rain on the back of her hand. By imagining a massage, she can make her shoulder muscles loosen. She watches her breath for hours. If she meditates across modalities, her perceptions transform, mutate, open new dimensions. The paradigms of the world freshen and shift. She discovers strata of life the entire human race seems to conspire to ignore.

One day, as she sits in a cafe near her house, reading the rental ads and drinking a cappuccino, she sees an image float across the air. The air-picture is a crouching lemon-yellow child with crimson saucer eyes. When the man at the next table gets up to leave, the child evaporates.

The next time this happens she is with Axel. They are discussing why she doesn't want him to help her select her retreat house or stay with her during her first weeks away. She is drawing boundaries, even with Axel, even with her listening Joseph whom she loves more than music. He doesn't care, he says, he's just worried for her safety. A blue fist floats around the room during their disagreement, then disappears when they change the subject. He was lying, she realizes, he does mind.

What other people won't allow themselves to think is becoming visible to her in stark, primal images, stained in the variegated hues of human emotion. She suspects the air teems with such images, cast adrift by owners who reject what they mean, images hungry to be viewed. She is afraid they will swarm around her, like moths to light, and she will lose her own sight, so fragile, so new. Yet her fascination is stronger than her fear. This is where she has to go. This is the world she must learn.

Meditation powers her down passages into vistas she once called imaginative, fantastical. She might meditate on a person, using one word they utter, one facial expression, one gesture. If she holds the meditation in mind the next time they meet, there's a shift, unpredictable, sometimes minor, but always discernible, always there. The whole phenomenon makes her feel strong, omniscient, and a little bit crazy. Or silly. Like the day she concentrated on the smell of a vanilla bean, and felt wild with the intensity of odours when she went for a walk. A man drenched in men's cologne strode past her, followed by a sulphurous cloud of flatulence and fear she was sure contained every fart he'd tried to hide in a very long, very proper lifetime. She decided to table her meditations on scent. She wasn't sure she wanted to whiff every rejected scent in the world.

If she dwells on the meaning of any of this, on the general and not the particular of it, she calls herself a fool or a nut-case and tries to reattach her senses to the mundane. Get real, she chides, you're hallucinating. Maybe she's just trying to ditch herself, yet again.

She decides to see a therapist. She collects names from Axel, Baker, the Women's Centre, her family physician, and calls around for an appointment. Most of them act as if her call is an annoyance. They are abrupt, seem to think whether or not they have openings is a medical secret. They never ask anything personal, though they are quite willing to discuss their fees, the status of her budget, and the extent of her health-care coverage. Finally, a Dr. Duerf agrees to see her for a consultation appointment and she takes it, though she would have preferred to see a woman.

She can't decide what to wear. Probably every outfit will mean something symbolic: pants that she wants to be a boy; a mini that she wants to seduce him; a suit that she wants to *be* him – there is no solution. Really, she just wants someone to support her year of solitude, to validate the nuanced, though weird, perceptions opening to her.

The doctor's waiting room is plush, yet spare and windowless. Operatic sounds bleat from the radio, hiding a faint hum from the heating system. Magazines like the *Smithsonian* and *Architectural Digest*, the tofu of reading, devoid of sex and politics, fan across the coffee table. She is definitely in the wrong place.

She hears the swish of a distant door opening and closing, the ting of a small bell. Her heartbeats drown out the opera. The door to the dim room opens, and on the threshold stands a smallish man with a grey goatee and eyes that twinkle. A vermilion breast floats above his head.

He introduces himself without extending his hand, bows her through the door, and sweeps an arm towards two leather chairs in the corner of the spacious room. The chairs are darker than the breast, more burgundy than red. The breast bobs gently above his head as he crosses the room.

"Are you worrying about the person you just saw?" she asks. Not a good start.

"Why would you ask that?" The doctor sounds genuinely curious.

"You look, well, a little distracted." The vermilion breast is starting to fade.

She finds it disturbingly difficult to talk about herself. Every time she mentions something important in her life – Axel, Karl, not remembering, the dra-wounds, Survivors – she loses her voice. Images must be zooming over her head. She wishes the doctor would talk a little.

He doesn't probe the air-images, or even her silences. If he notices either, he gives no sign. This isn't for her, she thinks. You have to be able to *talk* to get anywhere in this kind of therapy. Baker might be able to use it, Axel might be able to use it, but Kendra cannot. She's never been a talking kind of person. Language seems too final, nails down events like vows or promises. And she's clumsy with it.

Dr. Duerf can't tell her anything that might help, not after only one session. "It takes a long time to understand anyone enough to help them," he says. "Years. And you need help, my friend," he says. *My friend.* "You're in deep trouble." Some part of her leaps forward *he knows we're here* and tears spring from nowhere into her green eye. She tells him her plans then, her intention to venture into solitude. The words slide out, as if the tears have lubricated the way. He seems to approve; at least he doesn't caution her against the dangers. He invites her to come back if she wants, anytime, to tell him how she's doing. He would be happy to see her again. As she walks out, a tumescent, ultramarine penis floats above his head. She wonders if this has something to do with her or if Dr. Duerf always thinks in genitalia.

Axel talks to her with such tenderness, and touches her as if her skin were parchment, or spun glass, but the blue fist bobs around the room more and more often. Sometimes, its fingers come to life, pointing or beckoning their long blue messages, shaking a gesture of reprimand or shame. Kendra has never known a fist so eloquent. It clenches and opens, shakes and threatens, storms across the ceiling, swoops like a bustard towards some object, then glides right through it. It has features on it like the moon.

Axel picks up a china figurine from the mantel and strokes the folds of her gown. They haven't spent one night together, since Vancouver, he says. He wants to try. The crease between the fingers of the blue fist broadens into a smile. He traces the wreath of flowers around the black porcelain hair so that not a single fragile petal could be disturbed. The fist sails through the air towards the china. He doesn't care if they have sex or not; he can't even begin to express how distasteful unreciprocated sex is to him. He places the figurine near the edge of the mantelpiece. The blue fist circles around it, trembling.

They lie next to each other and her skin turns to porcelain, a cold thin glassy shell. When he touches her, like he promised he wouldn't, the blue fist evaporates.

ↄ ↄ ↄ

Look, whispers the Little One. See what happens.

Billie and Gabriel peer into the farmhouse. The redheaded toddler has stopped arranging the pieces of puzzle and watches the broad man in the plaid armchair. He beckons: come to Daddy. She tosses her head, no, stubborn, like him.

In a flash, he is up. He scoops her with two hands, one

shovelled under the patch of white, the other one gripped around her stiff shoulders.

♪ ♪ ♪

Axel massages Kendra's stiff shoulders. She wants to scream at him: Don't. You promised. She lies still.

♪ ♪ ♪

He carries her up the stairs, massaging the white patch with his giant thumb. He lays her down on the crocheted afghan in the middle of his huge bed. The wool feels itchy against her legs.

♪ ♪ ♪

Axel turns her over on her back, kisses her porcelain lips.

♪ ♪ ♪

He crawls up the afghan until his legs, the rough bark of tree stumps, fork over her face.

♪ ♪ ♪

The blue fist, the creased moon of its face a quivering smile, smashes into the ceiling and raises two fingers in a long blue *V*.

31

In spite of several gruelling trips into areas where snow clearance is minimal, to track down promising tips from her real estate agent, Kendra has not been able to find a cottage. Axel insists on taking her to Isabella's to talk to Ebe. Ebe can always help, he reminds her. Irrational as it is, Kendra doesn't like Ebe, doesn't want any of his favours. "He's a good man," Axel says. "Look at his arm, look at the numbers. Helping people is his *raison d'être*, not a way to trap you or make you obliged." Shame doesn't make her like Ebe any better.

"Wait," she says, when they arrive. "I need coffee first." She particularly dislikes asking favours from a man who reminds her of Karl.

Axel carries over two glasses of steaming latte. She likes the way Ebe serves them, in ordinary glasses with the coffee layered by colour up to meringue-like peaks of whipped froth. Axel has also brought over a stack of the enormous cookies Ebe stocks from the bakery down the street.

"I don't want to ask him," she says, halfway through her coffee.

"I'll do it, if you want."

"There's something about taking help," she ventures, "that tilts the whole purpose. Makes it, somehow, not mine."

He changes the subject, but not quite. He's spoken to his father about her plans. His father agrees, she shouldn't go live alone, not in her state of mind.

She stares down at the table, back to the brilliance of his eyes. "I have to," she says. "It's that simple."

"Then take a phone. Take a radio. Take something."

She shrugs. She hasn't made up her mind what to take, though she isn't taking him. "I'll bet he told you to break up with me," she hazards. "If he didn't, I'll bet your mother did."

"She did," Axel says. "He didn't."

"What did she say?"

"You know what she thinks. That I should find a Jewish girl. Someone like her."

"I agree," Kendra says, almost in a whisper. "Don't wait for me. They're both right about me." There's no telling how long she'll be, or how safe.

"I'm waiting," he says. "But I'm coming up too. I won't leave you alone for so long."

He has forgiven her for fucking Frank, like an overheated bitch in the park, or so he has said. He called it an error, like writing a dud of a song. She found it hard, not fighting with him, or being punished. She dreamed of men with beards of hemp and seaweed, their fins prickly like mace, breaking open the scales of mermaid girls as they tried to swim through oceans of semen, rupturing their silver skins until entrails of womb tissue streamed behind them in a translucent wake.

Axel fetches Ebe, who sits at their table. Ebe's face is a ruin, cratered and scarred into a caricature of agony. His eyes look like grottoes. Yet his smile sits flush on his distortion of a face, not ten feet in front, nor a mask, though lord knows he could use one, but as real as a snowstorm, or the table, or love.

"I will look," he promises, when he hears her story. "I think I have a line to a place in Muskoka."

She thanks him more profusely than she would if she liked him. Saint Ebe, she thinks, but doesn't tell Axel. Ebe is Jewish. Axel and Baker both like him to excess.

The cottage Ebe finds for her is on a rugged island just off the shores of Lake Minerva, a few hours north of Toronto. A slender causeway connects the island to the shore, making it accessible by car or foot, flawing its isolation. But it is a breathtaking site, better than she has dared to dream. The cottage sits on the crest of a rise of land at the nose of the peninsula and is surrounded on three sides by forest. Even the lake side sports a straggle of birches and pines. The island itself is the centrepiece of an archipelago of tiny islands, most of them undeveloped.

Kendra picks her way down the icy jetty to the small deck at its end. There's not another cottage in sight. All she can see is an expanse of frozen lake, the same colour as the sky, extending all the way to a fringe of trees, small on the horizon. The floating dock, a stone's throw away, is ensphered by a crust of winter ice. She climbs down the glazed rungs of the ladder and walks out onto the lake. Bits of snow slide into her boots. She turns to examine her cottage. It is larger than she pictured, not massive, but solid. A Muskoka verandah wraps around three sides of its split-log exterior. The afternoon sun glints from the windows in mellow golds, like the honeyed light of angels' faces, or Christ's. Ebe said under the dock was a boathouse, equipped with a motorboat, a canoe, a laser sailboat, and cross-country skis.

The heart of the cottage is a large room, overlooking the lake. A fireplace of Muskoka stone dominates the room and its rich, dark log walls. The furnishings are sparse and practical: a long table along the lakeside window, a sofa and chairs grouped around the hearth, a tiled area setting off the kitchen. The bedrooms, not insulated for winter, are closed off. The jewelled light

of the sun tints the room with amber, the same tone as the high-
lights it makes in her hair. Ebe says if she wants the cottage, it's
hers. The owners will approve his choice. Kendra was beginning
to think she'd have to take off, travel from park to park across the
country, tenting, using an assumed name. Yukon – no one uses
their real name in the Yukon. She began to try out new names:
Astor, Billie, Amelia. It had its appeal. Now, in less then two
weeks, she can move in.

Baker, of course, offers to look after everything in Toronto.
She will take charge of subletting the condo, get the money to
Kendra, to Ebe too, if she wants.

Kendra's going-away dinner is with Survivors and Axel, the
people she thinks of as family. Lena has gone wild with Indian and
island foods. The selection of wines only Axel could have picked.

The air is as laden as the table. The blue fist shakes a finger,
as if warning her to be good. A plum fire blazes from the corner
of the ceiling. The fire seems, though she's guessing, to be stoked
by Survivors' instruments, splintered and fragmented like her
high school guitar. Someone must be ruing the demise of their
group. A naked red toddler, swinging a rucksack, scampers round
and round on the walls. This image, she feels certain, has been
cast out by her.

Kendra drowns her sensibilities in champagne and cassis.
Bourbon would be faster, but reminds her of Frank. She drank to
feel normal that night too. Normal is senseless, then? Kendra
studies Angel, Baker, Lena, Axel. Baker is sucking down martinis
again, and tasting each appetizer. She doesn't stare off at a window, or the ceiling.

"Hey, babe," Baker says, feeling Kendra's eyes on her, "here's
to you. Friend of my life." She raises her glass. They all do.

"Whatcha gonna do, up there in the wilderness, without
me?" Baker asks.

"It'll be tough," Kendra says. "I'll think of you every day."

"You can even see me," Baker says, "any time you decide."

"You have to come back once for me," Lena says. It's odd, Lena asking for something.

"For us," Angel corrects.

"Did you do it? Are you pregnant?" Baker is jouncing with real excitement.

"Just a minute." Lena returns with a small vial. It is empty, a blank label held around it with an elastic. She holds it up for everyone to inspect. "We're collecting," she says.

"Wow," says Baker.

"How long can you freeze it?" Axel asks. "Before it loses its potency?"

"Did your brother come through?" Kendra remembers how badly Angel wants her own genes to contribute.

Angel shakes her head. "The ass."

"We're trying not to freeze any. Fresh is the best," Lena tells Axel.

"Wanna kick in, honey?" Baker asks him. She knows he'll say no, one more proof of her theory about liberation and men.

They pile food onto their plates. Caribbean fish stew, and curry, tandoori baked chicken, paratha, chapati, rice, salads. Baker pinches a finger's worth from each platter before she ladles out a helping. Angel lets Axel take charge of the wine. Even Lena, serving or seated, doesn't peer into the air. Is transparent air normal? Maybe Kendra's ability is the old separation between her senses she felt as a child. She hasn't told Axel about his blue fist, skittering about in this other dimension. Axel is never angry, except playfully, or at issues. He'd say the fist was hers, her idea of him, her rage. And she doesn't know, she couldn't argue.

The air-pictures have faded. The world looks bleached, her friends colourless, encased, separate. Everyone gorges and drains glasses of wines. The bouquets alone are enough to intoxicate her senses, too extended by far. They laugh and tell stories, preferring their past to the present. No one mentions the tour, or Frank, or Vancouver. No one mentions "The Incest Song."

"What are you really gonna do?" asks Baker. "Up there by yourself? I'm serious."

Kendra still can't talk. "I'm going to live," she says, "just live."

Lena looks sad now. "What I meant before" – Lena addresses both the blue and green of Kendra's eyes – "is I want you to be with me when I inseminate the first time. Will you come?"

"I'd be honoured."

"And me? What about me?"

"Of course you," Lena says to Baker.

"We've got plans for you," says Angel. "We need you to gather the sperm on the day. Too much running for one."

"Really?" Baker says. "You've got it." She starts to clear, her face mauve with pleasure, and pain.

Angel passes out liqueur glasses for *eau de vie* and cognac. Lena brings a tray with coffee and tea. Axel arranges presents near Kendra's seat. Kendra ruffles up his curls when he leans in front of her. His muss of curls makes him look like Jack Pumpkinhead. Baker tarahs at the door. Her face, still mauve, flickers in the amber lights from a forest of candles stuck all over the cake she is carrying. "It's your rebirth-day," Lena says.

"Make a wish. Make a great, wonderful wish," Baker says, as she places the cake in front of Kendra. Guidance, Kendra wishes, blowing with all her breath, give me guidance. *I will tour you through the night.* What a confident voice.

Eager, loving, dancing eyes glitter at her from around the table. She slices up the cake, a gorgeous Dufflet creation, a gazillion calories of raspberry, dark chocolate, whipped cream, espresso mousse. Baker hands her the first present. Kendra suppresses the unkind thought that she is trying to simplify her life. The box is large, heavy, stuffed with swirls of shredded paper and an assortment of tissue-wrapped packages. Ursula LeGuin's *The Left Hand of Darkness*. Doris Lessing's *The Four-Gated City*. Jane Austen's *Pride and Prejudice*. UrsieDorisJane, my daughter.

There is also a gift certificate to Isabella's Library and a bound journal with a silver cartridge pen clipped to the cover. The wrapping on the last package unwinds like gauze from a cast. Underneath, it is bubble-wrapped, then another layer of tissue. Inside, finally, is an antique china doll. She is a ballerina, one leg extended, arms over her head. Tiers of lace cascade down from her tight bodice. She looks like a Degas creation, fragile, yet in command. Baker knows it's Kendra's favourite. It was Baker's favourite too.

Lena hands Kendra a flimsy package wrapped in Xhosa African cloth. The cloth itself would look beautiful laid on a table or chair back. Inside is a piece of material spun from filament as fine and silvery as spider's lace, a gossamer shawl, suggestive of the lining of clouds and the sun side of rainbows. "It's a meditation shawl," Lena says, "like the one I used in Jamaica." The shawl shrouds Kendra in a transcendent arc of beauty. She closes her eyes for a moment and hears *I can keep your truth safe*. With Lena, Kendra doesn't have to find words. *She knows too*.

Angel thinks gift-wrap is a waste of time, like rooms filled with flowers, or people in ball gowns. She hands Kendra a khaki knapsack. "For your more mundane needs," she grunts. It is heavy with tools and hardware, everything Kendra will need to repair what Angel calls "household grumbles." From the knapsack's back pocket sticks the handle of a hatchet. There is also a single-bladed axe to split logs for the fireplace. Axel's jaw grinds at the sight of the blades. He has lost that kind of confidence in her, as has his father. Kendra felt like a burglar at the Mountain Co-op when she replaced her Swiss Army knife. The old one is in the bottom of Howe Sound, thanks to Baker. She hides the new one, especially from Axel.

Axel watches with uncertain eyes as she tears his recycled wrap from a large carton. She slits the packaging with scissors and lifts the cardboard flaps. Inside are Styrofoam boxes of varying shape and dimension. She untapes the first box. In its recess rests a grey metal box the size of a book. She's not sure what it is, a gadget of some kind. "Press the latch on the front," Axel urges. As she tugs at the lid, he leans over and swings it wide, revealing a small dark TV screen. She still doesn't get it. "It's a laptop," he explains, "a computer." "That pish of a thing's a computer?" she says. She has avoided computers for years, though Baker is nearly a hacker. Axel depresses a key and the screen lights with a ping. A cartoon mannequin dives across along the screen and turns to face her, making her whoop. A bubble materializes over the cartoon's head – computers have air-pictures – "Welcome to Macintosh." Enthralled, Kendra starts pressing the keys, following the instructions that ping and bubble onto the screen. Soon she can move a rocket around on its launcher and open a file folder in which to store information. Axel unpacks the rest of the carton and explains the use of each item – discs, external drives, CD-ROM, instructional booklets. It's as confusing as falling in love.

As they drive home, Axel smiles a huge smile, shy yet triumphant. He has done it. He has given Kendra something she never dreamed about. He has escorted her into new territory, opened for her new vistas, altered the shape of her life. Of everyone there, and they all love her, only his gift has tapped a new vein, reached an unmined part of her shadowed interior, given her passion. She, Kendra Quillan, the Ice Woman, has been influenced by Axel Berne, the maverick intellectual.

How he wants to fill her interior with the rest of him, make her green eye weep while her blue eye rolls and shimmies, melt the bleak, frozen wasteland in her compliant body, get her out of control because of *him*. He knows now that she is never there for their lovemaking, never there with Axel Berne, but off somewhere he never reaches, no matter how tender and kind, how omniscient and understanding.

The long blue fingers tap restlessly on the ceiling. On the floor, their puce shadow drubs an accompaniment. The shadow tapper chills Kendra. Axel's rage is growing, and the fingers are pointing to her.

Energy boils through his fingers as he caresses her. Inside, her ice thickens and she shakes him away, unclothes herself under the cone of light so he can watch her transformation into the slut-whore she feels his eyes make as they rake her body. She strips, piece by piece, sliding each garment along her skin in a mockery of sensuality that heightens its effect. A red chasm like a canyon drops between them. She walks across it.

⌐ ⌐ ⌐

The thug slinks through the night to his destination. His footsteps pound like thunder in Miles' ears, yet fall like twigs in the forest. I'll kill him, tonight. I'll kill him. I'll sever the branch at the fork, then hack the stumps to pieces.

The thief pulls off the covers and laughs. Such a little knife. He slips the knife from the knot of Miles' hand, lifts Miles' night-gown to her shoulders and balances the hilt from her genitals. Do you want one of your own? He waggles the blade to and fro, a silvery flash in the air. I'll give you mine. You'll like it.

Daddy, don't.

⌐ ⌐ ⌐

"Axel, don't."

"I thought you wanted me."

"I thought so too. I'm sorry."

"Shit, Kendra. I wish you wouldn't wait till the last minute to tell me."

"I didn't know this was gonna happen."

"Again."

"All right, again. It's why I'm going away. I can't keep doing this to you."

"Fucking right. I can't take any more."

"I know. It's frustrating. I'm sorry."

"Stop apologizing." He jumps out of bed. "I'll never be able to sleep now." His wine-coloured robe flaps around him. "Want something to drink?"

"No thanks."

Ha, a voice cries, *got him.*

32

Everything is nearly packed. As icing, she has saved Baker's gift certificate. Kendra is no reader, yet she's been savouring this trip to Isabella's, this dig through the dusty shelves for something other than music. She's been cataloguing ideas, disallowing old barriers and inhibitions, planning to buy mysticism and fiction, to plunge herself into words she has never understood. On the face of it, words seem to funnel polyhedral realities into a unitary face, whereas music burgeons under its surface, but perhaps she's been wrong, perhaps those thin lines of print are mere surf songs, its whole as oceanic as the blues, or Beethoven. *Come sing a song of joy. To peace and understanding.*

At Isabella's, Kendra meanders through books, reads a few lines and the back of the jacket to decide if the writer speaks to the questions, not yet moulded, in her mind. It is hard to tell. She concentrates on books about women, alone. She selects *The Bone People* by Keri Hulme, a book about a woman who secludes herself in a tower in New Zealand. The woman talks to herself, in odd, quirky voices, and she stays away from people, except a small boy. She picks *Journal of Solitude* for the musings of its author, May Sarton, who has chosen to live alone. Kendra wants light reading too, and takes mysteries by Sara Paretsky and Sue Grafton. Both their detectives are women; both live alone. She spots a writer whom Axel has recommended and looks at the first paragraph: "Human memory is a marvellous but fallacious instrument." She must have this book. She takes short stories by Alice Munro and Sena Jeter Naslund, then makes herself stop. She already has a bunch of meditation and yoga books at home.

At the cash register, Ebe sees she is devouring *The Drowned and the Saved.* "Will you permit me to add one I think you will like?" His smile is gentle against the cruelty of his face. She has seen him do this with others, but they always seemed broken-winged sorts of people, quite different from her. He ducks away at her startled flutter of assent, and is back before she has time to consider. He doesn't put the book inside the bag but hands it to her for approval. Kendra could never say no, not to this book. It is a trilogy about the camps, and God, written by a survivor, Elie Wiesel, who won the Nobel Prize, not for literature but for peace. The first volume is called *Night.*

Kendra has kept her packing simple. Basic wardrobe of athletic gear and jeans, warm outdoor wear, piles of jockey shorts, teeshirts, long-johns, enough to stave off visits to the laundromat as long as possible. She has packed a travel clock, flashlight, linen, candles, enviro-soaps, cleaners, lotions, sleeping bag, blankets, pillow. She has taken stationery supplies, her tools and journal, the computer Axel gave her, and a great store of books. No TV, no CD player, no cassette player, no answering machine, though she has agreed to maintain a phone line (but not to answer it), and Axel installed e-mail into the computer. For leeway, she has allowed herself a clock radio and her acoustic guitar. She can strum away most demons with an old English ballad or the throb of the blues. For Kendra, that's as safe as it gets.

Of course, she packs her Swiss Army knife.

Seventeen years later, and she is leaving again. Nausea gurgles around in her throat.

That night, Kendra and Axel walk for miles, mostly in the Annex, her stomping grounds for many of her years in Toronto. They walk down Queen, past the clubs where she played, first with Baker, then Survivors. When they got their first gig on the strip, Kendra thought it was the pinnacle of achievement, never dreaming of festivals, recordings, or tours. Success was never her dream, only peace, only freedom. She and Axel weave north, arms entwined, and pass the art gallery, where she spent many hours in the stone silence of its high-ceilinged rooms, gazing at Renaissance paintings with floating cupids and luminescent shafts of godlight, reminiscent of the awestruck moments when she first apprehended the immutable beauty of the Church. Pasted to each other, they stroll up to College, through the University of Toronto campus, past the Sigmund Samuel Library and Hart House. They gaze into the dimly lit windows of the second-hand and antiquarian bookshops along Harbord, Ebe's street, and wonder how such extraordinary shops could cluster on a single city street, a street in their Toronto, not Paris, not New York – though Atticus has a branch in Paris, and Caversham, the psychology bookstore, has the feel of Manhattan. And still, there is the Women's Bookstore, and Isabella's, and the pungent, savoury air that drifts from the Harbord Bakery and the Boulevard Cafe, all the way down the block to the leather shop and the kundalini yoga studio, where Kendra studied for years.

They meander up Brunswick to Bloor, just south of the big rooming house where she first lived. Those were her days as a street musician, playing in subways, at markets, on street corners. A rap musician with kiwi-green dreadlocks and an orange tuque is spinning off lyrics in Kendra's old spot. She shoots a twenty into his case, and he improvises a tribute, her last send-off. At the corner of Spadina, they catch the subway for home.

"When will I see you?" Axel says, resting his glass on the coffee table.

"Please. I can't promise."

"Is this it, then? Is this how you plan to live from now on?"

"I don't know . . . all I know is I have to do it or I'll die . . . actually it's more like the little deaths I did all along will be . . . eternal and I'll live my life as a half person."

"I'll be your other half. Once upon a time, it was supposed to be like that."

"Axel sweetie, I think Karl is my other half. I think the dead parts are his. I'm going away to find them, can you understand?"

"No. Explain to me."

"In my head are voices like tiny people . . . sometimes I can hear them . . . they live in the air . . . they come from tortured places – *lagers* and camps for the disappeared. They have stories to tell me. I have to go away and listen. They are me, I am them. I can't hear them when anyone else is with me. They remember, Axel, they remember you and me."

"Will you tell me their stories?"

"Axel, Axel, I love you so much."

She can't get close enough to him. She nuzzles and stretches and arches her body flush against his. She is sure, if they lie plumb, their skins will peel away like a layer of clothes, or an orange, and their guts will entwine *the rose bush and the briar* in a thicket interwoven forever.

She leaves before dawn. The 401 highway is empty as she speeds west along the collector lanes, curving north onto the 400. The charred sky ebbs over the distant horizon as the rising light of dawn laps waves of rose and gold and platinum across the heavens, just as it did on that seventeen-year-ago night when she escaped the U.P. Only a few truckers are out this early; she will be out of the city before traffic pollutes the views. Patches of snow quilt the countryside, thickening into winter down as she gets further from the city. Cottage country will probably be blanketed like the U.P.

199

As she hurtles up the 400, the car's shadow, elongated by the rising eastern sun, darts beside her Prelude. The light is too diffuse to etch the silhouette of her profile in the second window that scoots along the asphalt. The night she left the U.P., a hunched shadow crept along behind her, terrifying her until she made bunny ears under a streetlamp and found the shadow was her own. She hoos encouraging words to the shadow of her self now appearing on the pavement. "Hey hey hey, we're on our way, we're going to make it now my friend, my shadow friend. The sun is rising, come bask in the light."

The drivers who picked her up expected to be entertained. Even then, Kendra was no talker, chatter having eluded her as much as girlhood, so she sang to them or played ditties on her guitar. One salesman liked her music enough to give her money. Her first gig. She used most of it to buy a pocket knife from a bait 'n' tackle shop near her next stop. She fondles the Swiss Army knife in her pocket, its metal skin so reassuring to touch. Her first Swiss Army knife came years after she'd arrived in Toronto, when she spied a showcase of them arrayed in a circle, a mandala of knives, with blades and openers raised from their sides like tiny arms. The one she selected had a compass, a magnifying lens, a toothpick, and miniature scissors. She has never loved any knife as much.

Except, maybe, the one in the bottom of Howe Sound.

Why didn't she feel its scrape and jab inside her? It didn't hurt her.

It hurt me.

That voice is speaking to her. Kendra veers onto the shoulder of the highway and closes her eyes. Who are you? Blank grey space, devoid of sound.

She pulls carelessly back into traffic and a truck swerves, horn blaring like a foghorn, shouting at her. Her easy concentration

jams and she tails him, pressing her high-pitched horn in a con-
tinuous bleat. It's his fault.

That grey space was deliberate.

There's a lot going on I don't know about.

The highway forks to the west and Kendra leans into the
curve, attuned to her machine like a biker. A few farmhouses are
scattered across low, rolling acres. She feels exhilarated by the size
of the landscape, as if she can exhale the bloat of the city and
return to a scale calibrated by nature and sunlight and God. She
can hear whispers, not shouts, like wings in the trees, or that
voice in herself. Success has fit her no better than a second-hand
coat; you have to feel bigger than trees, more important than
wind, and she can't. She is small and human, the right size in the
landscape. Small and human and *hurt*.

The causeway is shorter than Kendra remembers, no longer
than an elongated jetty. She's forgotten something, and she U-
turns back towards the nearest town. The town is really a hamlet,
just a gas station, laundromat, cafe, and convenience store. She
checks out the convenience store, sees they are the post office,
newsstand, grocery, and video store. The cafe has a menu stuck
in the window. Old-fashioned fifties food: burgers and fries;
grilled cheese; hot sandwiches on bread that will gum in the
gravy; bacon, lettuce and tomato, no doubt slathered with mayo.
Perfect, though the menu is yellowed with age. Down the highway is a freshly Bavarianized town Kendra would like to avoid,
but the only library in the area is under the arcade of its trees.
The supermarket on its outskirts still closes on Sundays. Kendra
drives back to the causeway in just a few minutes. When she
reaches the island side, she stops the car and tosses her wristwatch
down a crevasse in the ice.

The only sign of life at the cottage is her old footsteps in
the snow and animal tracks, small ones, near the garbage bin.
She follows her own bootprints to the house, the crunch of the
snow and the *kathunk* of her heart juxtaposed like the quick

rhythm of mid-beat clapping. The key gets stuck in the lock, of course. She pulls the door towards her and twists the key. Nothing. She's forgotten the particular secret formula for this door, this lock. She twists the key as far as possible the other way, holds it down. Nothing again. Her hand is getting cold with the glove off. She kicks the door three times with the hard tip of her boot. Her calm was a lie, the eye of a tornado. She rattles and pounds at the door, yanking back and forth on the knob, and twists the key so hard that it cuts into her finger. Shitshit shitshitshit.

Calm down, fair adventurer, and try again. Nice and easy now. Nice and easy.

The key slides around, gliding over a little bump that was the resistant spot.

There now, you see, calm conquers all obstacles.

Kendra kicks the open door with her heel. Don't tell me to be calm.

Inside, it's damp and musty. Ugly brown cobwebs drape across the corners of the ceiling. The picture window is covered with watery streaks and white circles of birdshit. The sofa feels damp to the touch. She didn't notice any of this two weeks ago. She drops the bag she is carrying onto the floor with a thud and slings her coat onto the sofa. Looking out through the grime and the birdshit, she kicks her feet into the air and dances around the centre of the room: mine mine mine mine.

The fire she lights fizzles while she's hauling in the first load from the car. She restacks the logs with extra newspaper and kindling, and tries again. The logs are too moist and still don't catch. She slumps down on the sofa. She doesn't want to go into town, not yet. She balls the sports section into tight little globes. That should work. She weaves the kindling into a tottering net, its openings as small as chain-link, and tops it with the smallest logs she can find. This new life is going to take a lot of work.

She makes a hill of her belongings in a corner of the room,

stacks the groceries on the counter. The small logs have caught, yielding a paltry warmth, like a daytime moon, which she sits in for a few minutes, gathering her strength to scrub out the kitchen before dusk.

What's your hurry, Quillan, you've got nothing but time. Don't kill yourself, woman, don't work till you reel. Use your gut to measure time.

Don't forget to meditate.

That's not my thought.

Kendra whirls through the work, turns on utilities, scrubs shelves, unpacks, washes every dish. She finds a dry woodpile stashed in an alcove and lights the wood stove. A toasty warmth seeps into the room and into her limbs. She scatters musty cushions around the stove, pulls out the sofa bed to air and dry.

Don't forget to meditate.

In the crescent of warmth by the hearth, she leans back against the sofa base. She is filthy, tired, close to happy. Outside the late afternoon sun glimmers *a yellow brick road* across the snow on the lake. She folds her legs into padmasana, a full lotus, closes her eyes, thinks about which sensory focus to choose.

Sharohm sharohm sharohm   her mantra   SHAROHM SHAROHHHM sharohmsharohmsharohmsharohm fasterfaster weaving light through her arteries   sharohhmmm   her breathing slows a lump in her shoulders relaxes sharohm I should have cleaned the fridge ohm shar ohm will you tell me your stories shar ohm shaarrr *It hurt* me

it didn't hurt you 'cause it hurt me

who are *you?*

the one who holds the hurt

what hurt?

all the hurt   the then hurt   the now hurt   you stabbed me   you made more hurt

you sound so young are you young?

a chafing burning pain in her vagina yeeooow it hurts burns like fire ohgawdmary can't take it sharohm sharohm SHAROHM SHAROHM SHAROHM can't drown the pain tears streaming whose tears her green eye's tearing yeeeowzer where's the voice where is it

Blank grey void.

Whoops forgot I was meditating sharohm sharohm letting thoughts go

Her sharp hunger has slowed enough that she bothers to cook, and savours the meal. Afterwards she stretches on a mat by the fire. The baked air seeps into the yawn of her pores; her muscles liquefy in the ancient kind of warmth from the fire.

Open my heart, hearth. Warm its frozen chambers.

Her muscles pass beyond liquefaction and disappear. Except her heart, which rises out of her body and floats above the blazing hearth, its ruby colour muted by the sheath of ice around it. Droplets form on the ice, like water beads on a summer glass, feed into rivulets which slide down its translucent sides, tinting pinkish as the ice shield thins. When the shield is transparent, it is clear that the ruby heart has been shattered into a myriad pieces. The ice shield was all that held it in place.

NO, Kendra screams. The word holds no sound.

The shield cracks like an eggshell and her heart falls apart, shards of crystal and water spuming in all directions, some dropping into the fire, some floating off in the air. Crimson trails and ruby puddles form everywhere.

She is truly a heartless bitch.

Axel's blue fist was merely trying to punch through the ice around her cold, cold heart.

This is what happened. He broke her heart.

The apparition of her heart fades away, leaving her muscles

liquid and limp. A paler version of a heart looms in front of her eyes. The tip of the penis is a pale, faded heart, is the heart of the man. Her mind has turned to river, carrying away her thoughts. She hears her own thoughts in small, faraway voices remote though not secret, like a chat in the library or words from a balcony three storeys up, her own private thoughts a galactic distance from the control of her mind. Even this thought is a distant echo.

Something else is tumouring in her mind, a billow of greyness that envelops her brain and dims her reason.

Listen, Kendra, listen now.

I am listening. But my voice is so small.

It's okay. We have changed places.

I can't move.

I have the body. Think to me if you want something.

Move my arm.

Her left arm rises towards the ceiling. She can't feel it, but sees it waving like a plant in the air.

Wow.

Need more proof?

Not at the moment. Who are you?

My name is Billie.

Billie. My favourite name.

Yes.

You called me Kendra. You know me?

I have known you for some time.

How long?

A while ago I would have said since Axel. Now I think it's been longer than that.

What do you mean?

Axel and you are the mirrors. But I have been doing this thing all your life.

What thing?

What thing?

WHAT THING?

Her solo voice echoes in the canyon of her skull. Billie is gone. It's a lonely, empty feeling.

She tries to get up, but her body and mind are yet unconnected and she cannot budge, the physicality of her weakness like foam, or scum, in her blood, enervating her into a pool of flesh.

Marymaryquitecontrary Ipledgeallegiancetotheflagofthe unitedstatesofamerica Her strength is returning. Thelordismy shepherdIshallnotwant hemakethmetoliedowningreenpastures heleadethmebeside She gets up slowly. thestillwatersherestoreth mysoul Jellylegs. She stumbles on the corner of the toasted sofa cushion. Jillbenimble.

She's so tired. She barely manages to unroll the sleeping bag over the bare mattress before she throws herself onto the bed.

In the morning, she wants to die. It doesn't seem like a strange thought, just one that's there. There are so many ways she can do it. If it were summer, she could fill her pockets with rocks and swim into the womb of the lake. Now, she could wander out in the cold in few clothes. She could tie a rope to a beam in the ceiling. There are the halyards to use in the sailboat. She could buy a rifle. She knows how to use one. And she has her friend with her, her new Swiss Army knife, in its sheath of crimson. She fishes in the pocket of her jeans and takes it out. Its blades are folded, like still wings. It is reassuring to touch. She slips a blade out and rests the tip on the skin of her wrist. She feathers it across, and it feels like a caress. It makes her feel safe, just the fact that she can if she wants to. She doesn't have to live. It's her choice. She touches her Adam's apple. She could carve a big smile from one ear to the other, send herself off with the happy face of choice, of selection.

She leaves the blade of the knife open. It looks like a wing, poised for flight. She places the knife on the mantel, beside the figure of the dancer. Now she will always have choice.

She conjures the warmth of Axel's arms around her bare skin, their insides entwined in umbilical closeness. She would miss him.

Maybe coming up here wasn't such a good idea.

Axel, don't

She remembers why she came. It's just so fucking hard.

There you go, feeling sorry for yourself, Quillan, you spine-less sod. Get a move on. Get your flaccid, lazy body out of this house, this minute. Splash cold water on your face. Stoke up the fire. Get out and explore. But stop this infernal whimpering shit.

Exercise pulls her out of morning depressions. She flexes through yoga stretches, does pushups and sit-ups and warm-ups for running. She decides to run the cottage road, all the way to the causeway.

The iron-hard ground crunches under her runners. The pace of her body is sluggish and forced, the worst kind of run. She constructs a visual image of herself in a springy run, steadies it in her mind until her limbs catch on and slide into the peculiar, bouncing lope of her comfortable gait. She begins to notice the crisp air, its cold slap on her cheeks, its sting in the stale air of her lungs. Then everything is there: the white lattice of winter forest, the brown noses of roots and logs and sodden humps of leaves poking through the snow; the distant sky with its wispy trails of clouds, the last rosy tints of sunrise. And the woodland quiet: the absence of motors, propellers, of footsteps, children, snowblowers, sirens, telephones, jackhammers, power saws, beepers, garbage trucks, air brakes, car alarms. She hears a twig snap, the rustle of a dead leaf in the wind. Nothing smells as infinite as pure winter air. A smoky scent wafts into the purity, like a harmonic. Someone is enjoying a morning fire.

A small cluster of black objects is soaring along the road, about ten feet above. Six, seven, eight, maybe more. Kendra's never seen so many air-images at one time. She can't tell what they are, even closer up. They're shrouded, that's why. Each one is draped in black sackcloth material, as if their contents are too grievous for anyone's eye. A footfall thuds into her reverie. She has forgotten that her floating sensoria come attached to people. About fifty feet down the road, Ebe jogs laboriously towards her.

He is clad in worn navy sweats with the hood hanging free, a black wool tuque pulled over his ears. Away from the bookstore, in this setting, he is as thick as two tree trunks and as solid as granite. But his face is what gets her. She stares without restraint. Every inch of his skin looks pulped, though the bone lines and the hook of his nose show underneath. His cheekbones are flat planes, exactly like Karl's. Folds of hide hang in unintelligible lines, as on a bulldog, though the slackness may be from running. Pink scar tissue gleams above his eyes and again in the gnarl of his chin. His eyes are sunk into sockets as deep as wells.

Ebe is so ugly she is tempted to absolve him from ordinary responsibilities, as if ugliness places him in a dimension beyond human measure. What is he doing there, planted in the solitude he knew she was after? She has halted to gape at him in awe mixed with anger. In the end, it is he who absolves her for intruding.

He smiles with his smile that roots on his features, raises one hand, and runs on. As he passes, she is released from her thrall.

She wonders if he is staying in the cottage where the fire was burning, then decides he can't be. It would mean he was staying with others. As far as she knows, Ebe hasn't a friend or a relative, just patrons and people he helps, like herself. She can't imagine Ebe with a woman, a lover. His presence is dense with gloom; he could only live alone. She can hear Baker chiding her: *Ken*dra (she'd accent the first syllable). Any man can find a woman to live with— that's the booty of the war between sexes. Soddy old geezers, gone bald at their gizmos, still have the appeal of just being men.

Not that old man.

That one's gloom would break a woman in a day.

She runs all the way to the fork near the causeway without seeing another soul. Glorious, glorious solitude. Her being expands into the big space, throws off Ebe and his ominous cluster of shrouds, and reverts to her own life track. She walks home, sweaty and hot in the cool winter sunshine.

33

Ebe's face returns to her, bloated and close. Her third eye, peering from her calm mind, looks down into his sockets and sees nothing. His eyes are too deep to fathom. Suddenly, her diaphragm convulses; each breath foments a spasm. The greyness closes over her mind as fast as racing clouds.

Calm down. Calm down. Calm down.
What's scaring you? says the calmdown voice.
It's him. HIM.
Who him?
This is weird listening to a conversation in my own head.
The one who hurts us. With the big ugly face.
No, that's not him. It's a different big ugly face.
I've heard that panicky voice before. That young young voice.
Let's compare faces.
The calmdown voice is new.
Show me the him you think it is.

A face so huge it runs off the edges of the mind. Red leopardy splotches. Cavernous mouth. Bulbous nose breathing hot putrid gases. Thick coated tongue dripping white juice.

KARL!

She's outta there. Into the kitchen, lights the stove, grinds the coffee, mixes up cereal grains, heats the water, sweeps last night's ashes, rolls the sleeping bag, transforms the bed back to a sofa, fluffs the pillows, cleans shelves, cleans floors, arranges, rearranges.

Karl.

She won't think about it.

She can't not.

She draws the guitar from its plush bedding. Her one reliable source of harmony.

Her fingers are too uncoordinated for even simple chords. They are small and chubby. She can't play.

Karl.

I'll go to town, that's what. I'll drive up to that Bavarianized piece of tourist twittwaddle, snoop around the library, maybe have lunch in a cafe. Get some books, drink watery coffee, listen to the cheery chatter of the waitress and the regulars.

Weakness knocks her legs from under her.

I'll lie down on the sofa, that's what. I'll lie down, just for a few moments.

34

Ebe's cylindrical body looks sturdy, almost young, from behind, though something laboured in his footfalls suggests age and fatigue. He is running towards the causeway just ahead of her. He may be her nearest neighbour. At least she has a neighbour, even if it is someone she doesn't like. Kendra starts to circle past him. *Don't let him see us,* a voice pleads.

I can't run behind him the whole way, she thinks back. He's too slow.

She sprints forward but hesitates when she sees the black array, as much part of him as his limbs, though more intimate, a black halo not only of size but of consequence. When she musters enough courage to pass under it, the light stays constant, yet she feels an evening chill until she exits into the slant of the sunlight. She runs with urgency to escape the circle of gloom cast by this man, her rescuer, and his foliage of shrouds.

Rocks shoulder through the snow, exposing the barren land underneath. Muskoka is Shield country, where the earth's bedrock breaks to the surface, harsh and wild and beautiful. Ebe almost seems part of the land, or perhaps they have grown to be like each other, his face and the rocks. He is going to be part of my life, this man with a sideshow on his face. As surely as I am running down this road, I cannot escape him.

The road is deserted on the way back. An acrid rottenness lingers in the air. She thought she inhaled it when she ran under the black foliage, but its foulness, though unique, was mild. Beyond decay, it smells like evil.

At home, she tries to capture the cacophonous weave of agony and melody emerging from her interior. A fragment, a riff, a chord would be enough, a start. She needs new techniques. Neither the graceful repetitions of folk nor the grinding rhythms of rock are complex enough for what she's trying to render. She needs jazz, she needs symphony. Perhaps words. She has been practising with the computer, toying, exploring its range, but she isn't ready to use it for anything serious. Music is still the voice of her soul – or voices, now multiplying so quickly she can hardly keep tabs. She wonders if her talent, or her confidence, is up to the task.

The afternoon's work suggests otherwise. Nothing works, not one improvised bleat. She can't play even a solitary voice – Billie, calmdown, Little Miss Scared – much less discover how they blend. It may take more than a songwriter to capture the near-quiet, the whisper of the chaos, she's trying to get. It may take a composer, a real musician, to know how it all comes together into so much silence. Maybe she will never be able to reach that far inside herself and get out again, and she needs to get out.

The seat in the cafe is warm in the tepid way of food at a party. Near the window, young though tired parents try to interest a snot of a child in more than ketchup and fries. The woman's perm droops a hand-span from the top of her hair. A bulge no thicker than a beer can pouches near the belt around the man's waist. They look like Eagle City people, though their clothes are a sporty kind of casual. The waitress looks like someone Kendra might have known in high school.

A lump of electrician's tape over the springs forces Kendra to sit near the wall of her booth. She studies the gravy-stained menu, trying to decide between a hot turkey sandwich and a quarter-pound of who-knows-what burger. The way the waitress balances the order pad against the flat of her hand gives the impression of age, yet her face, under the crust of bleached-out hair, is as smooth as an overused coin. She couldn't be much older than Angel, or maybe Kendra when she worked the streets. The coffee is watery and has no aroma.

A familiar smell pools above the table. Kendra sniffs at the cup, at the air towards the front table, but the smell doesn't intensify. It's acrid, like the rot of an egg, and would be unbearable if it were strong. The urge to bolt, as if she could absorb diseases, or burdens, from a warmed-up cafe seat, waxes.

When she was at the pinnacle of wanting to be Ken, Kendra chopped off her auburn curls, piled them in an ashtray with a snippet of flesh from her shinbone, a quail wishbone, and three fingernail clippings, and set the whole pile on fire, murmuring phrases from Grimm and Oz and the Bible. She thought she would be transformed, much in the way Glinda the Sorceress had transformed Tip the Gillikin into Ozma, ruler of Oz, except Kendra would become a boy, dra-less at last. But nothing happened, except a caustic stench had billowed through the house, and Karl, who loved her rusty curls, went into a frenzy. Burning flesh or fingernails, or any bad stench, reminds her of the cruel side of Karl.

↗ ↗ ↗

He taught me how to make fire. Miles is telling the story. To rub two sticks together, up and down, up and down. Pieces of bark flew off. The underwood was white and fleshy. The sticks sparked against each other.

Harder, he yelled, when they didn't catch fire. Faster.

The rubbing took forever.

The friction had a smell.

The blaze, when it caught, flared up the open flue, searing the walls of the hearth. I thought my organs would scorch and char.

It smelled like that ashtray, or the hill of wreckage where we took our old trash.

In the mornings, I searched for ashes in the bowl before I flushed.

ℰ ℰ ℰ

Kendra opens her eyes in a hurry. The voices have talked for a very long time, describing things as if she won't get them, won't listen, as if she's like her own mother. The white bread on her hot turkey sandwich is squashed and sodden. The viscous gravy has congealed into a membranous skin.

Jaheesus, I don't know when the waitress brought this. Or how long I was out.

Kendra glances around. The family is gone, their table cleared, wiped, spotless. Two other tables are occupied, one by a couple of truckers, the other by a thin man in a baseball cap.

Ten minutes maybe.

She can't remember a thing. She doesn't know if she did anything, said anything, even ate anything, though she doesn't think so when she looks at her plate. She lost track of everything, including her surroundings, exactly as she did with Axel. She knows there were voices in her head, but what they were saying, the details, has disappeared. She had it for a moment, right afterwards, but now it's a complete fucking blank.

The waitress is carrying two steaming platters to the truckers. They must have ordered some time ago. If anyone was watching, Kendra must have looked like a zombie, or a whacked-out addict from the city. Of course, Canadians are too polite, too cagey to stare, and small-town people know how to get their gossip sideways. She should do what people do in a restaurant, eat something, try to look normal. The gravy on her plate is starting to separate like diarrhoea. She raises a finger to signal the waitress.

"Something wrong with the turkey, hon?" The waitress's voice moos across the room.

Sshhh, please.

"I can bring you something else. Maybe some dessert. We have lemon meringue pie, ice cream, apple crumble."

Kendra shakes her head, feels her brain knock against its container. On the bill, the waitress's scrawl is illegible, as bad as a prescription, though it's not her handwriting that's the problem. The letters and numbers won't coalesce. Kendra slides a twenty under the saucer. Better to be a big tipper than have the waitress come lowing after her.

All she wants to do is get home. At least there she can let the voices take over. At least there she can look at her knife.

How many voices, how many alternate sets of perceptions, how many parallel universes might be rattling around inside her, besides the one she thinks of as her own? When a voice talks to her, she hears her own history retold, as if her own discourse were no more than a fiction, a tale of domination, a conquest of will.

Shit. Those smarmy little buggers took over with Frank. Bailed out before morning, left her to awake with her hand in the till. Not even knowing if she'd asked for a condom. Here she's been thinking, the poor little sweeties, taking all this shit for her. Thinking she didn't have a legitimate voice in her own life, was a shell, a container, a hull of a person. She's driving across the cause-way. She can't figure this out with logic. They'll tell her what's up, as she lets them get stronger. If she can believe a word they say.

She accelerates her meditation program, applying the same intensity she once used on the guitar. A solidity composed of absolute stillness forms around her chaos, making it look small and silly, like white space around jittery words. She runs every morning. In the afternoons, she reads, cooks, explores the island and the towns, practises on the computer. She is not as afraid of her voices.

Her stillness can wrap around a rock or tree and absorb something from its essence, a sense of the vastness of life. Sometimes, when she lingers, or wears her meditation shawl, a vaporous shape, almost an air-picture, drifts out of the object and into her vision. Everything is rich and deep, with a life of its own.

Including the voices inside her. She can identify a few of them: Billie, the Little One, the calmdown one with a voice of honey, a bundle of rage called Miles, a swashbuckler called Amelia. Once, in the middle of the night, she awoke to see them fluttering, like bird shadows, all around the room.

She feels saner than she's ever felt in her life.

She is having more blank periods. They can crash over her like a breaker, knocking her out on the spot. Or lap over her slowly, though completely, when she is around other people. No one has spoken to her or reproached her for something she does not remember. Not yet.

Two days before Axel's first visit, a wave of blankness tumbles her in the kitchen. The counter breaks her fall, changes it more to a slide than a full-scale plummet. She knows how to handle this now. She tests the strength in her limbs with pushup-like motions. When these fail, she crawls to the sofa and clambers onto it. Storm clouds close over her mind.

↵ ↵ ↵

Stupid bitch.
I hate her.
She just doesn't get it, does she?
I want to kill her.
I've got a better idea. Make her hurt herself.
Nodontdothat, dontdothat.
Shut up. We'll take care of you.

What do you suggest?

How 'bout she hangs herself?

Nice. Just before he comes?

She can wear the cowboy hat.

You want us all to die? Let's just cut her up a bit. With glass.

Calm down, calm down. She's trying. She's spent her whole life not knowing. Give her time.

Fuck that. I want to watch her squirm like she used to with Him.

You donkey. If that gives you pleasure, you're just like Him.

You bet I am. And proud of it.

Don't listen to this mule gas. Let's just ask her to cancel the visit. She's cancelled everything else in her life for us.

Agreed.

Agreed.

The bitch wins.

ᕐ ᕐ ᕐ

It's a long time before she can move. She doesn't know if she caught the whole conversation, never knows. Well, *they* may not want Axel to come, but she does. She hasn't seen him for two months, two long months. She picks up where she left off, making pasta from scratch. She takes a sheet of pasta dough and runs it through the vermicelli blade. She doesn't pull her hand back from the edge of the dough, not until the last minute. It won't hurt, she finds herself thinking, though, god knows, her vagina hurt enough. Cunt, he used to call it, a word like a cut. She drapes noodles over the back of a chair. The dough looks like strands of dead hair. The knife's on the mantel, its blade like a wing. There is something beautiful about blood, like liquid rubies. She starts to push her hand through the pasta cutter.

Whoa, Quillan, enough. You heard them. Maybe you should reconsider making pasta for Axel at this moment.

She shrugs into her light parka and starts for one of the trails towards the lake. The sun is high and arcing west. Tendons of clouds skate across the blue. The April melt has not yet started, though moisture softens the air. The trail requires concentrated hiking. Hunks of granite-like rock, Muskoka gneiss, bulge from unexpected places and, with the ice, make the path treacherous. Under the thinning snow, the textures of gravel, roots, runnels and pits, and the muck of leftover leaves, drum against the soles of her boots. She picks her way, gathering sureness but never speed. Rarely is there firm, solid earth under her feet. The trees are clustered like buddies, or families, along each side of the path – pines and birches, hemlocks, maples, old folks and saplings. She could hang herself from one of their muscular branches, extended wide in the wings of a welcoming hug. The image repeats in her mind like the phrase of a song. A lynch mob of trees with beckoning branches. A stump of a stool to kick out from under her. The hood on her parka at one angle, her neck at another. Strange fruit.

Light cleaves through a break in the trees on top of a knoll just ahead of her. Ivory winter light with the diamonds of spring. She climbs towards it.

From the crest of the knoll, the lake stretches in front of her like a second sky. She could walk on the sky.

Muskoka has thousands of skies, all frozen in winter, pooled on this bedrock of Precambrian land.

She scampers and skids her way down the steep path on the lake side of the knoll. The path ends in a cove, a private wedge of beach that during summer she hopes will be her own. She shimmies herself deep into a crevasse that splits the side of the hummock. Someone has hauled a slab of granite into the base of the crevasse to serve as a seat, so she can cosy into this nest of stone and look out across the shimmer of the lake to the misty, shrouded islands low in the water like a pod of enchanted whales.

It's a seat for the gods.

Only a builder of pyramids could be strong enough, or desperate enough, or visionary enough, to haul this rock, this granite more ancient than glaciers, into this godforsaken, god-blessed hole in the wall.

Someone who knows one moment like this is a reason to live.

35

Axel unloads boxes of things, gourmet sauces and spices, old sheet music from Isabella's, frozen meals from Lena, a trove of second-hand clothes discovered by Baker, and wines of his very own choosing. Kendra trots alongside him, a silly banshee who forgets to help. The cottage air is toasted from the big flames of the fire. Loaves of fresh bread are cooling in the kitchen. Axel nicks pieces from the end of a loaf, the aroma of rosemary and basil on his breath when he draws near. His eyes, their complexity like the facets of winter, look as beautiful as yesterday's view of the lake. In them are the hue of the pale winter sky, the sparkle of granules of snow, the glitter of quartz in the rocks. Kendra breaks into the infantile wails she vowed no one would hear. How lonely she has been.

A tic starts to twitch between his eyebrows. He cradles her into his chest and rocks back and forth. Her banshee sobbing solidifies into a sheet of sound.

"You should come home, Kendie."

She yanks herself out of his arms.

"It isn't good for you to be so far away from the people who love you."

"They're just tears, Axel. They're not dangerous."

She wants to weave in him the beauty of her favourite places. To show him the millionth shade of grey in the watery sky, the way clumps of ice cloud over the water and reflect the pastel mists of dawn or sunset, mirror to mirror to mirror. Maybe a glimpse of the frozen shallows, where the fish will find shade in season, will reassure him that she is not just hiding, but maturing in the chrysalis of nature. But Axel's environmental eye fastens on the glints of debris. He notices acidic discolorations, patches of industrial scum, oily slicks, broken bottles, crumpled foil. She points out the lichens she has identified, a rosette in the bark of a tree, the tripes along the sheer face of a scarp beside the trail. "Lichens," she says, quoting from one of the books she's been reading, "are the ground cover of the tundra and taiga of the north, the highest-growing plant in the Himalayas, the hardiest form of life in the world, yet unable to endure the pollution of cities." This piques his interest.

She doesn't take him to her berth in the knoll.

A grey jay, the scavenger, the survivor, of the north, whistles a raucous, overconfident call. "They're my everyday company," she says. "They remind me of Baker." He didn't hear a sound, he replies.

Kendra chops the long green stems of chives to sprinkle, along with walnuts, on a purée of carrots and ginger.

"You never used to cook like this in Toronto," Axel says. His long fingers insect-dance around her waist, to her cunt. "I miss you," he murmurs.

"Axel. I'm working."

"So, stop." His hands tickle up towards her breasts.

He sashays and rotates against her, a rolling pin adrift in a pizza of dough. The bones of her pelvis press against the counter. He revolves her nipples like a slow clock.

The knife slips out of her hands, though she adjusts the stove to simmer and remembers to grab her glass of Merlot.

        ♪ ♪ ♪

dontlethimtouchme, dontletHimtouchme
Calm down, calm down.
I want those hands torn off her, joint by joint, beginning with the nail on the pinky.
She likes those hands. Watch her limbs. Medusa's hair.
Let's get out of here. Let's fly.
The waxwing flies point, then treads air at the rim of the sky so they can all go through together.
Welcome, my friends.
Gabriel. Gabriel. Where have you been?
I can't cross the border, the one at the skin. But never mind that, how have you fared?
Slow, Gabriel. She's a turtle, a terrapin.
Yet you are succeeding.
How, Gabriel? How?
You talk to each other. You're here together.
A big, mean one refused to come.

        ♪ ♪ ♪

Axel's fingers seem to curve from his palms like the talons of a hawk. Red feathers between the talons ciliate into tufts of red hair, ear hair on fat freckled fingers.

        ♪ ♪ ♪

The mean one will lie to us.
He will try. He will cloak the old tale in a miasma of jokes. Find the one place he doesn't joke. That's the door. That's the door.

        ♪ ♪ ♪

The blue fist is in paroxysms of pounding.

Axel gazes at her in a miasma of love. Who does he think he loves, who the hell does he think he loves, when he knows me so little? His eyelids droop, weary and heavy with satisfaction. His breath is starting to wheeze.

No way, you bastard. You're not going to get away with this.

"Wake up." Kendra jostles his shoulder with punches. "It's too early to sleep." Usually she draws the covers in a nest around his neck.

"Axel, I have to talk to you."

He looks at her stupidly. "It can't wait?"

"I might forget. It's important."

He rubs his eyes with the bunched fists of a child.

"I think I know why I don't remember. I think I've finally got it."

"Yeah?"

"Your hands become Karl's hands. I disappear."

"Hm."

"I don't know if I know if it's you or Karl. Or anyone."

Axel's eyes are shut.

I could squash that pillow till every wheezing breath hurricanes back down your throat, you goddamn stupid pervert. Joseph, yeah, right. Only if the Holy Ghost comes a-whispering to you in your dreams. That's the only way any goddamn man listens. You have to augment your message with the voice of God.

He listens better than any man you know.

NOT GOOD ENOUGH. Just 'cause none of them listen doesn't mean half an ear should make me grovel in gratitude. Oh thank you great holy male creature, oh thank you for thirty seconds of listening to me.

I'll scald his face with carrot ginger soup.

He's lucky it isn't urine.

What birds can only whisper

Karl pinches her nostrils until she gasps. A thin, warm stream pours into her mouth, different from the fat frothy stuff that comes in bursts.

How can she believe such ridiculous stories? Karl took her fishing, taught her how to hunt. Karl steered her through the woods and paused to listen to the call of the birds. When Karl poked fun at the pious, she laughed like a weasel. She slams her hand on the counter. Absurd. Karl loved her.

The mid-afternoon sun slants its tilted light across Axel's face. He rubs his eyes with a small-child gesture, as if he can refocus the scene into something familiar.

Kendra massages his scalp with sad, tender hands. There is nothing to say.

Axel's melanin skin looks jaundiced in the afternoon glare. He paces in and out of the syrupy light, back and forth across the room. His body, stiff at the shoulders, and too naked, has a bounce to it, like he, too, has absorbed the spirit, the exuberance, of the country. At the mantel, he picks up the knife.

"What's this?" He holds the knife up. Its silver blade flashes a snail of yellow light.

"It's not the same one," she says.

He snaps the blade down into its sheath.

"I'm taking this with me," he says. He walks over to the heap of his jeans.

This she can never explain. The solace from knowing she can die. The courage.

She puts out her hand. "I'll just get another one," she says.

36

Kendra hears screaming across the grey chasm. Lovemaking is the one intimacy she hasn't withdrawn from Axel. Not this too, she begs inside, he'll leave for sure. The screams subside. Axel moves his hand along her abdomen. Nausea burbles up her throat. "NO," she explodes. She runs to the bathroom and hunches over the sink. The retching slides back down to her gut.

Axel, propped against the pillows, stares vacantly at the windows. His right hand is balled in a loose fist.

"Are you mad?"

"No."

"I'm sorry."

"Sorry. Sorry. All I hear is sorry." He moves the fisted hand.

She jerks her palm open in a wing over her face, folds her forearm across her breasts.

"Christ. Do you think I'm going to hit you?"

"No." But she can't remove her hands.

He takes her wrists. "Look at me."

She must control the tremors. *She must.*

She drifts through the greyness to the space where the voices talk, and listens to the bruises they call stories. So many stories. A thousand and one, at least.

"KENDRA. LOOK AT ME."

don'tlook don'tlook he'llsee he'llsee She opens her eyes.

"Christ."

"What's wrong? What'd I do?"

"Your eyes. They're full of terror. And pleading."

"Not my eyes."

"Excuse me?"

"Those aren't my eyes."

"They go with the voices?"

"One of them is looking out of my eyes."

"Whoever she is, she's terrorized."

No shit.

"Talk to me. Tell me what's going on."

"My voice doesn't go there."

"Try."

" "

"Did you try?"

" "

"Have you seen your fucking face? Come, look in the mirror."

I've seen it. Ugly dirty filthy face.

Now Axel won't make love, won't even touch her. She's too dirty, even for him. "I don't want to make love to a terrorized child," he says.

"But you have," she says nastily. "Every time you're with me."

"But now I won't," he says. "Even if you will."

He's right, she doesn't see him as himself. Her ideas about men, about perverts, keep interfering. Yet it's Axel she loves. A man's-gotta-do-what-a-man's-gotta-do she would have dumped in the dust years ago. She tells him all this. She finds a voice who can.

37

The mantra rockets around her head at the ferocious speed of a spiralling toy plane, launches her free from the racing babble of her mind, free to just listen. Great clapping ensues. Everyone's glad Axel's gone. Now Kendra has time for them. They giggle and gurgle, whoop with pleasure, and she joins them, laughing at nothing but the sheer joy of being alive. Snatches of the weekend roll by in familiar clips, and replay in new ones. Not everybody had the same weekend. On the far side of the grey, Billie and Miles and the Little One wait.

✎ ✎ ✎

Come with us, Billie invites.

Where?

To the year Miles was born. Came into being, split from the rest.

The Muskoka sky is swallowed into the infinite blackness of a Michigan night, starlit by the companions of her childhood. Auriga, the charioteer of the southern heavens, lame yet compassionate, would scoot up and rescue her if she could only deserve it. (God, through Auriga, had made her this promise.) She made it her business to memorize the heavens. She started with Sirius, bright and reliable even when a full moon strolled across the sky. Next, the warm orange fire of Betelgeuse. Then Orion, the warrior, with the sceptre dangling from his belt. The seven sheltered Pleiades. Taurus, the bull, who some said was Jupiter in disguise. No rescue there. Jupiter was a difficult god to please. The twins Castor and Pollux, brothers of the woman with the face that caused wars. The face of the heavens was pocked by the stars, on some nights especially. Yet the Milky Way always looked like a river, and she would drift, drift on its currents, on a raft through the heavens.

I wanted to yank that starry cutlass out of the sky. The hell with rescue. So much anger makes Miles sound older than five.

They slip through the farmhouse window and hover near the ceiling over the bed. Four Kendras lie below in various poses.

The dollgirl, unzipped, in an ooze of white slime. She's me, Kendra thinks.

Us, Billie amends.

A boy waving his hand like a wand, or a cleaver. Stabbing the air with invisible knives.

That's me, Miles says.

Us.

An embryonic ball who rocks, cries, sucks her thumb. Me, says the Little One. I never got older than two.

A giant shadow darts swiftly at the dolly on the bed, pecks at the fruit of her cunt.

A trembling strobe pops out of the doll and hides under the bed.

Billie flies at the Four-Taloned giant. The Hawk is the one like Father. Billie is old, a grown-up.

I'LL KILL HER. I HATE IT WHEN SHE RESISTS ME.

It's finished now, Billie repeats.

The predator claws the dollgirl across the face. Her heels hook over the sides of the mattress. Her hips start to gyrate. A pool of gummy liquid drips from her shiny vagina. She fucks the air.

SEE HOW SHE BEGS FOR IT. SHE WAS ALWAYS LIKE THAT. I USED TO WATCH HER.

How'd you do that?

I'd step carefully to the edge of the body while he gobbled us with his greedy, lusty eyes. I'd leap out of our blue eye and hover just behind his skull. That's where I'd stay and watch. Like a little brain shadow. Every time he moved, I moved. It got so I could think exactly like him, anticipate a move before he made it.

You're one of us, then. A Kendra.

DON'T MAKE ME GO BACK. I'M NOT HER. I'M NOT. The shadow disappears into the dollgirl.

They consult for a while about what to do next, how to get everyone out and back home. No one wants to go back into the body, not because of the bruises, the bleeding, the jackhammer trembling, but because the love of Karl makes the whole of the story too painful to bear. Because it was the adoration, the worship of Karl – the nectar, the ambrosia, in his sweat and his spirit – that made this place heaven before it was hell.

The body on the bed starts to quake and shiver the way Kendra remembers from the cottage. Every limb has a seizure, but separately, a round robin of epilepsy. A thrum of energy propels her and the others into the convulsing body.

NEVER has she known such fear. She would do anything, kill her mother, or a bishop, live in Riyadh, anything to get away from that bed. Should I slip under it, hide? No, he'll kick me out with the tips of his boots, or the claw of his toes. Under the pillow, so he won't know I'm here? No, he'll squish it over my face, one, two, three. In the closet behind the clothes? You know what he does with coat hangers and flannel. No no no please don't come in.

Auriga, where are you? Oh Jesus. Oh Mary. Oh Mom. Oh Mom. Oh Mom.

The pasty, freckled, *hairy* hand holds hers, guides it down the slope of his body, stretched like a plank above her. She, no Miles, jerks her hand away. Move, warns the Hawk, and she rolls her head. He, Karl, clouts the side of her face. Her ear rings like a tin whistle stuck on a note. He curls her hand around the spongy mass of his thing, his penis. She rubs it up and down, tickling the tip, his heart, with insect-fingers before she bears down like he taught her. It's so big, she can only rub one side at a time. When it stiffens, it feels too hard to be human, like the horn of the devil, or the tail, full of gristle, like the tail of a dog or a chewy piece of meat.

His body is pink, cylindrical and broad. He skis forward on his elbows and knees. Stumps of legs, like a sawhorse, scissor over her face. With the axe edge of his hand he presses her throat, forces her mouth open to gag and breathe. She swallows her nausea, the vomit, the sounds. All sound disappears, sucked down with the world. There is only his penis, as big as a planet yet moist like a strawberry, its roots far away in a thicket of hair. A thicket the colour of oak leaves in fall, surrounded by a continent as white as Alaska, or the north of Michigan on this dark winter night.

Kendra and Billie fly back together. Where are the others? Kendra asks, though she can hardly hold a thought in her head. Miles and the Little One and the Four-Taloned Hawk?

They are back where they live, on the bed, in the dollgirl.

We can't leave them. I know what it means.

♪ ♪ ♪

Penis blues. Maybe she can write that song after all. Penis blues: the laughter fucked women glue over their faces. Maybe jokes are pinpoints of light from stars already exploded. For this, she needs words, the exactness of words, and their silence. The unwritten page is a universe of space, and a vacuum, a void in which to place her words.

Axel has given her not technology but music, a new way to play. And words break apart, into sounds, into rhythms, each letter a beat, or a note, each sentence a song, if she learns how to play. Language is about music, surrounded by space. Not meaning, as she thought when she was afraid. She sits for a long time in the space of a page.

On her way down the trail to her seat in the crevasse, she stumbles over rocks and roots, now snowless after the meltdown of spring. She is in such a hurry that she bumps against the trunk of a tree. Too eager, Quillan, slow down. She slows into the exploratory steps of a five-year-old. Everything on the trail looks fresh and exciting. *What's that?* a voice asks, as her eyes linger on the flimsy papyrus of a birch. "A birch tree," she replies, aloud in the deserted forest. "A hardwood. Good for fire logs and mediocre lumber. Possessor of extraordinarily beautiful white peeling bark." *What's a tree?* "Have you never been in the woods?" *I've never been out of the bedroom.* She is so buoyed by the excitement and curiosity of the voice, of Miles, that her heart won't plummet. Miles stares at the trees and the daytime sky, the roots and the rocks, the sudden shafts of sunlight. The freedom to enjoy anything whatsoever that piques his interest, he finds an extraordinary experience. She explains all she can about the forest, its narrow needly conifers that absorb the light, the deciduous branches that web the sky. She explains where they are – on a trail – what forests are, and lakes, winter and seasons, about the cottage and Muskoka and Toronto and the guitar. She isn't quite sure who has surfaced enough to listen. Miles for sure, maybe Billie. Billie sometimes knows more than Kendra herself.

When they reach the clearing, Kendra fails to sense something is different. She clambers and slides down the knoll, talking aloud to Miles, and settles her gaze on the lake, so the whole, incredible vista can trickle through her splintered mind. Only then does she turn to the granite (though it's actually a stone called gneiss) seat.

It's occupied.

Ebe roosts in her seat in the rocks. He nestles in the cleft, the embrace, of the crevasse. His eyes are half-closed. Not one shrouded object floats over his head.

Fury convulses her. She picks up a rock, rolls it around between the flats of her palms. So much ugliness in her place of beauty. The rock has a crest like a spear, or a skull. Ebe's brain would mash into ooze, grey and white and red, the colours of her helplessness. *I hate you. Die. Die.*

GO WAN HE'LL LIKE IT

She does a breathing meditation on a flat rock overlooking the lake. A small space forms between herself and the frenzy. "Are you okay?" she asks Miles. *No, I hate him.* She, or he, heaves a rock across the ice-caked water, another and another. Each rock slaps against the ice skin of the water, then disappears down a centre of orbiting ripples that never seem to end. He never did go away. He pinned her or held her or gagged her or slapped her or fucked her. There was *never* any space for her.

Ebe approaches with his slow, sad tread but stops at the point when one further step would puncture her safety zone, the large elliptical space around her, a fence of skin projected in air.

Even words could violate her. Ebe is silent. He selects a flat rock from a pile beside him and makes it hop across the ice and water. *Wow.* Miles of the woods is back. *How'd he do that?*

Miles finds a flat rock and plunks it at the lake. It doesn't bounce once. Ebe slows the motions of his next toss so Miles can imitate him. They stare at Ebe from the corner of their blue eye. Ebe skips another, as if their effort and his are unrelated. This toss is slower still. Miles tries, exactly the way Kendra played her first chord. He tries and tries. Ebe neither instructs nor praises. Miles skips a rock in one smooth motion, and another. Kendra's ellipsoid skin collapses and she moves closer to Ebe. "Hi," she hoos. Ebe smiles his rock of a smile, his eyes nectar deep in their sockets. She can't remember why she thought him ugly.

They sit in silence, each gazing across the lake. It is the silence of meditation and mantras, the silence that turns chaos to a whisper, the silence that encloses, yet unveils, all things. It is a silence deep enough for the silenced inside her. She is as comfortable as when she is alone, perhaps more so. Miles stirs inside. He has not ducked into the grey but is asking questions about the lake, the ice, skipping stones. Even with Axel, no one stays around, much less chats. Maybe she won't always be false with others, true only when sequestered in solitude. Maybe.

Ebe leaves before she has a chance to ask why he's there. She scoots up to the slab of granite in the hill. Ebe put it there? Ebe? He's the one who knows about reasons to live?

They didn't even speak to each other, not really, nothing of consequence. Yet she feels less alone at this moment than after thousands applaud her, than when she's cuddled with Axel, or praying in church.

Ebe was different today than he was on the causeway. She didn't feel the fear, or the violence, or sick with disgust. *The shrouds*, Billie prompts, *there were no shrouds*. The umbrella of shrouds with their stench of the devil was gone today. Nothing at all emanated from him. He was just there.

The next morning, she awakes and she doesn't want to die. Her inner landscape is more visible, more defined, as if the glance of a witness lit a lamp in the fog. She does a dancing meditation, like a dervish, in which her energy spins and stays still as a rock.

Miles can't wait to skip stones with his new buddy. She sets out early in the afternoon, lopes down the rocky path until a stumble slows her down. Miles has been thinking of nothing but Ebe.

She skis down the gravel on the hummock. *He's there.* Ebe is sitting on the rock overlooking the lake. She doesn't know a thing about him, except he owns a bookstore and has a tattoo on his arm. How does she know he won't hurt her? A terrorist could get a Holocaust tattoo as cover.

She huddles on the far side of the rock. Ebe has piled a few choice stones in the centre of the rock, between them. She flips one from hand to hand. Her hand jerks forward and the rock hits the lake with a splash. Miles. *Pretty feeble throw, kiddo. It was not.*

It's okay, Kendra. The man's okay. She trusts Billie's judgment. Kendra moves within talking distance.

"Were you waiting for me?"

"Of course." She has forgotten the accent of his voice.

"You knew I'd come today?"

"I was prepared to wait many days."

"Why do you help me so much?"

"Have you read the book I gave you?"

"A little. It's frightening. I don't want to go there. Even in books."

"I did not mean to frighten you."

Ebe is silent for a long while. Miles picks up some stones, deals them to himself and Ebe. They ping across the water, then drop without sound.

"Perhaps you will do me the kindness to answer me one question." Ebe's politeness is without rhetoric, almost courtly. He would not press her for an answer. It makes her want to have an answer.

"Why did you run a long circle around me when you saw me on the road? Not the first time, but the second?"

This, like the blade of her knife, she doesn't know how to explain. She wants to lie, yet she doesn't want to lie. A lie will ripple between them like a skipped stone. Ebe looks at her from the nectar of his compassionate eyes, so at odds with a face so brutal. He expects nothing for himself. He is asking for her.

"I was avoiding something I saw above your head."

"Shrouds?"

"A packload. You know about them?"

"Of course. When I sit there" – he nods towards the gneiss throne – "I can think about them. Otherwise I have to keep them at a distance from myself."

"We were destined to meet."

"Yes."

"You knew that, didn't you? Back in Toronto when I bought the books?"

"Before," he says. "When you described the cottage."

The ripples on the lake make a sound like a crackle, though muted and low. The last glacier of ice from the winter is breaking apart.

"You know," he says, "only one other person has ever been able to see the shrouds."

"Really? Who?"

"My second wife. A Buddhist."

"Not your first?"

"I don't know if she would have. The shrouds were not around when she was alive."

"They were so different, your wives?"

"She was younger than you when she died. Isabella. A bud who never opened. I *will* tell you, you know."

"What?"

"What's under them."

She looks to see if he is mocking her and is unprepared for the sobriety in his eyes. He shows no trace of the artifice she expects in the glance of a stranger, or a family member.

"Your eyes differ in colour to an astonishing extent," he remarks. "The right is almost Dresden. The left is emerald green."

"My mark of Cain."

He fingers the scars on his face. "Perhaps Cain is the mark of the chosen." He lumbers to his feet.

Every day she returns to the cove. The trip becomes part of her routine. Ebe is never there. Nor does she see him on the road to the causeway. She believes he promised to come. If their meeting was fated, as they both had agreed, he too should arrive at their afternoon hour, compelled by the magnitude of their connection. Miles is disgusted, *what a jerk*, and the Little One sobs. He'll come, he'll come, Kendra assures them. He has his reasons. He has his life. She refuses to lose faith at his failure to show. She thinks the cottage she is renting actually belongs to him.

38

Baker answers the door when Kendra arrives for Lena's insemination. They waltz around the room, as close as a couple of bad-ass kids on a dance floor. "Oh I've missed you, I've missed you, how I've missed you," Baker says. In spite of these protestations, Baker looks as if she has benefited from time away from Kendra and Survivors. While thin still, she has gained a bit of weight, feathery, comfortable weight, cushioning the zigzag of arrows and bones underneath. Her lightning energy hasn't abated.

"They're upstairs," Baker says. "I've been coming and going so much all day, they don't know it's you." She calls to Angel and Lena.

Lena is adding touches to the bedroom. She is bringing in spare pillows, clothing them in new cases she has sewn. Each pattern is significant, she says, holding one out for Kendra to see. It's another Xhosa print, but in shades of burgundy, mauve, and cameo pink. A beautiful arrangement of cut flowers stands on the ledge of the bay window. "A Hog's Hollow touch," Angel acknowledges. Her blush is a pale version of the pillowcase.

Angel suggests Kendra go look in the fridge. "Not dinner," Baker explains on the way down. A pharmacy of insemination vials, like the pouch of a hypochondriac's suitcase, covers the side of one shelf. Each one is labelled with a name and date and even a time. Baker is acting as courier, picking up the samples on the day, so they're fresh. It has taken a while to find donors, not just because men are reluctant to part with their sperm but because everyone had to have two AIDS tests, six months apart, to be certain. Angel's brother has not come through.

They have decided to mix semen from no fewer than four donors for each try. Two might spawn a child similar to one of its fathers, an identifiable copy of a man. Three does not solve the problem of race. Lena wants one black, or at least non-white, donor per batch, which complicates the issue of anonymity. They are keeping a file for each donor. In it, they record names, birth dates, and vital statistics, like weight, height, hair colour, skin colour, marital status, number of children (a fertility check), education, employment, hobbies and passions (listable), medical history, donor dates, and xeroxed proof of AIDS results. Lena adapted the list from the donor sheets at the fertility clinic. Baker says they get more information than she ever does, especially about marriage. Baker is not involved with anyone, hasn't been for two whole months. Maybe that's why she looks plump with radiance.

Lena places candles around the bedroom to send auras of light around all their chairs. Angel puts a CD in the small system she has built into the closet.

It is a tape of the call of loons. While Lena is changing, the three of them practise with the syringe in the bathroom. Baker already knows how to use it. She has grown closer to Angel while Kendra's been away.

Lena is floating around the room in a gown of gauzy cotton with long bell sleeves. In front of the candles, she bows her head and mutters a couple of phrases. "To keep the duppies away," she says, when she looks up. "I'm afraid they'll be attracted by a process like this." Angel hands Baker a stack of files. "Let's do one last check," she says. Lena props herself up against a stack of pillows, colour-coordinated with her gown and the bedspread. Beside Angel is a cooler containing the vials.

"Axel Berne," Baker reads. Kendra grabs for the file.

"Just kidding," Baker says. "Mustafa Hamid. Age twenty-seven. Born June 17, 1970. Place, Somalia. Five foot ten, black eyes, black hair. Single, no children. There's a note here. Reason for donating, too many people to support back home. Jesus."

"Got it." Angel pulls a vial half out of the cooler. "Check his health certificates."

"All clear," says Baker. "Both AIDS tests, and a copy of all his entire medical history. A little bias here?" she says.

"Can't be too careful," Angel says. "My father says they lie to get in the country."

"Antonio Pesaro. Age thirty-nine. Born 1958. Five-seven, one hundred and eighty pounds. Bit of a tub, that one. Bet he rounded it down. Clean on the medical. Hey, get this. Six children."

"Good Catholic boy. He hopes it's in his genes," Kendra says.

"Nice track record," Angel says. "He may be the man."

"Boy kids or girl kids?" asks Lena.

"Doesn't say," Baker says. "Shall I move on?"

"What does he do?" Angel asks. "I've forgotten."

"You won't believe this. He's a fitness instructor."

"I remember. Gold's Gym."

Angel offers cold drinks, lemonade or iced tea, from the cooler. Lena asks if James John Kendal is on the list.

"What's with the name thing?" Kendra asks. "I thought you wanted everyone anonymous."

"A precaution," says Angel. "We might need to know."

Baker reads Kendal's vital statistics. He's from Barbados and a civil engineer. Six foot two, unmarried, dimple on the left cheek of his tush. She picks up the last file. "Wow," she says. "I'm taking this one." Angel leans back in her chair. "Alain LeMontagne. Occupation, musician. Blue eyes. The visage of a poet. Great mass of hair."

"We'll auction it off," Angel says. "Never have to work again."

"Or split it between us," Baker says. "Think of the songs."

"Cut it out, Baker." LeMontagne is a heartthrob of the folk scene.

"Ah, well." Baker opens the file. "Bouchard probably wouldn't let him donate outside Quebec."

The last one, she says, is an Ontario boy. William St. Clair Dayton, born and bred in Timmins, twenty-three years old, a computer programmer and a chess player.

Angel removes the first vial and transfers its contents into a glass bowl. The semen is cloudy and viscous, difficult to pour, but not the gummy white ooze of the dollgirl. The contents of the next bottle are translucent, close to the hue of champagne. It takes a spatula to ease it all out. The variety in the colour and texture, and even amount, of the semen is surprising to Kendra. Also, its beauty, the flecks that sparkle like the metasediments in the dull granite rocks of the Shield. Semen twinkles at her, like Axel's eyes.

Angel mixes the sperm and suctions it into a syringe. Lena arranges herself with her hips high on the pillows. Angel bends towards Lena's face and whispers, then plunges the syringe deep into Lena's vaginal cavity. Lena guides Angel's hand, and halts when the syringe has passed her cervix.

Lena raises her hips to almost a shoulder-stand, bounces and twists and dances in air. "I found a way," she says to Kendra. Her face is lascivious with power and victory.

"Do the second one, Kendra," she says.

"Me? Why?"

"I want to glut my baby with love."

Kendra takes the syringe from Angel.

"Mix it first," Angel says.

Kendra stirs the mixture, inhaling its brackish, musky scent. It is thicker than vichyssoise, or the gravy on a hot turkey sandwich, and pasty, like thin bread dough. She folds it and kneads it with the base of the spoon. The syringe is slow to suction full.

Lena has dropped her hips back on the stack of pillows. Kendra can't see her face, just her legs and the gauze of her robe at her hips. Lena's hands are cupped around the beard of her labia, her slender fingers like the feathers at the tip of a wing. At a signal from Kendra, she will open – unzip – the flaps of her skin.

Kendra positions the syringe the way she practised, her thumb-tip on the plunger, her hand on the hilt. She nests the tip on Lena's eyelet, the colour of a plum.

"Now!" Kendra says, and plunges the syringe into the passage.

There's no resistance, just a tunnel of water, or a ripe avocado, and no sound to be heard. Not a swish. Not a breath. Kendra moves her hand around, stirring for contact. She pictures ripples in water and leaves in the wind. A kiss on a strawberry. The slope of a heart.

A hand rests on her arm. It's Baker. "Good enough," she says. "You can stop."

"But I haven't done anything yet," Kendra says. "I haven't put it in."

"Just push the plunger."

This is as close to being Ken as Kendra ever will get. She wants to pummel and wallop this thing on the bed. Lena likes it. Just look at her. It won't matter if the syringe makes her weep blood. Every bad feeling, every wound, every slight can surge up from Kendra's gut, from her heart, from her groin, into her arm and her thumb, purged through a plunger into the cells of another. She depresses the plunger, and drops, comatose with exhaustion, into her chair.

"Will you sing to me?" Lena asks, after Baker has taken a turn. "Sing to the baby I hope we will have?"

Kendra hasn't sung a note in months. She doesn't know if she can. Cruelty might warp her voice into the saccharine bleat of pop.

Angel brings in her bass, warms up a little.

Baker has a bongo and taps with her fingers and the heels of her hands.

Kendra's voice wavers and slips under the notes. Angel sits on the edge of the bed, her head bent over her bass. Baker pulls her chair close to Kendra, the drum held between her ankles. "It's okay, sweetie," she whispers. "You just didn't know." Warmed up, Kendra's voice grows full and rich, coloured and textured, can climb and descend through the octaves of passion. She sings old English ballads about love and courtship. She sings spirituals that she has never sung for anyone but herself. Baker taps out a jig, a Scottish reel, a strathspey. They play and sing until both Lena and Angel are sound asleep.

39

It is another month before Kendra sees Ebe. She spots him in the shelter of the rock, his eyes hooded and bruised in their sockets, his head covered in a bright red tuque in spite of the warmth. Hovering above the water are two shrouded objects, fading in and out of focus, from black to grey. Kendra tiptoes to the flat rock by the lake.

She decides to do an object meditation on the shrouds while she waits. She fixes the image of the larger one in the epicentre of her third eye. The draped object turns white and elongates into a human shape. The shroud rustles with the wind of breathing. A pinprick of light weaves a web of rays until the curtain lies in delicate, translucent folds.

"Stop."

Kendra was so transfixed, she did not hear Ebe approaching.

"I will tell you at the right time. Please, do not invade my privacy."

"I'm sorry. I was trying not to interrupt."

"You are angry with me for not coming." He lowers himself onto the rock.

"Well. Where have you been?"

"Sick." He pats the top of her hand. "I go through bad periods."

"I've been here every day. Almost."

"I know. But you can't count on me. I am not reliable. Though I think about you. I picture you here."

"You are the most reliable person I've ever met."

"When I am around, that is true. I want to come more often than I can."

Kendra asks about his illness, such a benign question that she is unprepared for the silence that follows. His breathing sounds laboured even when he sits, full of struggle. He waits until time and silence wrap a great space around the two of them.

"My given name is Ebriah Blum. I am originally Polish, a Jew, as you know. I spent four years in the place we used to call Oswiecim, which you know as Auschwitz. What you call a concentration camp and the Germans called a *lager*. Once, during a political meeting at Auschwitz, the former president of France, M. Giscard d'Estaing, and the Polish leader, Mr. Glerek, agreed that the ovens and gas chambers should be considered a 'symbol of European understanding.' I have been trying to understand them my whole life. I wonder how they found it so easy."

He fingers the scar tissue near his eye, rubs it while he watches the lake.

"I lost everyone at Auschwitz. Treblinka. The ghettos in Warsaw and Lodz."

"Isabella."

"Yes. And my two-year-old son."

All of her is listening, straining to be near. Ebe knows everything.

"I don't know what you have witnessed, *mein kindt*, but the shrouds were visible to you. You have been where no one should go."

They are gone, the shrouds on the lake.

"Your sickness," she says. "Can I help?" It's his, the cottage, her home. Of this, she is sure.

He pats her hand. Leaves his there.

"No, *mein kindt*. Memory is not a disease with a cure."

"Except love. There's love."

"That is what's under the shrouds."

The heaven before there was hell.

"I have one or the other. The wedding and the birth of my son. Or the camps. Never both. Not those I love on the same plane as evil.

"Those of us who bear witness to the excretions of evil, we are the contaminated ones. We bear the scars and the colours of Cain. To understand us is to be gripped in the bowels of knowledge. The doers of evil possess no such dilemma. They walk without shadows in the light of the sun."

Someone whose silence is graver than her own. Ebe does not need her to speak the whole of a nightmare that has neither ennobled nor redeemed, but simply diminished her. He knows how a defiled body can deform a soul.

He makes no effort to solace her tears.

40

Quodling, the half-world, is closer to thinkable since Kendra's friendship with Ebe. She has identified most of her voices, though a new one called KeeQue has appeared. Her air-pictures are receding as she acquires words. She still has trouble believing the dollgirl is her.

Fly KeeQue. Fly fast. Fly hard. Fly far. Kendra lets herself sink into the grey abyss.

⸜ ⸜ ⸜

Quodling is rimmed with rising and setting suns, its sky a fire of primary colours, fingers of dazzling light, which advance and recede, as if undecided between day and night. Glinda, in a chiton of material exactly like clouds, appears. The Grecian folds of her gown reflect back the colours of the heavens, but nuanced and subtle.

You have arrived, Billie whispers into Kendra's thoughts.

Where?

At the truth, says Billie.

We call it Quodling, Glinda replies.

A room appears, wet and grey, like the inside of a cloud. The dazzling lights shimmer through, but muted, occasional. Inside, a crowd is gathering. Kendra recognizes Miles, and the Little One, several little ones, actually. One of the tykes hollers in a predatory boom – the Four-Taloned Hawk, an inflated child. There is a girl in army fatigues, a tattered, homeless old man, two sylphs carrying messages from person to person, many others. The dollgirl lies on a makeshift mattress of wood chips and pine needles. Everyone surrounds a luminous child in the centre.

KeeQue.

A flash of mauve lightning strikes the room. The figures disappear in the dark aftermath. When the grey light resumes, streaked now with mauve, the figures are all Kendras: Kendra as an infant, Kendra at eighteen months, Kendra at two, three, four, several five-to-nine-year-olds, a cluster of preteens and adolescents. Miles is a five-year-old and the Four-Taloned Hawk can't be more than six. Amelia, in combat fatigues, looks seventeen and truculent. The homeless old man is a depleted fifteen-year-old in ratty old jeans.

They're all me. Kendra is mesmerized by the sheer number of tousled redheads.

One more surprise? Billie asks.

No. I can't take it.

I think you'll like this one.

Billie slides down a shaft of violet light into the room of Kendras. For a moment, head askew, belting out a song, she looks like Billie Holiday; then Kendra-now appears, in the buckskin skirt she cut to ribbons, her mouth wide in song and shock.

With a second flash of mauve, the room transforms again. Each Kendra contorts into a pose, one element from a composite of their memories. A Little One on her back, legs in a turtle flail, with a giant penis going in and out of her mouth. An infant with piss and semen on her face and neck and stomach. A five-year-old being fucked in the vagina, the hairless, porcelain vagina. A five-year-old dripping blood between her legs. A six-year-old kneeling like a doggie. A seven-year-old with a wood carving protruding from her rectum. A twelve-year-old licking a penis like an ice-cream cone. A three-year-old being smacked across the face. A four-year-old being smacked in the genitals. A fifteen-year-old sticking her tongue up a hairy anus.

Enough, Kendra cries. I get the message.

No, you don't, Kendra-now whispers, in Billie's voice. Look again.

The luminous child is still playing. She is surrounded by a wall of harmed Kendras. KeeQue is untouched.

ᒥ ᒥ ᒥ

Kendra thinks about Quodling for a very long time. About Karl, her mentor, and Karl, her tormentor. She could never have managed to grow up and know at the same time, to put the two Karls together. It is hard enough now.

41

The shrouds aren't air-pictures, but as much a part of Ebe as his eyes or his scars. Like smoke signals, they float above the knoll. Today there are five, not six of them. The other must be in his thoughts.

Ebe pokes his head through the rocky overhang above the seat. His face sags with strain, his scars more prominent than his features. The sixth shroud does not materialize.

The sorrow makes it his day to talk. Watching him struggle, Kendra wonders where he stores his words.

"Isabella told me a story I want you to know," he says. "In her Block were a young girl and her mother. The girl couldn't have been more than fifteen, but she was tall and strong and could pass for eighteen or even twenty, so she escaped the selections. Her mother was smaller and very frail. Everyone expected her to die, but she had her daughter to live for. They shared a bunk with each other, shared whatever clothing or food they could organize. The daughter was lucky – it took at least luck to survive – she got assigned to the kitchen and would bring turnip ends and potato peelings, to keep their strength up.

"Seeing their love survive in hell gave the others a whisper of hope, sometimes better than food. They wanted the girl to survive and bear children, to escape sterilization. No one in the *lagers* had sexual feelings. The men dreamt only of food or death. The women ceased to menstruate.

"Except this girl. Once a month, as regular as selection, she would bleed. It became an event in the Block, a group defiance of German will.

"Several women organized rags to staunch her flow, and they took turns washing them in the sewer called water. For once, spilt blood symbolized life.

"The block *kapo*, who people said was of Jewish extraction on her grandmother's side, hated all Jews, and the girl most of all. She mocked and tormented her, screamed out orders in German as fast as a shelling. The girl, an Italian, would rush through chores like a pantomime, for she understood little German, and disobedience could be punished with death.

"This *kapo* discovered the rags the mother was hiding. 'Who wants to see the Herr Doktor?' she asked. Mengele, or one of his ilk, was experimenting with sterilization without anaesthesia, in Block Ten.

"'Those are mine,' the mother said. She stuck the rags between her legs to demonstrate. The daughter started to push forward through the group but froze into a statue when the women closed ranks around her. Isabella muffled her cries with a hand.

"The mother was escorted to Block Ten. She never returned. The daughter became a Mussulman, a corpse waiting to die, for many days. When she awoke from this earthly death, she never asked for her mother or mentioned her name. The *kapo* became her best friend. She did not bleed again.

"My wife sent word to me, asking if I would find this girl if I survived. She knew only her first name and the small village they had come from, but eventually this was enough for me to trace her. She had married an American G.I., who found her beautiful and vague and probably ethereal – she never regained her memory of her mother – and moved with him to New York. They had four children, strong American children, the kind my wife would have raised. One of the children was named Isabella – an accident, for she did not remember my wife. I hoped God's hand was in her choice of name, for there was little enough of Him at Auschwitz.

"The girl was stunningly beautiful, as my wife had believed. She had gleaming black hair and laughter that rang out like the bells of the church she had joined. She had taken a German name, you can guess whose. Yet, life could drain out of her face in a moment, leaving a mask, a face without features. The family said she had 'seizures,' and avoided talk of the *lagers* or her mother or even baldness, as far as I knew. They warned me to keep my mouth shut, not to upset her. As if talking itself were the problem. As if memories would become dreams or phantasms if they were ignored. As if living an insipid half life could be better than a life disfigured by rage and the ethical weight of remembering. As if freedom could decorate life as a frill, and were not the lodestar of all that we are." He runs his fingers in the oyster of his scar. "There is no love without freedom, *mein kindt.*"

"You understand what I'm doing, then."

"I understand *nothing*," he shouts. "Every day less than the day before."

"Why the German name?" Kendra says. "I don't get it."

"Nothing else could protect her from the truth. She let her mother die for her. The nazification of her soul began there."

It was as if he had seen her with Lena, seen the perversion leap from her hand.

One of the shrouds is drifting between the lake and their seat, shuddering as if it's going to burst open before both their eyes.

"Go," Ebe orders.

"Why? Can't I do something?"

"Go. Leave."

The opacity of the shroud diminishes as it moves closer to Ebe. Several figures move about inside the egg of its curtain. Ebe's face whitens into a yellowish green, a sweat of mucus. "Go, go, get out," he shouts. His voice is fading into a laryngitic rattle. "I don't want you to see."

Kendra scrambles up the hummock and into the bushes. Only four shrouds are visible over the lake. The fifth must have forced its way into Ebe's thoughts. Its inhabitants had to be part of the story he gave her.

Two voices reverberate from the clearing. The laryngitic one is Ebe, but the other sounds young and foreign. "You brought me here," she is saying. "I wouldn't have come if you hadn't spoken so clearly of me." There is rustling and the sound of footsteps. Ebe's heavy tread, and no other, stumbles up the path from the clearing. Kendra trails behind him until she knows he is safe.

Memory is not as frightening as Ebe's story, as the nazification from forgetting, the repetition of cruelty, the ignorance. All her life Kendra has sought peace, but now she wants freedom, whatever its cost. She walks over to the mantel, closes the blade of the knife. She will find other wings.

There is no flight, no grey, for she has chosen. Everyone is right there, free, in the Quodling of her mind. Auriga offers the chariot she no longer needs. Glinda hands her the spiral notebook to read for herself.

Glinda reveals herself first. Her silvery white topknot uncoils into an auburn sunburst. She is the older version of KeeQue, and she laughs in the heart of her mind. "Joy," she says, "runs deeper than sorrow." She is touched by the wisdom of God, and is needed on the rest of the journey.

Billie is by Kendra's side.

"You sent me, Kendra," she says. "To find out what was going on after your first night with Axel. When you realized the stakes were so high. Come see what I found."

Woodrow, the rock dove pecking and stumbling around urban patches of turd-studded grass, is the tattered old man, the depleted adolescent Kendra in the ratty old jeans.

"I lay in the bed after he had raped us," Woodrow explains, "wondering how to live through another day in a home that offered no safety, no refuge, no peace. I tried to figure out where to go for a few hours, a few days, forever when the time came. Sometimes, death seemed the only way to go home."

"Who the fuck needs a home?" The girl, the waxwing with camouflage feathers, is kicking up a ruckus. "Stupid fucking ass.

"If you ask me," she continues, "home is where the war is. Who the fuck would want a second one when the prototype was a goddamn combat zone? 'Open up, honey. Let Daddy come home.' That's what fucking home was to me."

"Rough," Kendra says.

"Kiss my butt, cunthead. It wasn't rough. Not for this kid. I learned what to do and I learned fast. I could out-trick any meat on the street, outlast any whore in Amsterfuckingdam."

"Yeah, sure, kid," Billie says, "tell us more."

"You wanna know? You really wanna know?"

"Every single thing."

"You got it. Hold onto your puke, cuntheads. Listen to what Amelia did for you. I'd rub my hand over that flaccid curl of pigflesh until it grew into a hammer. Then I'd pop my cunt – *our cunt* – around him and dance to the salvation band. Or I'd lie behind him and lick his butthole until he squeezed a great big steamer into my mouth – *our mouth* – he loved to do that. That white puke would come geysering out before he got a chance to get in. Made me laugh, that tired old cocksucker, coming all over himself. He'd slap my cunt like a drum if he heard me. And get hard while he did it."

"You liked it, then? It was fun?"

"You stupid little puke. Like had nothing to do with it. I got good at it. I never had to be helpless. What I wanted was to drive a stake up his fucking ass. To smear every fucking piece of cum and shit and blood and puke all over him, then make him walk through the streets of Eagle City with a sign that read LOVING AMERICAN FATHER. No, you little puke, I didn't LIKE it. But I damn well knew how to do it. And I knew how to smile. A great big fuckin' smile that looked like lovin' it. Watch me."

Amelia licks her lips until they glisten with saliva, then spreads her mouth into a glossy smile, all youth and innocence and sparkling wet teeth.

Billie walks over to Amelia and wraps her into a mama-hug. She pushes Amelia's head onto her shoulder and murmurs things you'd say to a child. The big, white smile slides onto the ground.

Kendra turns to Crystal and Emerald, Glinda's messengers. "What about the two of you? Carrying all those messages. Fly fast. Fly hard. Fly far."

Crystal answers in her reedy voice. "I erected barriers and created grey spaces."

"And you?" Kendra turns to Emerald.

"I weakened and anaesthetized parts of the body. Held back bruises, made joints bend backwards, that kind of thing. If you want, I can show you a few you've still never felt."

"I believe you. It's okay."

"Copping out, you gutless piece of shit?" The predatory part of her nails her as soon as she shows a flaw.

"What do you want?" Kendra asks, in the truculent voice of Amelia.

"Amelia, poor sod, likes to think of herself as a Number One Bitch. Under that I-can-do-anything street-shit, she hasn't got a clue who she is. Perfect. What an opening for me. You lying little bitch. Those are fantasies. Nothing happened. You just wanted your daddy to pay attention to you. Now you're saying those

rapes really happened. Bullshit, you bitch. You dreamer. Go wan.
Admit it. You wanted him to ravish you instead of your mother.
And he wouldn't. So you fuck every guy on the block and holler
Rape, Incest, Abuse. To get even. To explain your failures with
men."

"That's exactly what he'd say."

"Of course, I am him. I can see every memory from his point
of view. How do you think Amelia got to be so good at predict-
ing what the old goat wanted?"

"So you really were helping?"

"The spy in the enemy camp: K.Q.'s intelligence and disin-
formation service reporting in, SIR."

"I thought you said it didn't happen."

"Ignorance is more foolproof than lies. Don't you remember?
'If you breathe one word of this to a living soul, honey, we will
have a hunting accident. Partridge pie. What was that extra-sweet
meat? they'd ask. Caught some namuh, I'd say; that's backwards
for human. And you know your mother. She'd request seconds
just to make me happy.' No better life insurance than not knowing. We went hunting with him often enough."

"He would have killed us?"

The Little Ones think so. They huddle and tremble just
hearing the thoughts of the Hawk with Four Talons, who is
Kendra at about age six.

It's Amelia who asks to hear their stories.

"I hafta talk for her 'cause she's too little," pipes a whispery
voice. She points to the tyke in the bedcrib and describes the
vision of the incest song.

Another Little One says, "I didn't understand he was doing
the hurt. I'd say, Daddy, Daddy, help me. I hurt. I sick. And he'd
say, There there, honey, it'll be over soon, you'll be okay. Then
one day I realized that the hurt and Daddy were the same.
Daddy, I cried, don't, I love you Daddy. Sweetie, he said, this is
what people who love each other do."

A new whisper breaks in. "I 'as scared. I 'ould lie there and lissen. Hear evry noise. Hear his steps. They 'alk to the fridge. Swssh. Open fridge door. Clink. Clink. Wssshhh. 'alk back to 'iving room. Voices, 'oosic. Click. Dark. I scared. Kathump. Kathump. Ssssss-whooo. He in doorway. He watching. I way under cover. Not move. Not breathe. Kathump. Kathump. KATHUMP. Help. Help. Help me Mommy. Help me. No no no. I scared all way through. He breathe a storm. Hhnnn hhnnn HHNNN HHNNN. Mommy Mommy Mommy Mommy. HHNNNN HHHNNN HHNNNNN. Daddy don't. I rip inside. I scared I rip in half. I scared the inside me fall out through big hole. I scared it never gonna stop. I want to 'cream. AAAAAAAAAAAAAA.

"I want my mommy to come and make me better. Mommy. I cry. I rock. I thuck my thumb. I bang my head. Mommy, Mommy, Daddy hurt me. Please, Mommy. Please find me. Please help me."

The next one is Astor. She is about seven or eight, and furious. "Did you recognize my story? About the cabin deep in the hills of Yugoslavia? The two sisters?"

"No," says Kendra. "Should I?"

"You're as bad as the girl in Ebe's story. You think he was only shtupping you, and not your sisters? Are you a moron?"

"Shit. Which ones?"

"Kimberly. She used to cry, and I was the one who'd go in and comfort her, listen to her stories. Sometimes he wasn't finished, and I'd have to watch."

"I am so sorry. My god, Kimmy too."

"It's okay." KeeQue's smile is a nimbus of radiant light. "Kimberly isn't hurt beyond repair. I know because I'm not."

She takes Astor's hand. "I'm the one who used to nurse us all back to health, when everyone else was unconscious or too depleted to move. I'd wash off the scum, put iodine on the bruises, bandage the cuts, and sing us to sleep." She hums a lullabye, rocks Astor and the Little One who just finished talking.

Miles appears, nestles against KeeQue and the others. "You?" Kendra says. "So little?"

"I HATED HIM. I wanted to pound my fists against his fat smelly body. GET AWAY FROM ME. GO. DIE. DIE. But if I tried even a little, he'd laugh and grind it in farther. So I hit myself. I pounded my thighs. I slapped and kicked and pinched myself. I bit my tongue till it bled. All so the hurt couldn't come from that bastard. 'Cause he liked to hurt us. It made him big and swollen. No man will ever do that to me again, this I vowed. Every man in the world is a Karl."

"Even Axel?"

"Axel asks. But he does the same thing."

"Ebe?"

"Ebe is not a man. Ebe is a god. Like Karl once was."

"No more gods," Kendra promises. "It hurts too much when they fall."

Kendra and Billie are just about ready to get some sleep when Glinda says there is a truth every last one of them has forgotten. In a mass, like one person, they all want to know.

Omigod. The dollgirl is still mute. As one, they rush to hear her story, to offer what comfort they can.

"DON'T TOUCH ME." Her voice is a naked whisper.

"Why not? We want to help."

"I don't want help from the likes of any of you. You left me alone when things got the roughest. Every last one of you. Now I can't stand to be touched. Especially by highfalutin' oh-we-want-to-help-you hands."

"What was the roughest?"

"What could be worse than what we went through?"

"You sound so bitter."

"You look revolting, all twisted up. Like you're crippled."

"What's that slime on your face?"

"You've got shit on your fingers."

"Close your legs. Have you no shame?"

"Yes, I have shame. I am shame. And I'll tell you the worst. The worst is being out of control of your body. To gyrate and bounce because every part of you has fled. The worst is obliteration as a human being. To be out of the equation. To not exist. To excrete watery shit without meaning to, or piss like a dog. To have your body jerk and flail in spasms called orgasm and be told it means you like what he's doing. And then, after you have been shamed so deeply that you never want to even have a face, he just might touch you in a way that feels tender. The worst is to still crave that touch.

"I do not wish to rejoin you in your journey back to the world. I wish to stay here and die from my shame. Please leave me. Please go."

They sit near her, their heads bowed in silence.

After a long time, the dollgirl stirs. She zips up her body. She pushes her waxen limbs into a seated position and refuses any assistance. She looks into the blue and green eyes of each one of them. "I will come," she says.

"Why?" KeeQue asks.

"The freedom to choose. Not one of you tried to force me, though your lives were at stake. Thank you."

They are all together now, and ready to live.

But Billie is panicking. She doesn't want to go. "Gabriel, Gabriel," she calls, "I can't go home without you. I thought you'd arrive on Quodling, on earth, and be part of us, but you've disappeared. Gabriel, where are you? Gabriel, who are you?"

"I am here, my friend." His voice resonates through their one mind.

"Are you coming with us?"

"I am not one of you. I must stay here."

"NO. Gabriel. I'll never see you again."

"Pray that you won't, my friend. But you can hear me if you try. Sometimes at night I will come and hover near your window. And you will never forget how to fly, even if you never go so far again."

"But you, Gabriel. What about your life?"

"We are different, my friend. Your torment is over. Mine continues. Go and see me sometime. In Chile and Argentina, Nicaragua and Columbia. In Cambodia, Nigeria. The homes of Saudi Arabia. You will find me, my friend. I am everywhere. Don't forget, my friend. Don't forget."

"Gabriel," Billie says, her voice different. "One last silly question before I leave."

"What is it, my friend?"

"What do I look like, Gabriel?"

His laughter stays with them long after his answer. "A cardinal, my friend. But the song of an angel."

42

When I came to myself, nearly two days had gone by. I was exhausted and ill, but happy, almost elated, if elation is quiet and still. Perhaps all my feelings were wrapped by the silence I once thought was a black hole. I puked and drank and bathed and thought. I let my new memory water my being, an underground river with banks of solid earth. I could talk now, because I had a story of my own.

When I went to find Ebe, he was dying. Only three shrouds were visible above his head and he had taken to his bed. His life was beyond even his wisdom, or the strength of his body, yet he had kept all of it near him under the shrouds. And managed, at the same time, to give to others, whose needs were less than his own. As with me. He opened his memory to give me a story, a parable that would allow me to live. A torrent of stories then eddied around him, telling themselves all at once. All the stories of his world, or the world, in his head at one instant. For such was his wisdom, as far as I could tell.

But it killed him as surely as the girl in the *lager* killed her mother by not making a move. I took his gift of a story, and now I have two lives to live, though lord knows I'm not worthy of the legacy from his.

I stayed with Ebe those last days, wiping sweat from the scarred sculpture of his face, and the molasses of excrement from his failing bowels. I massaged his body when he shivered and held him close to me when he wept. Or any time he would let me. I listened to the tales uncovered by the collapse of his shrouds, though they were often incoherent and fragmented. Sometimes stripped down to their basics, just a vowel or a consonant, not even a full word, and not always in English, sometimes Polish or Jewish or German or French. The tormented figures of all who had loved him, often frozen in the posture in which they had died, returned to be with him. Most were in blankets, their faces in tatters, but one I remember, in a robe of saffron and crimson, stopped to touch my face. As Ebe lay dying, amidst the debris of his loved ones, I kissed him. He thought I was his son and he died. In a whisper, I told him Lena would name her son Ebriah, though I knew he'd prefer Philip, the name of his son. All the people I loved passed through that room to pay their respects. Axel and Angel and Baker and Lena. I had much to go back to, a family, a home. Even my family in Michigan arrived one by one. I could see them all, in procession behind Axel and Baker, bend over and kiss him, as I had in his moment of death. For Ebe, a man who was intimate with evil, had given me life.